# TRIUMPH OF DHARMA

BOOK 3 OF SAMRAT YUDHISHTHIRA TRILOGY



SEMANTI CHAKRABORTY

Made with ♥ on the Notion Press Platform
www.notionpress.com

Naaraayanam Namaskritya Naram Chaiva Narottamam

Devim Saraswatim Vyasam Tato Jayam Udirayet.

[Having bowed down to Narayana and Nara, the best of men, along with Goddess Saraswati and Veda Vyasa, one should utter 'Jaya'.]

# Contents

## Contents

# Preface

The first two books of this series have witnessed Yudhishthira's rise to the imperial throne and his fall from it. This third and final part of the series will show his struggle to win his empire back, through the eighteen days long battle of Kurukshetra.

The war of Mahabharata is not an ordinary war. Within the sheer violence, there is a compassionate Arjuna who emphasizes with his revered elders even when they stand as enemies. There is a loving Bhishma who willingly reveals his way of death to his grandsons for letting them win. There is a dutiful Yudhishthira who lets go of his whole life's truthfulness to save his army from Drona's weapons. And an unarmed Krishna who becomes the biggest weapon in Pandavas' hands. The battle of Kurukshetra thus becomes a battle between all human emotions too, a never-ending struggle between the good and evil inside all of us. I have strived to take you to that battlefield through Yudhishthira's perspective.

With the completion of Emperor Yudhishthira's story, here ends a long journey that had begun more than ten years ago. With the blessings of Krishna and you all, finally I am here, presenting the third and final part to you who have supported my debut series since the beginning. I thank all of you, my readers, without whose love and support this could have never become possible. When the idea of writing on Yudhishthira struck me back then, I never thought that this would end up being a trilogy of about 230,000 words. That was a time when I knew nothing of the editing and publishing processes. I had no idea about how to turn my imperfect first draft into a published novel. Thanks to my stars, that I met Smt. Saiswaroopa Iyer at the right time. After that, there was no looking back. Saiswaroopa agreed to edit my manuscript and guided me through the publication process. She being a bestselling author in the Puranic fiction genre, her guidance and experience smoothened my journey as a debutant author in the genre. She is the very reason for the existence of this trilogy. I thank her from the bottom of my heart for everything she did to help me grow as an author.

My cover designer, Harsha Kaveripura, has been one of the greatest blessings in the journey of this trilogy. I met him soon after my first book was out, thanks to my friend and the bestselling author Deepak M R. Since then, I knew I had found the perfect person who can translate all my ideas into a visual masterpiece. I thank him for being there for me and delivering all the covers before time despite his busy schedule.

I wholeheartedly thank my friend and bestselling crime thriller author Neelabh Pratap Singh, for inspiring and encouraging me continuously for writing more and writing better. He has been a living solution for every writing problem I faced, and a helpful friend whom I can approach for any writing advice. I cannot end without thanking Sri Harikiran Vadlamani, the founder of Indic academy, who has promoted my first book by distributing review copies to the members of thousand reviewers' club. I really cannot thank him enough for considering a new author like me for this great opportunity. Along with him, I am grateful to every author friend of Indic Academy for supporting and reviewing my book. Those well-wisher and helpful friends indeed are blessings for me. A special thanks to Abhinav Agarwal, Ratul Chakraborty, Ranjith Radhakrishnan, Deepak M R, Nithin Sridhar and Arun Krishnan for helping me in multiple ways. I wholeheartedly pray to Krishna for their success and wellbeing.

I seek blessings from my mother, late Jharna Chakraborty, who had been there with me when I was writing my first draft of this book but left me before seeing the entire trilogy in print. I bow to my father, Late Narayan Chakraborty, who had wished to see me as a published author. I dedicate this trilogy to them, hoping that they will see from the high heavens and shower their blessings. I thank all my friends, especially Shivang Buch, Soumya Pal, Lavina, Debipriya Roy and Santosh Kumar Ayalasomayajula for supporting my first two books generously. Without their continuous support it would have never come this far. I express my heartfelt gratitude and seek their good wishes for this book as well. And most importantly,

I thank you, my readers, who have trusted a new author and encouraged her first writing endeavour. I offer this third book to you, hoping it to receive the same love and blessings.

Sarvam Krishnarpanamastu!

# CHAPTER ONE

Was it just me or did the clarinets of Abhimanyu's wedding sound like war trumpets?

It was the first wedding in the generation of our sons. Yet I could not connect myself to any festivity around me. Maybe none of us could. The delight of becoming in-laws was eclipsed by obvious concerns about war. Our new palace of Upaplavya, which king Virata gifted us on the occasion of wedding, seemed less like a festive assembly and more like a war camp.

Maybe that was for greater good!

"Welcome to Upaplavya, Dharmaraj Yudhishthira." King Virata greeted me.

I managed to bring a brief smile on my lips, reciprocating the namaskara. The king seated me on a gem-studded throne right at his left on the elevated dais, besides my brothers. On a smaller dais at the king's right, sat Abhimanyu with our sons. The Panchalas and Yadavas were seated on a carefully decorated ornate segment meant for royal guests. Everyone's face glowed in a mix of excitement and readiness, mirroring the bright morning light that bathed the spacious hall. Reflection of colourful gems that adorned the pillars and walls played on their silken robes.

I suppressed a sigh within as I watched Abhimanyu who had to leave his newly wedded wife to join the sabha. His handsome face looked even more radiant today. New bridegroom's jewelleries had not yet left his young body, but his eyes shone with determination and courage. His expression mirrored the gravity of the assembly.

"Honourable kings, princes and chiefs of Dwaraka, once again, I welcome you all in Matsya." Host king Virata addressed everyone. "I express my gratitude to each one of you for gracing my daughter's wedding."

Silence followed.

"As you all know, the five Pandavas and Samragni Draupadi have spent one year of incognito in my kingdom, and hence fulfilled their terms of exile. Now," he glanced at everyone once. "Samrat Yudhishthira wants to meet and interact with all of you about their next steps to regain their lost kingdom. I have called this sabha on his behalf." He turned to me. "Samrat, I request you to start."

Nodding at the king, I rose. All the pairs of eyes rested on me. Even the intricate curves on the pillars seemed to be waiting to hear me.

"Our venerable father-in-law king Drupada, all our relatives and friends of Panchala and Dwaraka," I joined my palms. "I thank all of you for supporting our mission and waiting for thirteen years. I apologise to you for refusing the help you have offered me then. But now the exile is over. Hence, I seek your wise guidance and advice to decide our next move."

"There is nothing to deliberate much, Samrat." King Drupada opined, his facial muscles stiffening. "You have kept your promise. Now the Kuru king has to keep his, by returning Indraprastha to you."

"But I don't think king Dhritarashtra will agree to do that." Satyaki frowned, crossing his arms.

"If they don't agree, we have to snatch back what is ours." Bhima's jaws clenched. His loud voice shuttered the quiet ambiance.

"Patience, Bhima." Balarama glared at him. "War is not the best solution to every problem. If this is what you had to do then why didn't you fight back then? Why wait for thirteen years?"

Bhima looked away, slamming his thigh. Balarama being his teacher of mace-fighting, I knew he would not argue with him. His fingers wrapped around the corner of his throne, crushing the golden layer.

"If you have cared enough to fulfil their terms of exile, you must care for peace too." Balarama advised. "It's always better to negotiate without bloodshed."

Balarama's sudden reluctance in war was surprising enough. But what he suggested was worth considering.

"I agree with you, Balarama." I nodded at him. "Before deciding on anything disastrous, we should give the Kurus a last chance to keep their promise. And that initiative should be taken from our side."

Bhima turned his head to me, his eyes crimson. Satyaki clenched his fist, shaking his head.

"I can send a trusted messenger to Hastinapura who will formally inform them regarding the completion of our term and remind them to return Indraprastha." I observed the reaction of my brothers. Their facial expressions turned sour like curdled milk.

Dhrishtadyumna shook his head impatiently. "In vain, Samrat. You too know that they won't agree. This is just waste of our time."

"And doing so will make you look weak in front of them." Satyaki added, exchanging a quick glance with Bhima who nodded with emphasis.

"Perhaps you are right." I agreed with a nod. "But not doing this will demean us in front of entire Bharata who will hold us responsible for the war. Also, don't you think that Duryodhana will utilise this to draw sympathy from the neutral kings and make them join his side?"

Dhrishtadyumna and Satyaki shook their heads and looked away, their fists hitting the sides of their seats. I exchanged a quick glance with Krishna who nodded subtly.

"And what if they don't accept?" Shikhandi looked straight at me. "Would you still prefer peace, Samrat?"

It presented a challenge. But I knew the answer.

"I can only make my proposal, Bhrata. Final decision will be theirs." My voice turned grave. "If they also prefer peace, peace will prevail. Otherwise not."

"You cannot say so, Samrat." Balarama's tone rose a little as he leaned forward. His fair face held a deep frown.

"Being the emperor it's your responsibility to save this mass bloodshed. Even if that calls for a compromise from your side."

"What's the matter, Balarama?" Satyaki raised his eyebrow. "What made you so insistent of peace suddenly? Weren't it the same you who was ready to fight for Pandavas just a few years ago?"

"Many things have changed within these years, Satyaki. Now both Pandavas and Kauravas are our relatives. I don't want them to fight against each other. I strive for the benefit of both."

"I am not against peace, Balarama." I calmly stated. "But to make that happen, Duryodhana must keep his promise first. I'm ready to make peace with them right now, this very moment, if they accept my proposal."

"Peace always comes at a price, Samrat. And you both should be ready to pay that."

Balarama insisted. I kept my gaze fixed on his face, still trying to realise what he wanted.

"If Duryodhana agrees to let go of the wealth that he won, you too have to be prepared for making a compromise if required. You should accept whatever they wish to return you, even if it is less than your expectation."

I was not prepared for this tone of Balarama. Not just that his way of speaking was too cold and unfriendly, those words coming from someone close to Krishna was shocking for me. For all of us.

Did Balarama never share Krishna's vision of Dharma sansthapana? What could have made him so desperate to stop the war even at the price of empire of Dharma that was Krishna's dream?

I took a quick look at Krishna. His natural calm smile was missing from his face.

"What are you saying, Balarama?" Satyaki voiced my unspoken thought. "Why should Yudhishthira compromise? He isn't desiring to snatch Hastinapura from them. He is just trying to get his own Indraprastha back. Is it his fault to ask for what belongs to him?"

"If it was his fault to gamble away what was his, now also it's not right to ask it back!" Balarama's raised voice threw a heavy blow on my heart after years. I froze for a while. His raised finger seemed to be pointing at my dark past.

“It is Yudhishthira alone who initiated this problem. Who told him to choose that king of Gandhara to play with?"

My tongue turned bitter. Who told him that playing against Shakuni was my choice?

I saw Bhima fuming, almost on the verge of bursting out. I held his shoulder, shaking my head. Arguing within ourselves would go against us only. Maybe that was why even Krishna was not reacting.

"Balarama!" Satyaki interrupted. "Don’t comment on something you don’t know."

"I do know everything, Satyaki." Balarama slapped his thigh to validate his claim. "Yudhishthira could have easily won against any other gambler but he insisted to play with that cheater Shakuni." His voice lashed out at every corner of the hall. "Now just because the game did not turn into his favour, he wants to fight against his own cousins? What kind of justice is this?”

I had overcome my initial shock by then. It was clear that Balarama had been misinformed. And it was also understandable who might have done that.

Krishna was right. Indeed, the wedding of Samba with Duryodhana’s daughter had changed things a lot.

"Rama! Have you gone insane?" Satyaki objected again, fuming.

“I am completely in my sense. I believe Duryodhana has complete right over Yudhishthira’s kingdom now.” Balarama continued in same tone. “If Pandavas want Indraprastha back, they have to stay low because the fault isn’t Duryodhana’s.”

“Stop it, Balarama!” Satyaki cried. “For the sake of Lord Somanatha, stop this false accusation!”

“What is false? Is it untrue that Yudhishthira himself gambled his kingdom and lost? Everyone in the Jayanta sabha including the Kuru elders advised him not to play but he did not listen. Now if Duryodhana refuses to give Indraprastha back, how can I blame him?”

"Enough!" Satyaki sprung to his feet. "One more word against Dharmaraj and I swear I'll forget my relationship with you!" he gasped. His frame shook in anger. A shocked Balarama could not even react. Satyaki then turned to the others, his eyes moved over everyone's faces.

"I have never imagined that someone can dare to insult Samrat Yudhishthira thus in front of his friends and relatives, and no one makes a protest against that!" he groaned. "My fellow Yadavas and the honourable Panchalas! How do you keep quiet and tolerate this accusation on him? Do you too believe that Balarama is right?"

"Calm down, Satyaki." I evenly said. "Balarama has said what he feels right. Everyone who is present here has right to put forward his opinion."

"But that doesn't give anyone the right to throw a false accusation on you, Samrat!" Satyaki fumed.

"Satyaki, listen..."

"Let me speak today, Yudhishthira!" he raised his palm to cut me off. "Otherwise all your friends will misunderstand you. And that's what Balarama's dear Duryodhana wants. To create misunderstanding between us."

The entire sabha stared at him holding their breath.

"Listen, son of Rohini!" Satyaki turned to Balarama. "I don't know from whom you have heard this wrong version of that incident. But that person did not tell you the truth."

Krishna exchanged a glance with Satyaki and nodded. His silent agreement seemed to have added to Satyaki's spirit. He held his head higher, moving closer to Balarama.

"To begin with, Yudhishthira did not play dice willingly." Satyaki continued with confidence. "He was trapped in the name of a friendly game. He did not insist to play with Shakuni, rather it was the exact opposite. The entire thing was pre-planned to rob Pandavas of their wealth."

I exhaled as my heart filled in gratitude. Satyaki did prove himself as a true friend, once again. I noticed that Krishna's smile was back, after long.

As if Satyaki was speaking what he could not.

"They cornered him, cheated him and defeated an unskilled player with their deceit and no one cared to stop that. The Kuru king himself enjoyed his son's open robbery and other elders supported it with their silence." He paused to breathe out and glanced at others. "Here are the other Pandavas, and Samragni Draupadi's natal family. Please correct me if I have said anything wrong."

"Each and every word of yours is true, Yuyudhana Satyaki." King Drupada agreed. "Pandavas were cheated in the open. Still, they have stuck to their promise and fulfilled the condition of exile set by the Kurus. Now no point of law can stop them from claiming Indraprastha."

"And neither can any other law stop them from raising weapon for their own rights. Either Duryodhana will return Indraprastha, or will die with his family. There is no third option left now." Dhrishtadyumna clenched his fists.

"I think Yudhishthira must start collecting armies from this moment on." King Drupada suggested. "The sooner you can do that, the better. Because Duryodhana also will do the same and kings tend to join that side who approaches them first."

Balarama had not spoken since Satyaki's strong counter. Now his facial expression changed. He stood up from his place, frowning.

"If that's what you all plan, count us out of this." He evenly stated.

"Dau," Krishna spoke for first time. "Have you thought of our dear Subhadra once? How will we face her after denying support to her husband and son?"

Balarama's gaze shifted to his brother. "I must remind you, Krishna, that we are not just Subhadra's brothers but Lakshmana's in-laws too. Both sides are equal to us and we must not discriminate. Either we shall help both, or help none."

Balarama's indication was clear. Krishna's face still retained his natural serenity. But I could guess what storm must have been going on inside him. Balarama was not just his elder brother. He was Krishna's closest companion and witness of all his troubles and successes. It pained me to see how their inner conflicts were coming up in the open.

"Hope you will agree with me, Krishna." Balarama added.

"I have never gone against what you felt right, Dau." Krishna softly said. "Even now I won't. Your younger brother will fulfill your wish." A smile played at the corner of his lips. "I promise you."

"You two might be bound by this weird logic of equality, Krishna. But I am not. I have no relation with that wretched Duryodhana. Hence," Satyaki sideglanced at Balarama. "Hope I'm free to take my own decision!"

"If your own stubbornness is greater than Yadava unity, then do whatever you wish, Satyaki!" Balarama retorted.

"Yadava unity?" Satyaki sarcastically laughed. "Where is that, Rama? A new necessity of maintaining so called equality between Kauravas and Pandavas has divided them already. Not just the Yadava kingdom but also within your own family. But you are unable to realise that."

"Honourable Yadava friends!" I found my words. My grave tone made both look at me.

"I request you to calm down. This sabha is not meant for fighting within ourselves."

I rose from my throne.

"I have heard all of your opinions. Thank you all for joining this discussion. With respect to all your views, I want to make one thing clear first. We do not want war. We understand the huge drawback of a massive war and we shall try our best to refrain from it." I declared as I turned to the Lord of Panchala. "Maharaj Drupada, you are the eldest among us and our well-wisher. I request you to send a trusted messenger to Hastinapura on our behalf."

"Sure, Yudhishthira." He nodded. "But you must prepare beforehand because this emissary's success is not guaranteed. Start sending messages everywhere."

I joined my palms to him. "I accept your advice, Maharaj. But before that I want to tell everyone that, we have invited you here for attending prince Abhimanyu's wedding." I fixed my gaze on the Yadavas who were still murmuring at a low tone.

"This invitation should not be taken as our proposal to join our side in war." I stressed upon every word, hoping to make my intention clear. "None of you are obliged to fight for us if you don't want to. We shall send out messengers later to all our friends, or at least the ones we consider being so." I glanced at Balarama. He sat expressionless now.

"It will be entirely your choice whether to accept that proposal or not." They were my final words.

# CHAPTER TWO

"Jyeshtha!"

I turned back. Krishna's face held a rare trace of darkness.

"You haven't slept yet?"

He shook his head. "I could not until I speak to you."

He stared through the window, at the sleeping Upaplavya. Today's discussions in sabha had kept him up at this midnight.

"Jyeshtha," he softly said. "I know you are shocked. And hurt. Please don't take my brother's words to heart. He is not himself right now."

"Forget about *me* feeling bad, Krishna!" I held his palms in mine. "Rather I feel pained for you, brother! I can only imagine your predicament! Now I have a clue about the trouble brewing within your own family, your own people! And I believe we have seen a small part of your true struggles today."

Krishna smiled. A hint of pain surfaced in his deep eyes. "Familial relations have never held me back when it came to a greater good, Jyeshtha. I have been seeing these since I was twelve."

"But it's always the harder when you have to face it all alone." I pressed his shoulder. "I cannot even digest the fact that Balarama, your constant companion of every phase of life, can fail to understand you today!"

Krishna smiled a wry smile. His fingers played with the flames of nearest lamp.

"It's not his fault, Jyeshtha. Dau is under an illusion now. And he does not realise that he is being played with."

"Who is doing that to him?" I wondered aloud. "Duryodhana?"

Krishna shook his head. "No. He just did the initial manipulation. The rest is done by his daughter."

"Lakshmana?"

"Right. Dau melts too soon. And when his favourite nephew Samba's wife draws his sympathy, that happens even sooner."

"Does that mean Duryodhana is using his daughter as a pawn in this whole game?" Bitterness reflected in my tone.

"He is misusing my brother's affectionate nature. He knows that Lakshmana's tears can be much more effective than his pleas. And here his strategy has been successful. Dau has promised Lakshmana not to raise weapon against her father and brothers." Krishna looked at me. "What you have heard in today's sabha was the consequence of those manipulations."

"How many more families Duryodhana will break!" I muttered, sighing. Krishna did not comment. The dark shadow of untimely clouds over the moon played on his face.

"I hope Dau will understand one day. Just that it will be too late by then."

"Krishna," I held his shoulder. "I know what Balarama is to you. I cannot forgive myself for causing this rift between you brothers. I tell you again, reconsider your decision once. You don't have to join my side being so hard on yourself."

"You are mistaking me again, Jyeshtha. You are not the cause. I'm not supporting you, my cousin. I support Dharma. I support what is right and beneficial for Bharatavarsha. And this is my own decision. Nobody forced me to do this."

I hid a sigh, nodding. I knew how determined Krishna was in his aim of Dharma sansthaapana. But Balarama, under Duryodhana's influence, would never understand this. As long as he kept blaming Krishna as being partial to us, I would never be free of this guilt.

"I don't regret my decision, Jyeshtha. Neither am I going to reconsider the same." Krishna's decision was clear.

"But it's also your duty to think of your daughter-in-law." I reminded. "You cannot ignore Lakshmana's natal family's wellbeing. Neither can you let her feel betrayed in her marital home."

"I understand that." Krishna nodded, looking at me. "Worry not. I shall not disappoint her." A meaningful smile played again on his lips. I knew he had a way out of this predicament. It just struck me that he had promised Balarama that he would fulfill his wish.

"What are you going to do, Krishna?"

"Anything but staying neutral. This is the battle of Dharma. The battle of re-establishing my dream. And I cannot stay away from it." He smiled more now. "But I assure you, I won't give Dau a chance to complain either."

***

"Thank you for accepting my request, Aacharya." I bowed to the royal priest of Panchala who had agreed to convey our message to Hastinapura. After a brief discussion with Maharaj Drupada, the king had suggested that he would be the perfect person for this task, given his wisdom and expertise in political matters.

"It's my honour that you and my king have trusted me to carry out this task." He smiled. "I shall try my best to validate your claim in front of the Kuru king."

"You are like Deva Guru Brihaspati in wisdom, and a skilled strategist like Shukracharya. I have no doubt that you will be able to explain our demand in the best possible way." I joined my palms. "Aacharya, I have one more request if you don't mind."

"Without a hesitation, Samrat." He encouraged.

"I have a feeling that the Kurus have already started assembling armies. It would be of great help if you can also bring us the information of war preparations that they are taking."

He nodded. "Stay assured. You will get every detail about every development at Hastinapura when I return. May all Gods bless you to get back your kingdom again."

As he left after blessing us, Sahadeva turned to me.

"Jyeshtha, I'm sure that Duryodhana has started gathering armies. We must start too. Sooner than later."

"I second Sahadeva." Nakula agreed. "We don't have many allies to begin with. And we lost Yadava numbers."

"Let it be, Nakula." My jaws tightened. "Smaller army with shared goal is much better than having a huge group that is always busy fighting within themselves. We need a united front. Not those conflicting Yadavas."

Bhima rubbed his chin, his brow curved. "But what about Krishna? He is not someone who breaks his promise. And he promised Draupadi to avenge her insult."

"You really think Krishna can support us going against Balarama?" Nakula shrugged.

"I don't." This time I replied. "Krishna loves Balarama, and he will never go against his wish. But he can still support us without opposing his elder brother." I smiled, glancing at them. Everyone's eyes narrowed in silent question.

"How is that possible?" Nakula voiced it.

"Even I don't know, Nakula. But Krishna will find a way."

"How can you be so sure?"

"Because I know Krishna well. As far as I have understood, he himself does not want to stay seized in this inner conflict between Yadavas. If he wants to come out of this, he will find a solution himself."

"Perhaps." Bhima nodded. "But right now, we don't have time to wait for Krishna's decision. It should not be too late to send away proposals to our friends and all other kings."

"Correct. Let's start with our relatives first. Bhima, send messengers to Kashi and Magadha. Nakula will write to Chedi king Dhrishtaketu and Sahadeva to uncle Shalya of Madra. Send a word to the Pandya king in south too."

"Alright, Jyeshtha, but what about Dwaraka?" Arjuna's eyes threw the obvious question. "Aren't we going to approach them at all?"

"I have not forgotten Dwaraka." I spoke. "But I won't send any messenger there. You personally will go there along with Subhadra. I believe Krishna will find his own way. But we have to ensure that nobody accuses him of being partial to us. Hence, this formal approach is necessary."

Arjuna nodded. Bhima was going to say something but before that, the guard announced Draupadi. My gaze stuck at the door as the empress hurried in, her face bearing signs of worry and a slight disturbance. I wondered what made her leave the discussion with Matsya's treasurers at the midway.

"What bothers you, Samragni?" I straightened myself.

"Subhadra's personal messengers have just returned from Dwaraka." She informed. "Krishna has declared in Sudharma sabha that he will participate unarmed in the war."

Unarmed? Weaponless in the middle of a battlefield?

It took me a while to let the words get inside. But as they did, Krishna's last words echoed in my head. My intelligent cousin was never to make a foolish decision. This had to have some reason.

"Unarmed?" Bhima repeated in shock. "Why?"

"Not just that. He has assembled his army of powerful Narayana soldiers to give them away to whoever asks for." Draupadi added, curves deepening on her brow.

I exhaled. Now it all added up. I could see what Krishna's intention was behind this.

"I'm not yet getting what Sakha is upto." Draupadi sank on the nearest ornate coach, shaking her head.

"Relax, Krishnaa. He is keeping his promise." I smiled now.

Everyone looked at me, disbelief large writ in their eyes.

"I told you, brothers, Krishna will find his own way. We have just heard his solution."

"How can staying unarmed in battle be a solution?" Nakula shook his head, shrugging.

"It will be. Because Duryodhana will never want Krishna to join his side if he refuses to raise weapon." I explained. "And this is why he declared it in open court."

My brothers exchanged glances for a while. I caught Arjuna's wandering eyes and nodded with emphasis. His eyebrows curved. Then, they evened, making his face lit up. Arjuna's lips curved into smile, followed by Draupadi who exhaled, nodding at him.

"Excellent!" Arjuna thought aloud. "Krishna has done this so that he can be on our side!"

"Without a doubt, Arjuna." I nodded.

"I see." Bhima straightened up. The next moment he leaned back, shaking his head. "But even then, an unarmed warrior can never be a part of an army."

"Charioteers can be, Bhrata." Arjuna reminded; his eyes were glowing in excitement. "I shall request Krishna to become my charioteer. I know he will agree."

"And let his Narayani army go to Duryodhana who will gladly accept it." I added, smiling more.

"Sakha's wisdom never fails to impress me." Draupadi's eyes spoke of admiration. "I never thought that he would come with something like this to fulfill his promise of helping both sides."

"And of course, to avoid hurting his own Yadavas on the other side. No doubt that this is the best decision he has taken. For himself, and for us too." I leaned back on my throne.

It felt much lighter now as the burden of guilt went easy my chest. Since the past few days, I could not come out of the disturbing thought that Krishna might end up facing more blame from his own people for supporting us. I was glad that he did not do that. Each soldier of his Narayani army equaled all Yadava warriors together in battle. If he gave it to Duryodhana, I hoped Balarama would never accuse him of being partial.

Choosing Krishna at this moment meant not just losing his army but also the assistance of his powerful weapons. Yet, I had no second thought regarding my decision. Krishna alone was much more than his invincible Sudarshana or Kaumodaki. It was his wisdom that once defeated enemies like Kalyavana and Jarasandha, not his weapons or army. His wisdom had once made us achieve the throne of Bharatavarsha. He did not need to change his role this time to make us win this war.

"A weaponless Krishna will become our biggest weapon in this war. A weapon Duryodhana would forever regret losing." I looked at my brothers. Arjuna sat straight, all ready to start his new mission.

"Let's not delay anymore. Go, Phalguna! Approach Krishna on my behalf to join our side as your charioteer!"

# CHAPTER THREE

Upaplavya felt charged with presence of illustrious Kshatriyas from all over Bharata.

Thanks to king Virata's flawless hosting and supervision, the entire city had become super active for the war preparations. Arrival of our ally kings had taken the strategic discussions to an advanced level. I could see each face glowing in excitement and determination. My brothers were finally satisfied and charged with confidence. And of course, Draupadi too. Her eyes seemed to have regained the lost trust on me, at least to some extent.

My both nephews, Ghatotkacha and Iravan, arrived even before we could have sent them message. They had brought large groups of Rakshasas and Nagas with them. King Abhibhu, the Lord of Kashi, who was Bhima's brother-in-law, arrived next with his valorous son and army. Lord of Pandya kingdom in the south had also arrived with his one akshouhini army. Chedi king Dhrishtaketu, the son of our late cousin Shishupala, contributed one akshouhini more, and so did Jarasandha's son Sahadeva. King Virata had meticulously arranged suitable shelters for all the soldiers and war-animals. His finance ministers had been on a regular discussion with Draupadi regarding the expenditures of war.

Magadha king Sahadeva, who was late emperor Jarasandha's son, did not share his father's aggressive arrogance. He was humble, loyal, and grateful to us for not usurping Magadha from him after his father's death. He had got his daughter married to my brother Sahadeva after the digvijaya, and thus strengthened our alliance even more. Dhrishtaketu of Chedi had a similar feeling of gratitude for us. His sister, Karenumati, was married to Nakula, and that made him one of our strongest supporters along with Panchala and Matsya. No doubt that their joining had generously added to our confidence.

But at this present moment, what bothered everyone the most was the smaller size of our camp compared to that of the Kurus. Tension was palpable in the meeting room as we gathered to discuss our present situation. Worry large writ in all the faces, especially the Panchalas.

"We have gathered only six akshouhinis of army so far." Dhrishtadyumna's brow had deep curves as he broke the silence. "Much lesser than that of Kauravas, I believe."

"We shall get a detailed information regarding their armies after our messenger returns." I spoke. "But as much as the spies have informed, they already received armies from Avanti, Salwa, Sindhu and Kamboja."

"Trigarta too." King Virata reminded. "Susharma could not leave this opportunity to avenge his defeat in Matsya."

"And not to forget Rakshasa Alambusha and Naga chief Takshaka and Ashwasena are also on their side." Iravan added. "Along with manpower, they will provide them illusive war strategies and special weapons too."

"I'm hoping a large part of Yadavas too will join Kauravas." Dhrishtadyumna looked at me. "What do you feel, Samrat?"

"I'm having a feeling that Yadavas mostly will stay neutral." I commented. "Balarama's neutrality is sure to affect his other brothers. Pradyumna and Krishna's other sons won't like to join because their love for Abhimanyu and Samba is equal."

"And that's not good news for us." Shikhandi rested his chin on his palm, crossing his arms. "Yadavas were sure to be on our side. Losing the warriors like Balarama, Pradyumna, Charudeshna and Satyaki is going to hold us back. Even if Duryodhana doesn't get them directly, their absence from our side will help him in indirect way."

"What about Kekaya and Shivi?" Dhrishtaketu enquired, looking at me. "They are your family relatives."

"They are. But both the kingdoms are split into two segments now and Duryodhana will take its advantage. During our exile he has influenced those north-western kingdoms enough when they were having frequent internal clashes." I said, looking at them. "The weakened kings then preferred to take Duryodhana's alliance for strengthening themselves."

"You mean even they won't come to your side?" Dhrishtadyumna turned his head to me.

"Even if they do, we cannot expect to get their full support anymore. At least one side of those kingdoms are bound to join Duryodhana. The side which is allied to him."

"Then the same thing can happen with Madra too." King Drupada remarked. "King Shalya also got Duryodhana's monetary help one time."

"Perhaps." I agreed. "I have sent messages to all these kingdoms. Still no response has come."

Dhrishtadyumna shook his head in despair. "This is not done, Samrat! Your own relatives and friends are siding with your enemies and you can do nothing to stop that!" His fist slammed the side of his seat. The sharp sound of his gold ring hitting against the throne echoed the frustration in his tone.

"This was bound to happen, Dhri." I calmly replied. "No one wants to be allied with those who have lost their kingdom and roam in forest for years. Our prosperity had attracted the entire Bharata to accept our lordship one day. Now the same prosperity in Duryodhana's hand is bound to make them inclined to him."

"That is not the sole reason, Bhrata." He was impatient. "Duryodhana is playing smart. He has not drawn Yadavas towards him through wealth but through trickery. I believe he has done the same to some other kings too."

I saw Shikhandi, Satyajit and Dhrishtaketu nodding, along with my brothers.

"Bhrata Yudhishthira," Dhrishtadyumna continued. "If you too cannot do the same, your loss is confirmed."

"No need, brother." I denied. "I want a united front. Gathering people who are unwilling to fight for me won't help us in any way. I shall gladly accept only those who will willingly come for me. For Dharma."

"A battle cannot be won with philosophy, Bhrata. Battlefield is not a place of emotion. Lesser army always comes with a risk of defeat."

"I know that, Dhri. I'm not talking out of emotion. We must focus on quality over quantity. A well-united, well-organised army with a clear goal can win over a much bigger group even being small." I encouraged him. "We need to work on that."

Dhrishtadyumna's frown did not ease. I paused to observe the others' reaction. Most of them still had deep curves on their brows. But I knew they were listening.

"Noble ones, our number might be lesser, but our unity, dedication and strategy have to be greater than theirs. All of us must have the same aim for Dharma's victory and there should be no compromise in reaching that." I raised a finger, glancing at everyone. "Such focus is sure to bring us victory."

Some of the faces lit up now. Some others straightened themselves on their thrones. I saw king Virata nodding, along with the king of Magadha.

"Makes sense, Samrat." Dhrishtaketu remarked.

Dhrishtadyumna nodded. "Well, I get you, but we still..."

"We can talk on this later. Dhri." I cut him off. "I have been informed that Aacharya has just returned from Hastinapura. Let's hear him first."

***

The entire meeting room held leaf drop silence as the priest of Panchala spoke of his experience in Hastinapura.

"My words seemed to have fallen into deaf ears, Samrat." He sighed. "The Kuru king said nothing regarding giving back Indraprastha. He only sent his blessings and good wishes for you all."

My jaws gritted. As expected!

"What did Duryodhana say?" I looked at my messenger.

"He accused you of lying." Aacharya's calm expression turned bitter.

"What lie?" I kept asking despite of understanding what it could have been.

"Yuvaraj Duryodhana said that the term of exile has not yet been completed. And demanding your kingdom before that is unrighteous." He explained.

The edges of my lips curved. I knew that this logic would come. This was why I waited five months more after the last year was over. Just to complete one year in both lunar and solar cycles. I did not have any expectation from Duryodhana and even his loving father. But I hoped at least someone from the sabha of Hastinapura would know that I was right. At least the elders. Even if they chose not to voice it in open.

"Dharmaraj has to learn about righteousness from that evil Duryodhana?" Bhima snapped. "Has everyone in Hastinapura forgotten calculation of years?"

"Samrat, Yuvaraj Duryodhana also added that if you demand your kingdom before the terms of exile is over, you have to fight them to win it back." The priest continued. "They would not let go of their 'lawfully won' kingdom otherwise."

My brow evened. I was expecting to hear this.

However I might try, peace did not seem to be there in my country's destiny!

"Did noble Bhishma express his views on this regard, Aacharya?" I patiently asked. A clearer picture of Kuru sabha was needed to understand their possible next move.

"He has agreed that your calculation is right. He admitted that one year of incognito had indeed been over before the day of Vijaya Dashami when prince Arjuna faced the Kuru army. Dronacharya and Kulaguru Kripacharya also supported him."

Well, so at least now they had managed to voice what they felt! *Better late than never!*

"But Duryodhana did not agree, I presume?" I asked again.

The priest frowned more. “It was Angaraja Karna who has spoken on behalf of the Yuvaraj this time.”

The very name churned the whole suppressed mountain of fire within me. I had to shut my eyes to send it back.

“He clearly stated that you have not yet fulfilled the condition of dice hall. Hence either you all must go for a second exile of another thirteen years or come to a battlefield to fight them.”

My fists curled. The fingernails dug into my palm, drawing blood.

“We are more than eager to meet them there.” Bhima curled his fists, clenching his teeth. "Their wish will be fulfilled really soon."

“Aacharya, what else did you notice in their sabha? Have all their allies arrived?” I enquired after calming myself a little.

“Most of them have, Samrat.” He nodded. "I saw the kings of Kamboja, Sindhu, Trigarta and Pragjyotisha present there. Kauravas have already gathered ten akshouhinis of army."

“I have guessed this earlier.” I muttered. “This is why Duryodhana and Karna are finding excuses for not returning our kingdom. Advantage of resources.” I crossed my arms.

"I have also reminded them about what Bhima and Arjuna along with the Panchalas can do to them." Aacharya said. "I explained why it would be better for them to accept your proposal rather than facing you in a war now."

My brows curved. "Did anything change?" Though I knew it would not.

He shook his head. “They are too overconfident for their own good, Samrat. Indeed, Hastinapura surprised me a lot. I have never seen such a royal court where Yuvaraj and his friend from another kingdom overrule the king and elders! That king of Anga has no connection with the Kurus. Yet, he seems to prevail upon the king and Yuvaraj.”

“This is how they have come to this far, Aacharya.” My breath raced as I struggled to suppress the anger within. “And they refuse to grow out of it. The king himself is seized in his love for Duryodhana. Karna, Shakuni and Duhshasana act as fuels for him.

And those aged and learned ones, have imprisoned themselves to that throne in the name of loyalty. I have no more expectation from them now."

"Enough, Jyeshtha!" Bhima looked at me. "You have fulfilled your duty by giving them an opportunity. They have refused it. Now only war is the way."

I slowly nodded before turning to the priest.

"Aacharya, did the king give no reaction to their proposal of war? Haven't he sent any reply to my message at all?"

"The king seemed a little disturbed when I spoke about the prowess of Pandavas and Panchalas. He admitted that your message is humble and peaceful enough. He also agreed that you have the power to win Indraprastha back, yet you have asked your uncle for returning it. He told Duryodhana that a challenge of war should not be sent as a reply to your peaceful message."

I laughed to myself. The king must have been too scared to send his beloved firstborn to Bhima. My brother's oath in the dice hall must have haunted him since past thirteen years.

"King Dhritarashtra has said that he would send his messenger soon to you." The priest informed. "With the reply of your message."

Bhima's eyes narrowed. "Don't tell me that it's invitation of another dice game!"

"Perhaps not, Yuvaraj. The king seems to be against war. Maybe he will try to make peace with you."

"Not anymore, Aacharya!" Bhima waved his hand. "Peace was dead when his son refused to return Indraprastha."

Nakula and Sahadeva too nodded in assent. But I could not share their opinion. It seemed wise to listen to whatever king Dhritarashtra wanted to say. Rushing to the battlefield without giving them an opportunity to speak would show us in bad light.

I waited for thirteen years for my Indraprastha. Some more patience for a few more days won't harm.

"Let the king's messenger come first, Bhima." Was my final reply. "We shall decide after that."

# CHAPTER FOUR

"Not this way." Abhimanyu corrected Anjanaparva's position. "Hold it to your left."

Anjanaparva nodded changing his direction accordingly, tightening his grip over the sword. His weapon clanged with Abhimanyu's. They locked with each other for a while. Their muscles strained as they kept on increasing the force on each other. After a while, Abhimanyu stepped back and struck a quick blow. Anjanaparva countered him with acute agility. Abhimanyu backed away and launched another huge blow disarming Anjanaparva.

"Excellent, Abhimanyu!" I clapped. "Just perfect!"

Both turned to me and bowed.

"Grandfather, I have learnt a lot from uncle Abhimanyu." Anjanaparva humbly admitted. "But still could not defeat him even once." His gaze dropped to the floor.

I smiled as I caressed Anjanaparva's bald head. This fifteen-year-old son of Ghatotkacha was the youngest warrior of our side, and hence, beloved of all. His uncles, though not much elder than him by age, showed utmost interest in training him while practicing together.

"Not even you, son. Even we, his elder brothers, could not do that yet." Prativindhya beamed, patting Abhimanyu's back. "He is Uncle Krishna's student. Unconquerable like him."

"Anjanaparva has improved a lot, uncle." Abhimanyu said, looking at me. "I'm sure he will surpass me very soon."

"I have seen that, Abhi. I must say that it's *your* training that is making him improve at this accelerated pace. Not just him, but all of your brothers too. No doubt that you are a great teacher just like your father and uncle Krishna." I patted his head.

"But Abhimanyu is not teaching us the method of countering chakravyuha." Iravan complained. "He avoids the topic every time we ask him."

"Don't you understand, brother Iravan? He doesn't want to share his special knowledge." Sutasoma chuckled, patting Abhimanyu's shoulders.

"Nothing like that, Bhrata Soma." An embarrassed Abhimanyu denied. "In fact, I myself am yet to learn it fully." He lowered his gaze.

"Didn't Krishna teach you that?" I was surprised.

"He did, uncle. But only the part of penetration. He has not yet taught me the strategies of exit."

"Why so?"

"Uncle's life had its share of twists and turns too. After my first lesson of penetrating the formation was completed, brother Samba's wedding happened, followed by completion of your exile." He explained, making his tone softer. "Neither of us got to start the next lesson."

I nodded, realising how hard it had been on Krishna since then. And on this boy, who had to leave his newly wedded wife to prepare for the first war of life, at this tender an age!.

"Chakravyuha itself is an advanced level of warfare that a few warriors know, Abhimanyu. Learning even half of it bolsters one ahead of other warriors." A familiar voice made me turn.

"Satyaki!" I exclaimed, seeing him smiling.

"You didn't expect me here, did you?" he smiled more, as if enjoying my surprise. "Well, Samrat Yudhishthira, I have come to join your army." He bowed with a mock seriousness.

"Thank you for coming to us, Satyaki!" I managed to smile but could not share his exuberance. Several thoughts kept passing through my mind as I led him to my chamber through the spacious corridor. The recent arguments between Satyaki and Balarama in Upaplavya's sabha rang in my ears. Satyaki's immediate decision of joining us was sure to create more clashes within the Yadava chiefs, making Krishna's situation even harder.

"What bothers you, Yudhishthira?" Satyaki held my shoulder.

"After Kritavarma joined Kauravas, I did not think that you can finally break away from Yadavas. And that too this soon." I softly uttered, offering him a couch beside the window.

His smile faded as he pressed himself against the seat. "Yadavas are no longer together, Yudhishthira. And you have already seen that. It does not matter anymore who breaks away and who stays. It's all about priorities now."

I stared at him. Didn't it hurt to take this decision? After all, it was his family, his own people. I hid a sigh. Maybe he too had grown Krishna's detachment within himself.

"Everyone at Dwaraka is free to take his own decision. Balarama has his own choice. Kritavarma has his. I have mine too." He added, his face showing no expression.

"Didn't Balarama object?"

Satyaki shook his head. "He should have seen it coming. Neither would it have mattered to me even if he objected."

I nodded. I still anticipated Balarama to try and pursue his brothers and nephews, even if he could not do so with Satyaki.

"Moreover, he doesn't have time to waste on me now. He is rather keen on explaining about the importance of impartiality to Krishna." He let out a soft chuckle.

"I believe that Krishna's decision of staying unarmed has shocked Balarama?"

"Yes, and notably so." Satyaki agreed. "He is trying his best to convince Krishna."

"To join Kauravas, I guess?"

Satyaki smiled. "Balarama keeps on insisting him to be neutral. But I can sense that he actually wants Krishna to side with Duryodhana. So that he himself can join them."

"I feel the same. Krishna has shown enough 'neutrality' already by declaring to stay unarmed and promising his powerful army to any side who asks for. What more impartiality does Balarama expect from him?"

“Correct. Talking about neutrality at this time shows what Balarama actually wants."

"He can never go against Krishna no matter what, Satyaki. Hence, he is trying to make Krishna join the side he wants to be in.” I thought aloud, a weird sense of annoyance filling me in.

I could have never thought that my elder cousin Balarama could give in to wrong influence so easily!

“But Krishna is clear about his stance. He will join them who will approach him first. Just as every other king would do."

"That’s better. And looks fair too." I nodded. No doubt, my intelligent cousin had left nothing undone to fulfill his promise.

"That reminds me," Satyaki leaned forward. "I hope you have already sent a messenger to him?”

“Not messenger. Arjuna himself has gone to Dwaraka to approach Krishna.”

“Great!” he appreciated with a nod. “That’s wise. I hope it shuts mouths at Dwaraka. Krishna can easily reply to them that he could not refuse Subhadra’s husband since he approached him first.”

“Subhadra is Balarama’s sister too, Satyaki. I wonder what his reply would be to Arjuna.”

He frowned. “Don’t expect him to join your side, Yudhishthira. That’s the last thing Balarama would do.”

“I have no expectation from him who supports Duryodhana after knowing everything. I just want to see how he fulfills his wish of staying impartial to both. Especially after Krishna joins one side.”

“Are you sure about which side Krishna is going to join?” his lips curved into a knowing smile.

“Aren’t you?” I smiled too.

"I know what he wishes, Yudhishthira. And I have always seen him making his every wish come true. Such is his wisdom, which is mistaken as something miraculous by many." Satyaki leaned back on his seat. "He won’t fail this time too."

***

My assumption did not go wrong; neither did Satyaki’s faith in his friend. Within a week of Satyaki’s arrival, Arjuna returned with

Krishna.

"I have been worrying for you." I said, greeting Krishna. "Hope no more problems at Dwaraka?"

Krishna smiled. "How can one avoid problems where internal conflicts are at their peak? But I'm glad that I could finally come out of it. Thanks to you and Arjuna for hurrying things up."

"Did Duryodhana also approach you?" I enquired. I had the news that he had also left for Dwaraka almost at the same time when Arjuna left Upaplavya.

Arjuna's face stiffened in a frown. "Not just that," he said. "He reached there just before me with his request. Looks like he has been spying on me."

"What did you do then?" I turned to Krishna.

"Simple. I gave him choices. Either my well-equipped, well-trained Narayani army, or me alone, unarmed." Krishna relaxed back on his seat. "Just as I declared in Sudharma sabha."

"And he chose the army. Just like you have assumed?"

"Just like we all have assumed." Satyaki corrected. "I told you, Yudhishthira, I know Krishna's wish." He smiled a winning smile. "Did it prove right?"

I smiled back with a nod. Heart felt lighter after long. I was sure that even Arjuna felt the same having Krishna on our side, formally and finally. His relief was readable on his relaxed facial lines.

"Thanks to all Gods that everything went well." Arjuna took a long breath. "Now even Duryodhana's supporters cannot accuse Krishna."

"But what about Balarama?" I looked at Krishna. "Is he pleased with this?"

Krishna's face darkened. "Maybe not. He wanted me to join Duryodhana even if I don't lift weapon. That did not happen."

"Didn't Duryodhana ask Balarama for his participation?" I wondered aloud.

Krishna nodded. "How could he let go of this opportunity? But Dau has not yet given him any promise. He said he would inform him about his decision later."

"Your choice might have shocked him, Krishna. And angered too." I muttered.

"I know, Jyeshtha." Krishna said in an even tone. "But this was bound to happen. If Dau has his promise to fulfill to Lakshmana, I too have mine to Sakhi Draupadi. And to this Bharatavarsha. I can't back out from that."

"Salutations to Samrat Yudhishthira." A guard bowed. "Balarama Vaasudeva seeks your audience."

I straightened up. An unpleasant storm seemed coming up. I had to be prepared to face it.

"Send him." I replied.

Balarama hurried in within a while, his jaws tightened in frown, his eyes turned crimson in effect of wine. I rose to greet him, but he impatiently waved his hand.

"No need of such formalities, Samrat." He said in husky voice. "I have not come here to join your side. I have come to inform my decision to everyone present here, including my brother Krishna."

"We shall listen to you, Balarama." I calmly said, holding his palms. "But please take your seat first."

"I haven't come to accept hospitality of those for whom Krishna has dared to disobey me." He snapped. "He tricked me to support you. Your addiction to dice has caused friction within your own family, and now, in my family too."

Was it me or Duryodhana who did both? I pursed my lips to send the repartee back.

"But Krishna is too dear to me." His eyes softened now as he glanced on his brother. "Whatever he does, I can never go against him. I shall support neither you nor Duryodhana. I detest watching this mass bloodshed that's going to happen between cousins. I am leaving for a long pilgrimage of banks of Saraswati. Do whatever you all wish!"

Without letting anyone speak anything more, he walked away like a storm blowing out of my chamber. I stared at the path he went along. A sigh escaped me.

Maybe this also had happened for good.

With Balarama's presence, it would have been hard to fulfill Bhima'a vows. Being the teacher of both, perhaps this was best for him to stay away from a moral dilemma.

Especially when he didn't have any obligation to participate like our grandfather and Gurudeva.

"Have a safe and peaceful pilgrimage, Balarama!" I prayed within.

# CHAPTER FIVE

"Welcome to Upaplavya, Sanjaya." I greeted Hastinapura's messenger. "Hope the Kuru family is well at Hastinapura."

"All is well by Mahadeva's grace, Dharmaraj." Sanjaya bowed. "King Dhritarashtra has sent his blessings for you five brothers and Devi Krishnaa Draupadi. He has thanked all Gods for your successful completion of thirteen years' exile and prayed for your long lives."

"We are honoured to receive his blessings." I evenly said with joined palms. "And eager to hear the message he has sent." I came to the point without beating around the bush.

Sanjaya took a quick glance at my brothers and Krishna who sat around me. "Samrat Yudhishthira, if you don't mind, I want to deliver my message in private."

I smiled to myself. Maybe he thought that it would be easy to persuade me in absence of my brothers and friends. Perhaps, it was the king's very instruction.

"I don't deem the matter to be that confidential, Sanjaya. It is something the entire Bharata is aware of by now." I replied. "Everyone who is present over here are my well-wishers and deserve to know the content. You can speak in front of them without hesitation."

"As you wish." He reluctantly agreed. "Samrat, my king, with all his heart, prays for peace to prevail between the descendants of Kuru. Hence, he has requested, nay, pleaded you not to do something that threatens that peace."

My jaws tightened. Even after my best effort to avoid war, he still felt that it was me who was threatening peace, not his beloved firstborn.

"He has asked you to remember the lessons of Dharma. He has said that you are noble, peace-loving, and obedient to your elders. Fighting a war against your own cousins doesn't suit your noble character. Hence, he asked you to listen to your old uncle's plea and discard the thought of war." Sanjaya finished.

Bhima clenched his fist. His raced breath was audible in the silence. Arjuna's brow arched. The Panchalas fixed their gazes on me, observing my reaction. Krishna's lips had inscrutable smile.

I straightened against my seat. Everyone stared at me, anticipation strong on their faces.

"When did I say, Sanjaya, that I want to fight a war against my cousins?" I looked straight through his eyes. "From where did uncle Dhritarashtra assume this?"

"Don't take my offence, Dharmaraj." He joined his palms. "But you have already started collecting armies. Is it not for war?"

"Pray, don't take offence from my side as well. But Sanjaya, wasn't it his sons who started preparations of war first?" I patiently looked at him. "Did they not respond to my messenger that they won't give my kingdom back without war? What should I presume from these then?"

Sanjaya could not reply. He looked away, wiping out sweat from his brow.

"No sane person wants a war, Sanjaya." I continued in same tone. "I am no fool to crave for a mass bloodshed unnecessarily. Why would I fight if my demand is fulfilled in peace? I don't want war. I want my Indraprastha back. And I have not said anything beyond this to the Kuru king."

My brothers exhaled. I saw Bhima leaning back, his facial muscles relaxed.

"Pardon me, Samrat. But morality is much greater than a mere kingdom. Dharma is far beyond materialistic pleasures." Sanjaya now turned philosophical. "Why does Indraprastha matter to you so much that you have to take path of violence if you don't get it? Don't you think, Dharmaraj, that an ascetic life in forest is far better than being a killer of own family?"

I laughed to myself. No doubt that king Dhritarashtra had tried his best. Little did he know that I was not the same Yudhishthira anymore who could have agreed to such peace-inclined words. That younger self of mine died thirteen years ago, in his very court. He himself been a party to it.

"You mistake me, Sanjaya." I calmly replied. "I don't want my kingdom back for my materialistic pleasure. The imperial throne is not my object of luxury. It's my responsibility to my subjects whom I had once vowed to protect. I cannot deny my duty to them."

"Causing such a massive violence in name of duty, is undoubtedly a sin, Dharmaraj." Sanjaya's voice was cold. "Are you ready to bear the burden of this huge adharma on your shoulder?"

"Since when claiming one's own rights become a sin, Sanjaya?" Krishna spoke for the first time.

"Now you and your king are judging on Dharma and adharma of Dharmaraj himself because of your own interest. Where was your knowledge of Dharma when Samragni Draupadi was dragged in the court by her hair?" Krishna's calm voice lashed out on every silent corner of the chamber. "Where was your morality when she was attempted to be disrobed?"

I closed my eyes to hold myself. Even after thirteen years, that cruel memory still felt just like yesterday.

"If king Dhritarashtra was fine with that crime, he should not accuse Samrat Yudhishthira as a sinner now who is demanding for justice." Krishna continued. "Or should I presume that the definition of sin changes for the Kurus, depending on situation?"

"Mistake me not, Vaasudeva." Sanjaya said. "My king has not accused Samrat as a sinner. He just echoed the words of all common people of this country whose fate is being played with in this conflict of kingdoms. People of Bharata will never forgive Samrat for causing this huge loss. He will get unending infamy till the end of his life."

"Are you trying to threaten me or curse me, Sanjaya?" I stared cold at him.

"I don't have that much audacity, Samrat." Sanjaya bowed. "I can only suggest you as a well-wisher. You have always maintained a pious, spotless character through your lifelong adherence to truth and justice. Pray, do not let that unblemished image get maligned."

"Thank you for your concern! But you don't have to worry about my reputation, dear friend. Infamy is imminent whichever way I choose. Either I shall be known as a coward for not fighting for justice, or as a bloodthirsty emperor waging war against cousins. Blame will find me either way and I don't regret that."

I paused, only to sense that my own voice was reverberating from walls of the silent assembly hall.

"My decisions are not going to be based on what someone says about me. I shall do what I feel right. Hope that is clear to you."

"I respect the strength of your character. But don't you have any duty to your own family, Dharmaraj?" he made one last effort.

"I very well do. And that is why I had sent my messenger to my family to ask for what is mine. Did I not? But the response makes me feel that peace is impossible despite my best efforts." I observed Sanjaya's reaction. He avoided my gaze.

"You say that uncle Dhritarashtra wants peace. But he fails to do what is in his hands to ensure peace among both sides of Kuru family. He has said everything else in his message except returning my kingdom. You tell me, what should I do in this situation?"

Sanjaya lowered his head. I heard him heaving a sigh.

"I admit that it was my fault to play the damned game and lose my kingdom. But I have fulfilled their demand of suffering for thirteen years for that. Is my claim unfair now, Sanjaya? Your king is well aware of how much we have suffered in exile. Does he still think I'm wrong to make a claim now?"

Sanjaya looked up.

"My king agrees that you indeed have suffered a lot, Samrat." He slowly nodded. "And he does admit that your claim is right. But he is helpless in front of his son's wish. He failed to convince Yuvaraj Duryodhana to return Indraprastha. Hence, he requests you to forgive him and his sons."

Forgiveness! *How on the name of Mahadeva can they even expect that from me now?*

"I am ready to forgive. But only when the other side is ready to accept my claim." My voice was calm yet determined. "Responsibility of protecting peace in the Kuru family is not mine alone, Sanjaya. The other side of my family too should contribute to it. Without their co-operation, peace is not possible."

"I can understand your point, Dharmaraj. And I assure you that I shall try my best to deliver your message to my king." Sanjaya joined his palms and bowed to me.

"Now I have to leave for Hastinapura." He spoke. "I seek your apology for whatever I have said wrong, Samrat. I am just carrying the message of my king. Pray, do not take my offence for anything that might have sounded rude."

"I understand, Sanjaya. Leave without a worry. Give our salutations to the king, grandfather Bhishma and all our elders. Tell them that Yudhishthira is ready for both peace and war. The choice is theirs to make."

I glanced at my brothers once. Each of them looked charged with unmoved determination. Their faces glowed with each of my utterings. Appreciation in their eyes told me that I was on right track.

"I can be forbearing, Sanjaya. I can also be ruthless if required. Now it's up to them as to which Yudhishthira they want to see." There was no uncertainty within as I uttered my final decision.

# CHAPTER SIX

"Feeling so relieved to see you all after so long, sons." Uncle Shalya beamed, giving his blessings to us.

King Shalya, the Lord of Madra, was our maternal uncle, the elder brother of late mother Madri.

"Gods have been kind that you have completed the terms of exile without a failure. I'm sure that you will get back your kingdom too very soon." His tone was encouraging. "Suffering cannot last long for those who follow Dharma. Good times shall make a comeback."

"We strive not only for our good times but for entire Bharata's, Matula." I replied. "Bless us so that our efforts bear fruits."

"I know, Yudhishthira. My blessings are always with you, five brothers. May you get back your kingdom like Lord Indra got back his Amaravati from the hands of Vritrasura! This blessing is all that I can give you!" he hid a sigh in the last sentence which I did not miss.

"Rest for some time, Matula." Nakula said as he rose. "We can talk later in the evening. Let me inform king Virata to make arrangements for your army."

Uncle Shalya's lips parted as if to say something but his gaze strayed away, almost unwilling to meet ours. "Don't have to stress yourself, Nakula." He managed to speak. "Army has not come with me. Neither can I stay here for long." His eyes betrayed guilt.

I watched uncle for a while. The more he hesitated, more it was clearer - His weird behavior and guilt surfacing in his eyes had almost confirmed that what I had suspected was true. I glanced at Nakula and Sahadeva once. Both looked surprised. I could only imagine what their reaction would be if my guess was correct.

"I didn't get you, Matula." Nakula stared at him.

Uncle Shalya lowered his head. I heard him sighing.

"My sons, the army of Madra cannot fight on your side!" he looked away, biting his lips. "Forgive your helpless uncle if you can!"

I leaned back on my seat, letting the sigh escape that I had held for long. I knew this would happen. I felt bad for my little twins who looked shocked and hurt. They were totally unprepared for this.

"I have come here to meet you all after thirteen years. But I'm unable to break my promise to Duryodhana and join you." He admitted. "Forgive me if possible!" he joined his palms, still looking away.

"It's alright, Matula." I held his joined palms. "You don't have to apologise to your own nephews."

"Yudhishthira, child," he struggled for words for a while. "I believe you know. At least you would understand what I have gone through in the past thirteen years!"

"I understand, Matula. I have heard it." I softly said. "Duryodhana had helped training the Madra army without taking any payment, right?"

Uncle nodded. "He approached me at a time when I was disturbed and weak because of the sudden division of my kingdom. Trade of Madra suffered due to change of weather. Duryodhana capitalised upon the opportunity to help me financially."

"But why did you let him provide you financial help in the first place?" Nakula snapped.

"Could you not take some other way to improve Madra's trade, Matula?" he continued in more raised voice. "Didn't you know what that Duryodhana had done to us, your own nephews? How could you let him help training your army?"

"I had no other choice, Nakula." Uncle softly replied. "I tried not to be in Duryodhana's debt. But he kept providing resources for Madra's flourishing, indirectly, sometimes even without my knowledge. When I came to know, it already was too late."

Duryodhana had proven again that his strategy of breaking our relatives away from us was successful. He had given his best to increase his own allies and reducing ours. The chunk of thirteen years had been very helpful to him.

"I still tried to pay him back for his help." Uncle Shalya continued. "But he refused. Instead of money, he demanded my participation in war. And I had to agree." He sighed again.

"He refused money because he doesn't lack that, Matula." I calmly remarked. "All he wanted was allies. Especially our allies whose support could strengthen him and weaken us at the same time. And I have to say that he is successful in his strategies."

"Yudhishthira, I still tried my best to find a way to get rid of him. But I could not. Duryodhana has shut all my ways to return to you now. He has bribed to draw my soldiers and my subjects to his side. My own people will stand against me now if I don't fight for him."

"Don't give such excuses now, Madraraja Shalya!" Nakula's dark face had turned crimson in anger now.

"If you wanted, you could have stopped this at the very beginning itself. You could have told him directly that it's never possible for you to stand against your beloved little sister's sons. But you did not."

"I do admit my mistake." Uncle's chin dropped to his chest. "But I have promised him, child. I cannot break it now."

"Promise!" Sahadeva frowned. "What is the value of promise made to such an evil mind who himself cannot keep up his own promises? Why should you stick to a vow that you were forced to take under someone's pressure? Or should we presume that you gave him your promise willingly?"

"Deva!" Pain resurfaced in uncle's eyes. "Pray, by the name of my dear Madri, I never wanted to..."

"Don't take our mother's name anymore, Lord of Madra!" Nakula cut him off, raising his finger. "Could you not even think of her once before doing this? Thanks to you! I cannot face our mother Kunti who raised us two with love. I have no words to tell my brother Yudhishthira who had asked for my life over his uterine brothers one day!"

"Nakula, trust me, son." Uncle Shalya held Nakula's arm. "With all my heart, I shall always be on your side and pray for your victory. But Kauravas have bound me with their wealth. I cannot break that bond of debt now."

One more elderly person with knowledge of justice yet bondage of debt to injustice! One more slave of Hastinapura's wealth in name of loyalty! I sadly smiled to myself.

When you fail to maintain balance of Artha, Dharma too gets misbalanced!

"You don't have to break it, Matula. You are not the first one to face this relationship." I evenly said. "We understand that with wealth in their hands, Kurus can now buy anything. They have bought our grandfather's sense of morality and our teachers' loyalty too. It's no surprise for us that your affection for your nephews has been sold as well."

"Yudhishthira, pray, don't misunderstand me! True that, I cannot give you my physical participation and my one akshouhini army. But I can help you in some other way despite of sitting in the opposite camp. Except joining your side, whatever else you want from me, I shall try to give you! Tell me what you want."

"Your blessings will be enough for us, Matula." I calmly replied with joined palms. "Nothing more is required."

"No, Yudhishthira!" he shook his head. "I cannot live with this guilt that I'm raising weapon against Nakula and Sahadeva, my own sister Madri's blood! The very thought is eating me up since years. I have to do something for you. Otherwise this regret will kill me."

"Enough of your favours, Madraraja Shalya!" Sahadeva's voice was harsh with sarcasm. "Pray, don't do anything more! We don't need your help. We five brothers are enough to fight against your entire army, however huge it is."

"I know that, Sahadeva. I know my nephews can win their battle without my help. But I still want to do this for my own peace of mind. Pray, let your uncle become free from this guilt!"

"What do you want to do for us, Matula?" I patiently asked. Something had struck me by then.

"Anything you trust me to do." His face brightened up a little. "I can provide you secret strategies of their camp."

"No need. We have enough spies to do that." I said. "If you really want to help us, then I request you to do that in some other way."

His eyes narrowed. "What way?"

Dhrishtadyumna's words echoed in my ears.

*Duryodhana is taking away all your friends and relatives to his side. Why can't you stop this, Yudhishthira?*

"Matula, you have to demotivate and distract a warrior during his battle with my brothers." I said, knowing well what I meant.

I knew I was never going to snatch an alliance from Duryodhana's side. Neither could I persuade Balarama or uncle Shalya to join me. But this was something I could still do. Deployment of Kootaneeti – Make the enemy taste their own medicine even if by a miniscule. If Duryodhana could play with Balarama's psychology and turn him against us, why couldn't I do something similar to weaken him? Why not to take this opportunity while uncle Shalya was also willing?

*Playing deceit with the deceitful, a key strategy to win wars!*

"Distract during battle?" Uncle repeated with question. "Whom?"

"Angaraj Karna, Duryodhana's dear friend." I voiced it. "I hope you know that he has vowed to kill Arjuna. I request you to protect my brother from his deceit. Whenever Karna will face Arjuna in the battle, you will insult him in such way that his concentration gets distracted from the war. Let him not be able to fight with his full might."

A part of me protested. But the rest of me shut it up. It was the same Karna who had called names of my wife one day. It was the same sinner who wanted to see Draupadi naked. I clenched my fist. He did deserve this! And I would do anything to see him dead, even if that was not a fair way!

*There is no sin in removing sinners from this world!*

"Alright, Yudhishthira." Uncle nodded. "I shall try to do this for your and Arjuna's sake if situation favours. I promise you."

# CHAPTER SEVEN

"Madra's army too is lost." Dhrishtadyumna massaged his forehead. "We are left with seven akshouhinis now, while Kauravas have eleven."

"I could not even imagine that uncle Shalya would betray us at the last moment!" Nakula pursed his lips.

"Don't be dejected, brother. Whatever has happened, will be for our own good." I patted Nakula's arm. "I don't want a single half-hearted warrior in my army. Madra's soldiers are grateful to Duryodhana. They could have never given their best for our sake."

"Even uncle Shalya will be half-hearted on that side, Jyeshtha." Sahadeva commented. "I believe his guilt is genuine."

"I know. And we shall turn it to our advantage." I said. "Now his contribution in Karna's downfall will ensure our victory."

"Was this necessary at all?" Bhima's brow arched. "Arjuna's valour and divyastras are more than enough for Karna."

"I have complete faith on Arjuna, Bhima. But not the slightest on Karna's intentions." I sternly explained. "There is news that he has taken an oath of not touching meat and wine till he kills Arjuna."

"Then he will have to fast from them till the end of his life." Bhima smirked. "I pity him!"

"I cannot take it so casually, Bhima. It's clear that Karna is now too desperate to kill our brother. How can I trust that he will fight a fair battle against Arjuna?"

"Do you think that Karna can do something that Arjuna cannot handle?" Bhima stared at me. From his tone I could sense that he did not like my plan. Maybe none of them did. My gaze moved to Arjuna once. He sat without an expression on his face. Maybe his mind also rebelled at my decision but he could not voice it out of respect.

"I don't know what Karna will do. But his extreme desperation is always a cause for my worry. The least I can do is trying to guard Arjuna from any possibility of deceit. And that's what I have asked uncle Shalya to do."

"I think we can talk about Karna later." Krishna interjected after a long bout of silence. "The next immediate course of action calls for more attention."

"Right." I concurred. "It has been almost a month since Sanjaya has left with my message. Still no response came from Hastinapura."

"No response is also a response in a way, Jyeshtha." Bhima remarked. "This means they still do not agree."

"And now war is the only response from our side." Sahadeva concluded, determination reflecting on his tightened jawlines.

"No." I shook my head. "Not this soon, brothers. Declaring war without hearing from them will show us as invaders of Hastinapura, not as their rightful heirs, unfairly deprived of what was theirs." I walked closer to them. "We don't want that."

"Then what's the way, Jyeshtha?" Bhima hit his fist on his thigh. "We have waited more than enough."

"And they chose to not respond." Dhrishtadyumna exchanged a glance with Bhima and nodded. "Will we keep waiting all life to hear from them?" he turned to me.

"We won't. If there is no response, we must force a response from them." I crossed my arms. "We shall send another emissary to Hastinapura."

"What is the point?" Arjuna shrugged. "The same thing will repeat."

"No. This time I shall send a different proposal to them. I shall ask for not the entire Indraprastha but only five principalities. Let's see what they do."

The entire hall remained silent for a while. I could hear them gasping in shock.

"Five principalities?" Bhima burst out. "Have you gone insane, Samrat?"

"Not at all, Bhima. This is my last effort to make peace. And the last opportunity for Hastinapura to grab it." I calmly replied.

"Haven't we already given the last opportunity to them?" Dhrishtadyumna grimaced.

"We have." I nodded. "But you all have seen its outcome. King Dhritarashtra is trying to play victim now. He is portraying that it's we who are selfish enough to declare war against his sons. I'm sure he paints the same picture to the subjects and all vassal kings."

"Let him." Nakula shrugged. "Why should we care for his false accusation?"

"We have to, Nakula. Because we are going to rebuild our empire once again." I patiently explained. "We cannot let the royals and Kurujangala's commoners look up to us as some tyrannical intruders. We want them to sympathise with our cause. For that, they need to know that it is the Kauravas who are against peace. Not us."

Silence followed. Bhima gnashed his teeth tighter. His fingernails torn the embroidered cushion of the ornate coach.

"With our power in their hands, they have already taken away many of our supporters. But if they now succeed to draw people's empathy also towards them, that will confirm our moral defeat even before the war." I added. "No empire of Dharma can stand over the foundation of mass hatred."

"Kurujangala's subjects are always in our support, Jyeshtha." Arjuna calmly said. "They had even wanted to follow you to exile back then."

"That's the incident of thirteen years back, Arjuna. Commoners tend to change with time, especially if the rulers are good at influencing them. Those who have power and wealth, do always have an upper hand to influence most people. We must point out the realty to them for winning their support back."

"I understand." Sahadeva impatiently nodded. "But is it necessary to make such a huge compromise for that?"

"This is not a compromise, Sahadeva. This is a process I'm following carefully. They have denied returning Indraprastha. Now we are making a viable proposal that won't cause Duryodhana much loss from his 'won' property but will establish that we are preferring peace seriously."

"And what if he denies five villages too?" Sahadeva snapped. "Will you give up your entire claim and go to forest then?"

"If they deny this, I shall make them lose everything in battlefield."

Nakula shook his head. "I still don't get what exactly you want to achieve by this!"

"I want to remove the illusion that Duryodhana has created on everyone's minds. Our aim is justice, not revenge. Let entire Bharata realise this." I raised a finger, glancing around. Frown on my brothers' faces expressed their clear disagreement. I knew that they would never feel convinced with this idea.

"Do you think it will actually work?" Dhrishtadyumna doubted aloud.

"It might not. But it can at least make us fulfill our final duty to all. If Kauravas deny sharing even this small piece of land, there will be no more trace of guilt left in us. We shall know that we have tried our best. And so will everyone who are staking their lives for us."

"Jyeshtha is right, brothers." Krishna agreed. "Entire Bharata needs to see who deserves to rule this country again. Every single soldier fighting on our side needs to feel proud that he is fighting for Dharma, for victory of the deserving ruler who cared for them." He beamed. "Trust me, it will keep all our soldiers motivated to fight for their Samrat till their last breath!"

"But at the risk of losing whole Indraprastha? And sparing Draupadi's wrongdoers? What kind of justice will we get from this?" Bhima snapped, shaking his head. "I cannot agree with this!"

"Justice does not equal to getting whole kingdom back. Justice equals to reconstructing of our mission. Our empire of Dharma."

"How are you going to establish that empire with five villages?" Bhima retorted, throwing a glare at me.

"Stay without worry, Bhima. We are going to lose nothing. Five villages will be enough for us to establish a new empire once again."

"Don't show us a false dream, Jyeshtha." Sahadeva's face stiffened. "It is not possible."

I smiled this time.

"You all once said building a city from barren Khandavaprastha is also impossible, remember? But we did build it from scratch. Why cannot we do that again?"

No one spoke now.

"We have ability to rebuild our new empire even from one small principality. Five villages will be more than enough for us. If our power knows how to destroy, it knows how to construct as well.

"We won't lose anything, brothers! Whatever might be the result of this emissary, we shall benefit from it. Either there will be peace with a new empire, or there will be war with our existing one. But in both the cases, Dharma will be with us. Bharatavarsha's mass support will be with us. And that's all we need."

"Duryodhana will mark you as a coward, Samrat of Bharata!" Bhima reminded. "They won't understand that you are giving them a second chance. They would laugh at you."

I turned grave. "I don't care about what Duryodhana thinks of me. Neither can I ignore my duty because of his carelessness."

"Bhrata please!" Dhrishtadyumna frowned. "Don't let the world misinterpret your nobility as weakness!"

"Real strength never needs a proof, Dhrishtadyumna." I was calm yet determined. "Let time decide whether I am weak or not. They will feel our strength soon enough if they refuse my proposal." I paused and glanced around. All the faces held frown.

"I need your cooperation in this mission, dear ones. The matter is crucial and requires a good messenger who can express my intention in a proper way. It would be better if someone from my close friends and relatives carries this proposal to Hastinapura."

A brief silence followed. Some of them seem thinking, some others exchanged determined glances. My gaze fell on Dhrishtadyumna first. He shook his head.

"Not me." He denied. "Neither do I think that any of my brothers will agree."

"My opinion is no different." Bhima declared, frowning more.

"Neither is mine." Sahadeva's nostrils flared. "And I'm sure that Satyaki and the others too feel the same."

"Samrat's noble mission will not go in vain." Krishna's calm voice made me turn to him.

"If no one else agrees, I shall be your messenger, Samrat." He volunteered. "I shall do this for the sake of Bharata. For the sake of Dharma."

"You have just voiced what I wanted." I exhaled, smiling. "Thank you, Krishna. You are not just our friend but our greatest well-wisher, and the wisest speaker among all of us. No doubt that you are the best person for this."

"I shall do this because I understand your intention, Jyeshtha." He affectionately said. "You want to restore justice without mass violence. Being a common relative of both sides, I feel a duty to try once for that." Krishna paused a little, and then added in softer tone, "But as you must know, this attempt has more chances of failing like the last ones."

I nodded. "I am prepared for this mission's failure, Krishna. If Duryodhana can deny his daughter's father-in-law even when he proposes only five principalities for us, there will be no reason to spare him anymore. It's now either five villages or entire Bharatavarsha for him. Choice is his how much he wants to lose!"

# CHAPTER EIGHT

"Five principalities? Has Dharmaraj Yudhishthira's self-respect stooped to this level now?" Draupadi's sharp voice lashed out at the silence of my chamber.

"If the Chakravarti Samrat of Bharata has to beg for such paltry compensations today, the next step will be letting go of the entire rights and retire to forest. Hope I did not speak wrong, Samrat?"

"Samragni, I understand the reason of your disapproval." I softly said. "But can we please reconsider the whole matter from a greater perspective once? We have accepted a barren Khandavaprastha once for sake of peace. Aren't five villages better than that?"

"No!" she strongly protested. "This time it's not just the matter of getting a kingdom to rule. It's about responsibility to restore justice in entire Bharata. Back then it was our personal interest alone. Now it's the interest of entire common mass of this country who has suffered under Duryodhana's rule." She paused for breath, and then added. "It's the interest of all womenfolk of this land whose honour is not safe in their hands." Her tone turned more determined. "Can we just take our own small share of land and forget all of them, Samrat?"

I knew she would say this. She was not just the empress of this land, she was, by heart, the mother of entire Bharata. And a mother would never agree to let her children live under Duryodhana's rule.

I held her palm. "You are never wrong, Samragni. But we cannot forget that the very common people of this country whom we want to protect, are also going to suffer if war becomes inevitable." I patiently explained. "And it's our duty towards them to try one final time before putting their lives at stake."

"Some greater price needs to be paid for a greater good, Samrat. I believe you too know this well." Her voice was firm. "Justice, even if comes at price of blood, will benefit both us and our subjects. Not some void, useless peace."

"Krishnaa, listen, Sakhi," Krishna tried to speak.

"I have listened everything, Vaasudeva." Her voice tuned too cold and devoid of emotions as she looked at Krishna. "I have never imagined that you too can support this pacifist nature of your cousin!"

"My dear friend," Krishna smiled, patting her hands. "Pray, don't misunderstand Jyeshtha. Whatever he is doing is for justice itself. How could you think that Dharmaraj will let go of justice?"

"What justice will come from five villages, Krishna?" she snapped. "Is this for what we have suffered for thirteen years? Is this for what Arjuna had gone through such a hard tapasya? Samrat is not just insulting himself but his ever-devoted brother too who has suffered much more than him."

It felt like sting straight to my heart. I looked away. She always had to reserve a special mention for Arjuna, no matter what!

"What was the need for all these hardships if we were going to give away our Indraprastha to them forever?" Draupadi's question whipped me again.

"Indraprastha will be yours again, Draupadi." Krishna said in consoling tone. "Keep faith on your husbands."

"Faith!" Her facial muscles cringed, expressing sheer anguish of betrayal.

"I did keep faith on them, Krishna. But they failed to stay worthy of it once again. I let go of the ordeal I faced in the fateful dice hall in order to 'keep that faith'. I have not objected Samrat's message to Hastinapura despite of knowing that my sinners will be unpunished if it succeeds." She closed her eyes, pausing to gather herself.

"I accepted my husbands' honour as a sufficient harbinger of justice. But your dear cousins never cared!" She added, opening her eyes. Teardrops running down her cheeks revealed how long she had suppressed them within.

It pained me. Not a single word of hers was wrong. It was true that we had thought only about getting back Indraprastha but not for punishing her wrongdoers. Only Bhima did, but it was I who silenced him.

The guilt of thirteen years chocked my throat. The dotting wife of ours who had not thought of herself but wanted only our good, our prosperity, were we going to disappoint her again?

"Krishna, all I wanted is creating a Bharatavarsha where no woman will ever face what I did." She spoke again. "Cannot I get this much justice too?"

"What you want is my aim too, Draupadi." Krishna said, wiping tears from Draupadi's eyes. "Re-establishing Dharma in this land is all we want. And I assure you that your husbands too are trying for the same mission."

I moved close to Draupadi.

"Give me one more opportunity, Krishnaa." I softly pleaded. "You have never lost faith on us, not even after the disaster of Jayanta sabha. I request you, trust me one more time! If I fail this time too as a husband, I shall leave the next decision entirely to you."

Draupadi observed my face for a while.

"I want to trust you, Aaryaputra. But it's you alone who leaves me confused every time I do." Her eyes betrayed anguish, her voice sounded almost like a whisper.

"Thirteen years ago, I could not understand how my righteous husband could stake me in dice. Neither today can I match the present peace-loving Samrat Yudhishthira with the person I saw in forest. That man who was determined to bring back justice for us, for himself, for this Bharatavarsha, - I don't see him in you now!"

I hid a sigh. It was time that I had to prove myself once again in her eyes.

"He has not changed, Krishnaa. I assure you, I'm still the same person who has prepared himself for war. I have not left the battle that has begun thirteen years ago. I just modified my war strategy a little. Sending this peace proposal to Hastinapura is part of my strategy, Krishnaa. Not escaping the battlefield."

"And what if this strategy fails, Samrat?" she stared at me patiently. "What if Duryodhana accepts?"

I shook my head. "He will not. Because he is more interested in our loss even than his own gain. No matter how more he gets, he always wants us to lose everything and roam forever in forest. His ego and envy will never agree even to part away with five principalities."

Draupadi's brow arched. I exchanged glance with Krishna, to which he nodded.

"I feel that you are going to make another gamble, Samrat!" She muttered. "Risking both your family and subjects, once again."

I smiled dryly, nodding. "You got me correct. I am playing another gambling game with Duryodhana. But situation is not the same now, Draupadi."

She looked away grimacing.

"Thirteen years ago, I didn't know how to play. Now I do. Duryodhana cannot trick me anymore." I said. Draupadi turned her head to me. Her large eyes were squinted in doubt.

"Stay assured, Draupadi." Krishna said. "Thirteen years ago, dice was in Shakuni's hand. Now it's in Dharmaraja's hand from the beginning itself." His eyes beamed in confidence.

"This time I myself am his dice, Sakhi. I shall ensure Jyeshtha's victory. You trust your sakha, don't you?"

Draupadi stared at Krishna for a while, and then, she subtly nodded. I heard her heaving a deep sigh.

"Dear friend, I have promised you that your wrongdoers will suffer their Karmaphala." Krishna added. "I won't break my promise. Just keep patience a little more!"

***

We gathered in the assembly hall again in the evening.

"I shall leave tomorrow morning, Samrat." Krishna formally said. "Give me the message you want me to deliver to the Kuru king."

The entire sabha maintained silence, looking at me. I sensed Draupadi's concerned gaze.

"Give the king my salutations first, followed by the elders." I began. "Tell him that I don't want to malign the names of the revered Kuru ancestors by declaring war within my own household. Though being a kshatriya it's my Dharma to fight for what is mine, I do understand that a battlefield never gives more gain than losses. If war happens, there is no certainty about who will survive and who will not. Weapons will never discriminate, and losses will be equal in both sides. Even a victory at this cost of dear lives will be equal to defeat.

"Hence, Maharaj, I do not want to drag our family's conflict to battlefield. If you disagree to return Indraprastha to us, we request you to give a minimum of five villages. Be it Pramanakoti, Makandi, Jayanta, Varanavata and another fifth one of your choice. I promise that peace will prevail. But not unless this minimum share of our late father's kingdom is given to us."

"Any reason for these specific places?" King Virata's brow arched.

I nodded looking at him. "Certainly. Pramanakoti is the place where Bhima was given poison. Varanavata has seen Duryodhana's attempt of burning us alive. Jayanta is the place where the game of dice had been played. In short, I'm asking them for the return of their own past sins. Let me see how they react."

"There is no doubt that Duryodhana will get angrier to hear this." Bhima commented. "There is no more way of peace." He shook his head.

"Since when *you* want peace, Bhrata Bhima?" Krishna softly chuckled. "I hope you haven't forgotten your vows."

"Not at all, Krishna." Bhima frowned. "It has been me who wanted war since that day of thirteen years ago. And it's me alone who still wants that, no matter what Dharma and Dharmaraj says!" he side glanced at me.

Krishna nodded with a slight smile, glancing at Draupadi whose face had lit up a little.

"You are not alone, Bhrata Bhima. I too am with you in this." Sahadeva said with a straight face. "I cannot support this proposal of peace that has a risk of losing our rights. I request you, Bhrata Krishna, discard this idea. We are going to get nothing from this."

"Maybe you are right. But I have to do my duty." Krishna said. "Anything more you want to tell them, Jyeshtha?" His gaze returned on me.

"Tell Duryodhana that it's better for him to accept our claim than fighting a war." I continued with my message. "Remind him that the ones he depends on, have lost in front of Arjuna alone just six months ago. Tell him that his best friend Karna might daydream on killing Arjuna but in realty he could never stand in front of my brother. How will these people help him to defeat Arjuna when he will be with us four and Panchalas? It should not be the case that now he refuses to give even five villages but after getting killed in Bhima's hand, he finally has to lose the entire world to us."

A brief smile played on Krishna's lips. "Alright. I shall try my best to make him understand this."

"He is a man who never understands what he doesn't want to!" Bhima groaned. "You are trying in vain, Krishna."

"That's his choice. I can only do my part." Krishna looked at Bhima and then he glanced at the others. "I don't know whether I can succeed in this mission or not. But I assure all of you that my emissary will not be fruitless."

Krishna rose.

"I shall make the entire Bharata see who tried to uphold peace and who denied it." He raised a finger. "At the end of everything, even if war happens, I shall ensure that no one can blame Pandavas for that."

"You don't have to stress yourself so much for our sake, Krishna." I held his shoulder. "You just see to it that our mission of Dharma gets fulfilled. That's all I want."

Krishna patted my palms, nodding.

"Don't go alone, Krishna." I said again. "Take Satyaki with you. Those people have no sense even of the norms of emissary. I cannot take a risk on your life."

# CHAPTER NINE

I had never seen Prativindhya thus.

He was among those warriors who never lose their calm even in front of hardest of opponents. Focus and patience was his innate qualities that I had always observed. But he did not seem to be himself today. Not just that he was missing targets one after another. The usually calm warrior in him was now too quick to lose his patience even after he tried a lot to hold it.

As if someone was playing with his concentration.

His fifth arrow deviated from its aim about by three fingers, much more than the previous four. His curled fists knocked his waist. He picked up the next arrow in much hurry. This time, it could not even reach near his target.

"Prati," I moved closer and held his shoulder. "What bothers you, son?"

He turned to me. That sharp gaze was not new to me. Prativindhya had inherited his mother's eyes. His gaze mirrored the same depth of wisdom and empathy, and now, the same anguish too.

For a while, it felt like Draupadi herself was staring at me!

"Why, Janaka?" he almost whispered. "Why this unfair compromise?"

I looked away, heaving a sigh. My guess was correct.

"You promised us justice." He continued, now a little louder. "To mother, to my brothers. Don't tell me you are going to break your promise now."

I let him vent out. For I knew how it hurts to suppress feelings within. I did not have my father to share my pains. He had his. At least now.

"I have not wasted a single moment in the past thirteen years, trusting that my mother would get her justice one day. I have never allowed myself to feel sad in my parents' absence, knowing that I have to prepare myself for the battle of Dharma. How can you crush all my sleepless nights under your mission of peace?"

I sighed again. It was true that I had failed him. I had ruined his childhood. He had complete right to complain against me. I had no escape from this.

"I feel you, my child." I softly said, caressing his head. "I know how hard it has been for you to become a guardian of your younger brothers at the age of ten. Your struggle has been much harder than mine due to absence of your mother." I patted his back.

"But trust me, son, I'm not going to deprive you anymore! As the empire of Dharma will be reestablished, you only are going to be the heir of it."

He shook his head. "That's not all I seek, Janaka. I want my mother to get her justice for which I have readied myself. Pray, don't sell that justice away in the name of peace!"

"What makes you think that I'm selling away justice?" I patiently stared at him.

"Then why are you asking for five principalities, Janaka?" His voice could not hide sheer frustration. "Is the price of my mother's honour so less for you?"

"Prati, I can understand your feelings for your mother. I appreciate that her honour matters to you above everything." I patted his cheeks. "But you are not an ordinary son, my child. You are the future ruler of this Bharatavarsha. You need to care for all commoners of this land as well."

Prativindhya's face turned grave. "I'm not ignorant of my responsibilities, Janaka. But even then I fail to understand how it's going to help our people. We are providing repetitive chances to those sinners. Isn't this delay a risk for the commoners as well?"

"Mistake me not, child. I'm not giving chances to the sinners. I'm giving chances of peace and prosperity to my subjects."

He lifted his surprised gaze at me. I knew he still lacked the understanding to discriminate between vengeance and justice. Maybe it was normal for his age to mistake one for the other. Growing up in Panchala might have added to that misinterpretation. If I had to prepare him as a future ruler of my empire, I had to start from the beginning.

"I would never have sent this proposal of peace had it been a conflict just between us, two segments of Kuru family." I continued, looking at him. "But it's much more than that. It's not just about our loses but of innocent commoners of this country. I cannot use their lives and wealth for my personal interest. If I do, I don't deserve to become their emperor again."

Prativindhya looked up. "Are you trying to prove yourself to your people with this?"

I nodded. "I am, because I owe them this. I know that Duryodhana won't give us even five villages. Still, I sent this proposal to do my final duty to this country. At least Bharatavarsha would know that their emperor has done his part."

"Maybe you are right from your side, Janaka." He admitted with a slow nod. "If that's what you aim for, I won't oppose you in that. Only one request to you. Let justice be your subjects' as you wish. But pray, let it be mother's too!"

"Justice will come, Prati. I promise you that it will. It might be peace or war in the worst possible situation, but it would never be peace or justice. I won't let it be!"

His keen gaze rested on me, as if scrutinising me from inside. Just like his mother!

"Our new empire will build. Be it with or without bloodshed!"

***

"News has come that a few soldiers in our camp have fallen sick." King Virata looked worried.

"It's expected, Maharaj. We mostly have armies from plains of Ganga and Yamuna who are not used to with this weather of north-west." I said. "We should have arranged more for their ease."

The king nodded. "I shall go personally to check the supply of food and water to all. Will ask the royal physician too for accompanying me."

"We cannot thank you enough for the endless help you are providing for us." I joined my palms. "Your friendship is undoubtedly a blessing for us within all these hardships."

He held my joined palm. "What are you saying, Samrat? It's my greatest fortune that I could come to some help for Dharma. My entire family will feel honoured to dedicate themselves for our beloved Uttara's in-laws."

"The very in-laws who failed to even provide a marital home to her!"

I turned back as I heard Sahadeva. His voice was unbelievably calm.

"I apologise to you, Maharaj Virata, for we could not yet give our daughter-in-law the home she deserves." Sahadeva joined his palms to the Matsya king. "But I promise you, it won't take long to rescue our kingdom from Duryodhana's sway."

"I have complete faith in your prowess, Rajkumar Sahadeva." King Virata rose and held his hands. "I know that my daughter will return to her home. Indraprastha will become yours again. The war will be fought." He looked at him with determination. "That's what we all are preparing for."

"You are right. The war *will* be fought." Sahadeva's jaw tightened, his eyes glowed. "If our emperor does not fight for his rights, for justice, I shall do that! Because," he paused a little. "Indraprastha is my home too. The woman who was wronged thirteen years ago, is my wife too."

"Sahadeva!"

"You heard me right, Samrat." He looked at me, his tone reflected the calm before a possible outburst. Even king Virata looked shocked.

"Being the youngest, I have tolerated enough of my elder brothers' 'Dharma' which is nothing but a misnomer of weakness." He vented out frustration. "This so-called Dharma made us fail as husbands, as rulers. But not anymore! If you four want peace, so be it. I shall fight for my wife!" His grip tightened around the sheath of his sword.

"You will, brother." I calmly replied. "But pray, wait a little more. We cannot take the final decision until Krishna's message comes."

"You keep waiting with the others. Leave me alone! If you have your Dharma, I have mine. I have waited for thirteen years to give justice to my wife, trusting that you won't fail her anymore. But I was wrong. It's time to correct myself before it worsens."

My chest twisted in pain. I struggled to hold myself, reminding that all misunderstandings would clear by themselves with Krishna's return.

"I shall wage the war all by myself, without your banner. You don't have to break your word to anyone."

"Do you think this responsibility is yours alone?" I felt aghast.

He gave me a stern stare. "I do not, Samrat. I still think that avenging Draupadi's insult is our joint responsibility. But I cannot keep quiet anymore to see that you are begging for only five villages to her sinners instead of punishing them! How could you even think that her honour's worth is so less?"

Lump formed in my throat. Even my own little brother wanted to break away! How would I even expect then that the Panchalas and Matsyas would not?

"Pray, release me from your bondage of Dharma, Jyeshtha!" Sahadeva fumed. "I'm tired in this prison now. I shall break all norms of morality for punishing them who dared to hurt my wife!"

"Alright, Sahadeva." I slowly nodded. "Do whatever you wish. If you think that breaking away from me will bring justice to Draupadi, then you are free to do that."

No one spoke.

"But remember, Draupadi herself kept us united when we were on the verge of breaking. She had followed us to the exile only because of preserving our unity. Now if you feel that your decision will justify her unnecessary sufferings of thirteen years, then do it! I won't stop you!"

"But I would!" Draupadi walked inside in measured steps.

"Krishnaa!" Sahadeva shook his head, frowning.

"Krishnaa Draupadi is never away from the five Pandavas, Prince!" her voice was calm yet determined. "Breaking away from Pandavas means breaking away from me. I want you five to fight against Kauravas, not against each other. This will not give me justice, Aaryaputra. This will make me lose my battle."

Awed and grateful, I stared at her. Now she was not the same woman who felt disturbed at the proposal of peace. Regality of the empress shone on her face. A different aura that could draw respect from one and all. A declaration that could never be opposed.

"I request you not to take any decision in haste until Samrat Yudhishthira declares war." The empress uttered.

"How can you say this, Krishnaa? Weren't you too against this proposal of peace?" Sahadeva looked aghast.

"I was and I still am. I do want you to fight this war and not to crave for peace. But remember, Rajkumar Sahadeva, you should gather your strength before fighting, not break away from it. Remember that you cannot win a battle without your brothers. Neither can they win without you."

My voice chocked in gratitude. I knew that my empress had finally realised my intention. The very fact that she was still with me was enough to provide me the strength I needed right now.

"Your unity is your biggest power that once transformed even a barren Khandavaprastha to a heavenly Indraprastha. You cannot afford to lose that power when you need it the most. Know that there will be no rule of Dharma even if a hundred of Indraprastha become ours, unless you five stay as one."

Sahadeva lowered his head now.

"I didn't want to hurt you, love. Pray, mistake me not." He muttered.

"I know, Aaryaputra." Draupadi's tone softened. "I understand your concern for avenging me. But you can never do that breaking away from your brothers. Keep a little more patience. Krishna has gone there with a plan. I believe he will not fail us."

Sahadeva nodded a subtle nod. Draupadi met my grateful gaze once, and then slowly walked back to her room. I exhaled after long as the tingling of her anklets faded away.

Our empress had saved us from breaking apart, once again!

# CHAPTER TEN

I could feel the storm that might have happened in the sabha of Kurus.

Krishna retained his usual calmness when he greeted us and took his seat casually, as if nothing happened. But his even smile held satisfaction of success. On the contrary, Satyaki was visibly fuming. Their contrasting reactions hinted that my guess had come true.

"I could not succeed in the aim you have sent me to achieve, Samrat." Krishna evenly informed. "They have not agreed for peace. Duryodhana would not share even the soil collected on the tip of a needle with you, leave alone five villages."

My fists curled at the height of arrogance. But the next moment my fingers loosened. Within all my strategy of making peace, I also had wanted this mission to fail.

It might seem to be my failure to the world, but in real, this was my success.

"As expected." I retorted. "With eleven akshouhinis gathered by his side, Duryodhana thinks he has become invincible. He forgot Arjuna's arrows in Matsya war that had left him and his best friend disrobed. He does not realise that he would have to fall dead on the very soil he denies to share now."

"Didn't the king say anything?" Arjuna narrowed his eyes. "It was his personal messenger Sanjaya who gave us enough lectures on peace just a month ago. Where did those peaceful words go now?"

"The Kuru king's mind changes according to his own interest, Arjuna. Or rather I should say, according to his beloved firstborn's wish." My jaws clenched. "Before sending Sanjaya he was worried for my brothers' vows and prowess. Now since he sees that our army is smaller than his, he doesn't feel the greatness of peace anymore."

Krishna smiled, leaning back. "I must admit that your understanding of the psychology of Kurus is flawless, Jyeshtha. Everyone has reacted to your message exactly as you have already presumed."

"Did our venerable elders give their opinion?" I enquired.

Krishna nodded. "They have tried their best to convince Duryodhana. But as you know, they are just voices present there to whom no one pays heed."

My lips pursed. "They have become 'voices' in present, Krishna. Have they been so in the dice hall, today could have been different!"

"I agree." Krishna admitted. "But I could also sense the guilt in them. They still wish you well. It's just that they cannot break the bondage of duty to Hastinapura."

Duty indeed! Such a duty that could subside their conscience every time Duryodhana wronged! Be it in the dice hall, or in stealing cattle of Matsya!

"Noble Bhishma and Dronacharya have praised you a lot for your message, Samrat." Krishna continued. "They are pleased to see that you are trying to stop the war. That made them even angrier at Duryodhana who denied your proposal straight on face."

I nodded, smiling a little. Krishna had kept his promise. He said that he would ensure that all the blames of war got shifted to Duryodhana. He was successful in it.

"And uncle Vidura? Didn't he say anything?" I looked at Krishna.

Krishna shook his head, sighing. "He has now completely silenced himself in the sabha. Whatever he has said to me, was outside the palace."

My heart ached. I could feel how much indifference and accusation uncle might have undergone before withdrawing himself thus. Maybe he had realised that all his efforts were going to be wasted. The sole voice of Dharma, the conscience of Kuru sabha had finally disappeared.

The last trace of auspiciousness too had deserted the Kurus! There was no doubt that their downfall was near!

"Uncle Vidura wants you to fight, Jyeshtha." Krishna continued. "He understands why you are trying for peace. But he believes that the Kauravas don't deserve your nobility anymore. He has advised you not to waste your energy in this and fight for your rights."

I nodded. I had expected this from him.

"Uncle has said what our true well-wishers would. I believe that even our mother has the same opinion?"

"Certainly. Aunt Kunti has sent her message to you all." Krishna said, glancing at my brothers. "She wants you not to settle up for so less and fight back for your kingdom."

"How is she doing, Krishna?" I whispered; an ocean of emotions churned within me. It had been more than thirteen years that we had not met her.

"Just like a lioness matriarch does when her sons are banished from their rule." He smiled a little. "She has waited long to see you on the throne of uncle Pandu, Jyeshtha. She won't be at peace unless you claim your rights."

"I know, Krishna." I slowly nodded. "Mother has suffered much since her young years. It's our duty now to give her kingdom back to her. And we shall strive for that."

"Is mother displeased with us, Krishna?" Arjuna muttered. I looked at him, knowing that he voiced a pain that had been suppressed within all of us.

"She is a Kshatrani, Arjuna. If she has to see that her warrior sons are reluctant to fight for justice, it's normal for her to feel disappointed. If you want to term it as displeasure, then maybe it is."

"Is this why she did not come to attend Abhimanyu's wedding?" I voiced it. This thought had been eating me up since months. The way mother had stayed away from us even after completion of our exile had spoken a lot about what she wanted us to do.

Krishna smiled again. "Maybe aunt wanted to see you all at Indraprastha and not at Matsya."

I slowly nodded. "I understand, Krishna. Mother is willingly staying at Hastinapura to remind us that our father's kingdom has not yet been ours. And she won't move from there unless we achieve our aim. She is making another sacrifice to encourage us to fight back."

"Hope we aren't going to disappoint her with another negotiation, Samrat?" Bhima gave me a stern look.

"No more question of further negotiations." I shook my head firmly. "Duryodhana won't give us anything and it's clear like daylight now. I just did my duty to them. I have given them choices, but they chose war. Now no more way is left." My fist curled. "Either they will die, or we will!"

"This could have happened much earlier." Bhima groaned. "You wasted time unnecessarily."

"Not at all, Bhrata." Krishna said. "This apparently 'failed' emissary has benefited us in several ways. The Kuru elders are now even more displeased with Duryodhana. Most of the court nobles are praising Dharmaraja's noble intention. The soldiers and commoners of Kurujangala are rooting for your victory now."

"What is our gain in this?" Nakula frowned. "They are never going to fight from our side."

"They aren't. But their hearts will be with you, always." Krishna explained. "Duryodhana has lost his moral support, brothers. Even his army will lack the rock-solid unity that we are going to have." He explained, glancing at me. "Jyestha's strategy could not win peace, but has won entire Hastinapura's heart for sure."

"Now I realise why Samrat insisted on this." Sahadeva slowly nodded. "I failed to sense it earlier." He looked at me with joined palms. "I apologise for opposing your decision, Jyeshtha. Your and Bhrata Krishna's diplomacy is always beyond me."

Sahadeva knelt down at my feet. I lifted him and patted his head, smiling. My little brother exhaled, his face lit up. Then, I turned to Krishna.

"I cannot thank you enough for this success, Krishna. Without your efficient emissary, this could never have turned into our favour. All credit is yours." I patted his palm.

"Not just all credit is Krishna's. All struggles too have been his alone, to ensure your welfare." Satyaki spoke for the first time. His eyes were still crimson.

"I stayed silent for this long on Krishna's request. But not anymore. Since he himself will never talk about his own problems, I have to!" He added, frowning.

The last sentence sounded concerning.

"Krishna, has everything been fine?" I leaned forward with concern, chiding myself for not asking for his wellbeing first.

Krishna just smiled. Satyaki took a quick glance at him and frowned more.

"How on earth can you stay so quiet about your own insults, Krishna?" he cried. "Why don't you let people know the cost you are paying for their good?"

"Satyaki, dear friend, nothing has happened to me." Krishna calmly held his shoulder.

"But something could have happened, Krishna!" Satyaki groaned. "Had your final words not scared that blind king enough, you would have been in the same prison Samba has lived in. But he had his own fault to be there while you did not!"

"What do you mean, Satyaki?" I held my breath. "They were going to seize Krishna?"

"Precisely, Samrat! You were right to guess it. Your cousins do not have the least sense of behaving with a messenger, let alone their own daughter's father-in-law!"

"Attempt to seize an unarmed messenger who carried the message of peace? Have they forgotten the norms of a royal court too?" I could not resist the outburst.

"They have just shown their real nature once again, Jyeshtha." Arjuna's eyes turned crimson, the corner of his lip curled in sheer contempt. "What else to expect from the ones who can humiliate their kulavadhu in open court?" His angry breath was audible in each of his words.

"And those noble elders of Kuru sabha did repeat their job of watching every injustice silently, right?" I muttered, my jaws gritted. "Their so-called loyalty to the Kuru throne did not even let them save the honour of a guest of Kurus!"

"Maybe they didn't even consider Krishna as their guest at all, Yudhishthira." Satyaki said. "His refusal to reside in Duryodhana's mansion might have displeased the Kuru elders."

I looked at Krishna. He understood and nodded. "I did what I felt right, Samrat. As a messenger of Pandavas, I was supposed to stay in Mahamantri Vidura's abode where my aunt Kunti lives. Not with their cousin who has snatched away everything from them."

I observed him for a while. His wisdom had another level which I could not even realise at times. A part of me was convinced that he did it deliberately to ensure that Duryodhana did not listen to his words of peace. That was his strategy which seemed to be a failure but in realty served our purpose. My only regret was that he himself had to suffer humiliation in the process.

Satyaki was right. There was no limit of Krishna's sacrifice for the sake of others. For Dharma. He had never hesitated to put himself at risk for his greater mission.

"You have done your level best for our sake, Krishna." I admitted. "Now we shall do ours. Enough chances have been given. Enough we have waited. But not anymore. Now they will see what Yudhishthira's anger looks like!"

I turned to Arjuna.

"Summon all the leaders of our armies, brother! We need to prepare for the journey to our war camp."

# CHAPTER ELEVEN

"You have been called for an urgent discussion, honourable kings." I addressed the warriors assembled in the sabha.

"As you all know, we had sent a proposal of peace to Hastinapura as the final effort to stop the war. But our emissary has failed." I continued, looking at them. "The next step should be sending a formal call for battle to Hastinapura, followed by our journey to a chosen battlefield. I hope all of you will agree with me on this regard."

"Without a doubt, Samrat." Satyaki spoke first. "There is no reason to waste more time."

"We have come to fight for your sake, Lord of Bharata." Chedi king Dhrishtaketu seconded. "We are with you in this."

"I second ChediRaja." Sahadeva of Magadha nodded. "We have been waiting for this decision. We shall do our best to make Indraprastha yours once again."

I shifted my gaze to the young boys sitting together on the other side. Though they were our sons and the youngest warriors of our side, their opinion mattered too.

"I have made up my mind to fight for my father's kingdom, Uncle." Iravan humbly replied, exchanging a glance with Ghatotkacha. "We both did."

"And so are we." Abhimanyu said. The other five boys nodded in assent.

"Fine." I exhaled. "First, we need to select a place. A spacious ground where chariots, elephants and foot soldiers can move easily and adequate water is available. And," I paused a little, and then added. "A space for cremating hundreds of corpses everyday."

The last part seemed to have caught everyone speechless for a while. But each warrior knew well that there is no certainty of their lives. Neither is there anything to get emotional about the realty of a battle of this large scale.

"I think Kurukshetra will be the best choice." Krishna broke the silence.

"Kurukshetra, the land of Samanta Panchaka?" I turned to him.

"Right." He nodded. "There are the five lakes that Lord Parashurama had created after his killing of evil kshatriyas all over the country. That place has his boon. People dying there in wars are beilived to ascend heaven."

"So be it." I agreed. "Kurukshetra is the place where Lord Parashurama had fulfilled his mission of removing injustice from this land. Let that be our battlefield of Dharma for the same purpose." I glanced at the others. "I'm sending my message to Hastinapura. We shall move for Kurukshetra in a couple of days."

"The choice of place is wise, Samrat." Pandya king remarked. "We would like to know under whom this seven akshouhini of army will march to Kurukshetra. Who will be the guide and director of all these illustrious Maharathas?"

"Pandyaraja is correct." Krishna said. "Samrat, you must declare your Senapati first. All of us, including the soldiers, need to know the commander-in-chief who will lead them."

The others too echoed his thought. I listened patiently. I already had someone in my mind as the Senapati of my side since I had begun planning for war. But it was difficult to declare my choice in front of all. The kings on my side were famous, valorous and experienced, all of them. Each of them had ability to lead my entire army, and maybe each expected to take that place as well. Choosing the one I had wanted might displease them, causing the unity of my army break. I needed to do it wisely.

"It is hard to choose one from all of you, honourable ones!" I said. "Each one of you is capable of ruling this Bharata, let alone this army. But the place of Senapati must be given to one person. Someone who will be able to lead from front. Someone who won't just be a great warrior but also would be there to motivate and unite other great warriors under his banner. Someone who would never give up till his death."

All sat erect, waiting to hear the next. But I was not going to declare the name myself.

"I seek your suggestions." I added, turning to my brothers. "Who do you think should lead our army?"

"Maharaj Drupada." Nakula said without pausing to think. "He is the eldest of our side and our well-wisher. He was student of our Guru Dronacharya's preceptor, and an equal to Gurudeva in warfare. Besides, he is an ideal king who can be the best leader."

I nodded, without commenting. I had no doubt on my father-in-law who had been a second father to me since my marriage. He always wished for grandfather Bhishma and Guru Dronacharya's death and I knew he would strive for that. But it was also true that I had seen him getting egoistic too fast, be it in the rift with Gurudeva or during sending messenger to Hastinapura. I feared that he would not be able to get along with king Virata and other veteran warriors like king Pandya of my side.

"Why not king Virata?" Sahadeva voiced his opinion. "He has helped us in our time of need. He is veteran and well-experienced in battles. I think he will be the best choice."

King Virata? His response to Kichaka in his own royal court flashed in my mind. I just could not think that helpless king as my Senapati. He could be leader of his own army, but not more than that. Someone else was needed who could direct him without disrespecting his position.

"I recommend Dhrishtadyumna." Arjuna suggested. "He has that fire in him that can show us light in the darkness of battles. He is always focused at his target which is an essential quality in a leader. I think he can guide us the most."

I took a deep breath. Arjuna had never gone wrong in reading my mind!

"I would suggest Bhrata Shikhandi's name." Bhima remarked. "We all know that grandfather Bhishma is the most fearsome warrior of the other side. And Shikhandi has vowed to cause his downfall in war."

I exhaled within my mind. It was good to see that my brothers too wanted someone from Panchala as the Senapati, just like I did. Panchalas were not just our in-laws. They were our best friends and always devoted to the purpose of this war. Their ages long rivalry with the Kurus would keep them charged to fight.

And I knew how eager they were to avenge their daughter's insult. Unlike Yadavas who cared so less for Subhadra!

"Krishna, what do you think?" I turned to him.

"I second Arjuna." He said, exchanging a quick glance with his friend. "Dhrishtadyumna has grown up with a strong determination and focus to kill Dronacharya one day. Our commander-in-chief needs to have a specific target like he has."

I nodded, and rose to my feet.

"I thank you all for putting your views on this." I said. "It's clear that majority of us wants Panchalas to lead our army. The reason is also valid. Panchalas are not just our close relatives and well-wishers, they are also enemies of the Kurus since generations. There is no doubt that they can fight against the honourable Kuru elders better than all of us."

Everyone listened with rapt attention.

"I want someone from Panchala family who will have the wisdom and zeal to bring victory. Someone who cares for our good so passionately that he would do everything to protect us. The one who understands his limitations and yet has such a friendly bonding with all of us that his leadership would never cause disrespect. The one who has been the most able Yuvaraj and Senapati of Panchala army since decades yet never caused any rift with his elder brothers." I gave a pause, looked at all and then extended my right arm to Dhrishtadyumna, smiling.

"I declare Panchala Yuvaraj Dhrishtadyumna as the Senapati of Pandavas!"

Dhrishtadyumna rose and bowed to me, followed by the other elders. Aacharya Dhaumya uttered the hymns of abhisheka, pouring water on his head. I greeted him with a tilaka. Krishna played his conch along with my brothers.

"I'm honoured, Samrat." Dhrishtadyumna beamed. "I promise to fulfill this responsibility to the fullest."

I reciprocated the smile, and turned to the rest of the sabha.

"Honourable kings, I believe that distribution of work makes one achieve his aim sooner and more effectively than leaving the entire pressure on a single person." I said. "Hence, I divide the seven akshouhini equally between seven major warriors. The first akshouhini from Panchala will be led by noble Drupada, our venerable father-in-law. And the second one will be under prince Shikhandi's care. I give the one akshouini of Matsya to king Virata's able hands. Yuyudhana Satyaki will lead his own army of Yadavas. Dhrishtaketu of Chedi will guide the fifth group, and Sahadeva of Magadha, the sixth. The rest one will be handled by king Pandya."

Silence followed. I took a look at my warriors. Their glowing faces spoke of consent.

"These seven commanders of seven akshouhini will ensure that their own armies can give their best." I continued. "Every day, each of them will have a specific target to reach and they will focus on that. Senapati Dhrishtadyumna will guide all these seven commanders and keep them united. And Rajkumar Arjuna will guide Dhrishtadyumna as the Sarvasenapati. He will be the Supreme Commander of our army."

"Hail Chakravarti Samrat Yudhishthira! Hail Dharmaraja Yudhishthira!" Everyone cheered. I breathed in relief to see that all had liked my decision.

"You have forgotten to allot task to me, Samrat." Krishna's eyes sparkled.

"I have not, Vaasudeva." I smiled. "I shall give you the most crucial task."

Krishna smiled, nodding. I knew that he was aware of his friend's wish. But I needed to declare it formally in front of all.

"Krishna, you will become the charioteer and guide of Sarvasenapati Arjuna. My brother's responsibility will be yours, and through him, my entire army's too."

"As you wish, Samrat." Krishna beamed. "In this battle of Dharma, I accept my role as 'ParthaSarathi', the charioteer of Pritha's son."

# CHAPTER TWELVE

The camp at Kurukshetra looked so different at night.

Rocks and trees stood still, wrapped in some mystical darkness. The half-grown moon looked pale in front of thousands of flambeaus that appeared almost like burning pyres scattered everywhere.

As if it were the very abode of Yama, the God of death!

I slowly walked ahead. A dark-hued figure was leaning on a tree beside my tent. His gaze was fixed on the moon hidden behind the clouds. I knew what bothered him.

Since Arjuna had heard that grandfather had become the commander-in-chief of Kauravas, he had almost gone into isolation. The reserved speaker that Arjuna was had retreated into silence now. He seemed to have been lost in some other world where nothing of these worldly problems mattered to him at all.

"Arjuna!" I softly nudged him. "Everyone awaits you in the meeting."

Arjuna turned his head to me, managing a nod. We entered my tent where all the major warriors were sitting. The first day's war planning was to be decided. But a weird quietness prevailed there. Curves of worry were visible on most of the brows.

"I knew that they would make Bhishma their Senapati." Dhrishtadyumna spoke first, rubbing his chin.

"Not to worry so much, Dhri. Choosing Pitamaha as his Senapati is Duryodhana's biggest strategical mistake." I calmly remarked.

"Mistake?" Shikhandi's brow raised.

"Of course. He should have targeted our major warriors first. Instead of that he has given the charge to such a person who has already set a condition not to kill us five." I explained, looking at them. "Duryodhana's error is surely going to work in our favour."

"That's fine, Bhrata. But we cannot ignore that Bhishma with weapons in hand is always invincible. Even in this age." Dhrishtadyumna reminded. "So much that his extraordinary valour and invincibility has been rumoured to be his ichchamrityu, the power of controlling his own death. We need a solid planning from the beginning to let him down soon."

"Only Arjuna can handle Pitamaha." I said. "He will be in the front. Yudhamanyu and Uttamouja of Panchala will protect his chariot wheels. Krishna will guide him as charioteer."

"But I don't think they would let Arjuna face Bhishma." Dhrishtadyumna remarked, shaking his head. "They also know that only Arjuna is Bhishma's answer and they would ensure that the two cannot meet."

"Correct. We have to stop them from blocking Arjuna's way to grandfather."

"So we need to divide our Maharathas accordingly with a particular target." Dhrishtadyumna said. "I shall handle Dronacharya. Father Drupada and Bhrata Shikhandi will keep Bahlika and Bhurishrava busy."

"Duryodhana will be in Bhima's share." I added. "Along with his brothers."

"Perfect." He nodded. "But Karna?"

"Keep him aside for the time being." I smiled. "He won't fight under Pitamaha's banner."

"What does that mean?" Dhrishtadyumna's eyebrows met.

"Spies have just brought this information. Karna have had a verbal fight with grandfather Bhishma. He has called Karna 'Ardharatha', half a Ratha. An insulted Karna had vowed that he won't fight as long as Pitamaha is fighting." I casually said, leaning back.

The news had relieved me enough. The less he would fight, the better for my brother.

Bhima smirked. "New way of escaping from the battlefield!"

"What else?" The edge of my lip curved. "If any other warrior was told thus, he would have rather vowed to fight more to prove this wrong. But the Lord of Anga is unique, in everything that he does." More anger welled up inside me as I talked about Karna.

*I too have vowed to see his chopped head!* I reminded myself.

"I shall deal with Shakuni then." Sahadeva proposed. "And Nakula can block Jayadratha."

"Uncle Shalya and king Susharma can be stopped by king Virata and our sons." I thought aloud. "And Abhimanyu can take Duryodhana's sons. Ghatotkacha and Iravan will fight with Alambusha and Ashwasena."

"You are forgetting Kritavarma." Satyaki reminded. "He is in my share." His jaws gritted. I nodded, knowing that Satyaki had been fuming since Kritavarma had joined the Kauravas.

"Alright." I said. "So this is the tentative planning for the first day. After that we can modify this according to situation. Do remember that all of us have to be very careful on the battlefield. Our unity and presence of mind only can save us with this smaller army."

Everyone exchanged glances and nodded.

"You haven't decided my task yet, Samrat." Bhuminjaya gently reminded.

I smiled at his enthusiasm. King Virata's youngest son shared the same excitement to fight this war as our sons did. Abhimanyu and Arjuna's trainings had honed his fighting skills in these months. The young boy who once wanted to retreat from his first battle, was now ready to fight for his sister's marital home. For Dharma.

"You will be in charge of stopping the Trigartas, along with your father and brothers." I declared.

"Thank you for trusting me with this." He joined his palms. "I promise that you won't see me retreating this time."

***

The first ray of dawn fell on the ground of Kurukshetra like blood dripping from wounded bodies. And maybe, wounded souls too!

I steadied myself on my chariot, looking ahead to the opponent army as far as I could see. The palm tree banner of grandfather Bhishma shone above the peak of crowd. Guru Dronacharya's golden banner waved on his left. On my own side, Senapati Dhrishtadyumna stood in front of the army. Arjuna stood on his right. Bhima and the twins stood beside Arjuna.

I saw Arjuna's face turning pale, his brow arched. Did his emotions weaken him again? I felt like talking to him but decided against, glancing at a calm, smiling Krishna holding his white steeds' reins.

I did not have to worry about Arjuna as long as Krishna was with him.

Kauravas' war cry was getting louder. They hailed their Senapati as grandfather took his conch in his hand.

I had one last duty to do before the first conch of war was blown.

I put aside my bow and took off my armour. Dhrishtadyumna raised his eyebrow in obvious question.

"Any problem, Samrat?"

I shook my head and went down my chariot. Now the murmurs began.

"Jyeshtha!" Bhima called. "Where are you going?"

I stepped ahead towards the Kaurava army. Murmurs were audible from my own side now. And laughter from the other side was even louder.

"Ha ha ha!" Duryodhana laughed out. "Feeling scared even before the first arrow could move, so called Chakravarti Samrat?"

"I told you, Jyeshtha, asking for five villages was only out of fear." Duhsashana smirked. "Now he finally understands that fighting against our Maharathas is not a word game to be played from the safe shelter of Upaplavya!" his lips curved in contempt. "Cowards!"

I did not even bother to respond.

"Jyeshtha!" Nakula cried now. "Pray, don't let Bharatavarsha call you a coward at this moment!"

"Return, Jyeshtha!" Dhrishtadyumna called. "I beg you!"

I sensed neighs with sound of multiple chariot-wheels coming closer, behind me.

They were following.

“Stop, brothers!” I raised my right palm. “Stay where you all are!”

“But Samrat...” It was Satyaki now.

“Do what I say!” was my firm reply. They were undoubtedly aghast. But no one argued anymore as they saw me kneeling down in front of grandfather.

“Pranam, Pitamaha!” I touched his feet. He could not speak for a while.

“No auspicious task can be done without elders’ blessings.” I continued with joined palms. “This war is a battle of Dharma for me. For all of us. I seek your blessings before that.”

“Yudhishthira! Child!” Grandfather muttered almost in a trance. I waited till he gulped his emotions.

“I knew that you would come to take my blessings before war.” His voice was half-chocked. “I would have rather cursed you for defeat if you did not!”

Curse for me, and participation for Duryodhana? Even after coming to the battlefield to kill me and my family? How wonderful, Pitamaha!

I sent the reply back to my throat. I won’t fight with words anymore. My weapons would do all the talking from now on.

“But now I bless you from all my heart and soul, my child. Vijayi Bhava! Be victorious!”

“Your blessing is invincible armour for us, Pitamaha.” I bowed. “But you too know that, we cannot achieve victory as long as you are fighting against us. You yourself will stand on the way of your blessings this time, sire?”

Grandfather thought a little. I sensed a slight movement of his jawlines behind his white beard, indicating a subtle smile.

“Smart you are, Yudhishthira!” he slowly nodded. “But you too know that I am bound by my promise. I cannot fight on your side, Vatsa. Except that, whatever you might want from me, I shall give you when time comes. Till then, let me pay my debt to Hastinapura."

I bowed to him again and moved to Guru Dronacharya.

"Pranam, Gurudeva!" I bowed. He came down from his chariot and raised me.

"Only you can have this humility to bow down to elders who stand as your enemies now." He patted me. "I'm proud of having a shishya like you, Yudhishthira. You do not need to ask for my blessings. Know that my heart and soul stay with your side alone, always." He paused a little, and sighed. "But I cannot join you physically, Vatsa!"

What else he could have said except this! The teacher who had not hesitated even to chop a young archer's thumb one day for the sake of his loyalty to Hastinapura, the Guru who could use his students to fulfill his vengeance, was expected to stand with his hosts only at this moment. I had no expectation from him anymore.

"Remember, Yudhishthira, when I first came to Hastinapura, starving from poverty, it was you who first promised me that the Kurus would feel honoured to serve me forever?" his lips curved into a sad smile. "Who knew back then, that this service would bind me to the lifelong debt of Kurus! They have fed this hungry mouth and in exchange, bought my loyalty." He shook his head. "I cannot leave them now!"

"I have not come to you asking for your participation, Gurudeva." I calmly replied. "They say a Guru lives in his successful disciples. And I already have you on my side in forms of your students."

His old eyes sparkled in pride now, as I saw him glancing at Arjuna once.

"True you are!" he mused. "May my students succeed in securing your victory, Yudhishthira! Vijayi Bhava!"

"I am honoured." I joined my palms. "But as you know, victory does not come with Guru's blessings alone. His guidance is inevitable for that." I looked at him patiently. "May I seek your advice for my victory, Gurudeva?"

"I knew you would say this." He smiled. "And as your teacher, I'm bound to respond.

"Listen, Yudhishthira! There is no one on this mortal world who can defeat me as long as I have weapons in my hand. You five and the Panchala princes might be my students, but still you will be unable to kill me unless I give up fighting." He looked at me meaningfully. "You are wise. I won't tell you more than this."

I nodded. "Thank you, Gurudeva! I shall remember your advice."

I moved to Kulaguru Kripacharya then. Taking blessings from him and uncle Shalya, I went back to my chariot. My brothers and friends looked relieved now.

"Let the war begin now, Senapati." I gave my command to Dhrishtadyumna.

# CHAPTER THIRTEEN

"Wait a bit, Samrat Yudhishthira!"

I looked in front, wondering who it could be. A chariot from the eleven akshouhini of the other side showed some movement. I waited till it reached me. A familiar tall figure stood on it.

"Yuyutsu!" I muttered.

"I have a plea to you, Lord of Bharata!" Yuyutsu bowed to me. "Please allow me to fight on your side!"

I observed his expression for a while. He was the only son of the Kuru king who had always been in our favour since childhood, as much as he could as a son of maid. But as we grew older, he had gone much quiet during his step-brothers' misdeeds to us. Neither did I see him speak a word in the dice hall.

Why this sudden change now?

"But you must know that such switch of sides should not be done on the battle field." I calmly said. "You have come here mentally committed to your father and brothers. You should be with them only."

"Don't take my offence, Samrat." He sighed, looking down. "There is no greater regret for a warrior than to feel forced to be on a side he doesn't want to be. Every warrior, irrespective of his class and ability, deserves complete freedom to take his own decision." He humbly replied and joined his palms. "You have given one last chance even to brother Duryodhana. Won't you give me one, to correct my wrong choice?"

"What made you surrender against your will, Yuyutsu? And what made you change that decision now, at this last moment?" I looked straight though his eyes. They betrayed guilt and pain now.

"It's my sense of duty to my father and brothers that had held me back for so long." He softly admitted. "But at the same time, not standing against sister-in-law Draupadi's insult and your exile has eaten me up. I have been torn between two duties of mine since thirteen years." He heaved a sigh. "I regret for being unable to see my Dharma earlier."

"You don't have to be so hard on yourself, Yuyutsu. I know you are with Dharma at your heart." I softly said.

He shook his head. "No, Jyeshtha. Being with Dharma just at heart benefits no one. Kumbhakarna knew that his brother Ravana was wrong to abduct Devi Sita but still fought for him. Neither his advice nor his sacrifice could bring a change in Ravana. For a greater good, Kumbhakarna's way does not work, Samrat. That requires being Vibhishana who broke away with his family for Dharma. And I too have come to you for the same reason."

"For which greater good do you want to break away, Yuyutsu?" I patiently asked.

"For the sake of commoners, Samrat. For the lowest class of people for whom no one cares." His eyes now shone in determination.

"In front of you this is not Maharaj Dhritarashtra's son or Yuvaraj Duryodhana's brother. This is a son of a Vaishya palace maid, a representative of working class people of Hastinapura who never got a good life since you have left them. I have come here on behalf of all Vaishyas and Shudras of Kurujangala. We need you, Dharmaraj! Only you can bring the change to us that we all look for."

Yuyuysu came down of his chariot and knelt down at my feet.

"I beg you, Dharmaraj! Allow me to fight for a better life of my community! For the people like us!"

"Arise, brother!" I lifted him.

"I respect your feelings, Yuyutsu. But being Vibhishana comes at a huge cost. I hope you know that what everyone will call you if you join me now?"

He nodded, smiling a little. "Traitor, right? Let them, Jyeshtha! I shall know that I never betrayed with Dharma. Let the glory of Vibhishana be mine that I never compromised when it came to justice."

"If you are this determined to fight for Dharma, I welcome you to the Pandava army with all my heart." I smiled. "You have done what many other illustrious ones could not, Yuyutsu. May the world never forget to hail you for being this strong."

Yuyutsu bowed and went back to his chariot. I instructed Dhrishtadyumna to show Yuyutsu a position that would suit him.

***

The dance of Mahakaala had begun on the field of Kurukshetra.

Dust flew from the feet of horses that seemed to blind not just our eyes but conscience too. Blood flowed from all the bodies, and perhaps, from all kinds of relations too that had been injured. All the known, even dear faces, went unrecognizable in the heat of war. Arrows shot in hundreds created darkness around us, as if even Sun God had closed his eyes seeing the violence going on.

Dhrishtadyumna had instructed Bhima to take the lead of Vajra vyuha we had constructed. Led by him, Abhimanyu and his five brothers launched the first attack on Duryodhana and his brothers. Dhrishtadyumna himself joined the group along with Nakula and Sahadeva.

I saw grandfather Bhishma rushing to protect Duryodhana. Along with him, came Guru Dronacharya and his son Ashwatthama. They surrounded my brothers and sons.

"Drive forward!" I ordered Indrasena, a sense of urgency entering my voice. Before I could reach my brothers, an arrow whooshed over my head. I ducked instinctively. The arrow hit my flagpost. The wood splintered with a sharp crack. My golden moon banner fell down on the ground.

I looked up. Uncle Shalya stood in front of me. My first opponent in the battle of Dharma!

My first arrow smashed his bow. Before he could take another, I pierced him with five arrows one after the other. He hurled a spear at me. My bowstring went loose. I found myself holding just the half of my bow. I threw the broken bow away and quickly picked up another. I had to stop his progress and decided to aim at his wheels. My arrows found their target! . His frame trembled in fury.

I did not stop shooting more. Soon king Shalya was covered with arrows, bleeding profusely. Still he managed to change his chariot. His next arrows struck me on my chest and both forearms. Those sharp edges penetrated my armour, drawing blood. I gritted my teeth in the sharp pain but did not waver. My arrows found their mark on Shalya's horses. They collapsed one after another and skidded in mud. Their deafening neighs blocked the noise of battles around me. My next arrow hit the throat of Shalya's charioteer. His head fell on the bloodied mud. His headless body did not tremble for long.

The Madra king looked perplexed. Before he could board another chariot, I shot another arrow on his chest. A surge of fresh blood spilled from his mouth. He sank on his motionless chariot, holding the flagpost.Bottom of Form

Wiping the dripping blood from my arms, I turned to the general battle. Bhima had taken the charge of Duryodhana. Dhrishtadyumna was having a hard time against Guru Dronacharya. Both were at their best, yet no one could overcome each other. My stomach churned seeing Abhimanyu battling against grandfather Bhishma. He was the youngest of the children and there was his opponent, the valourous Kuru patriarch whose age showed no effect on his prowess. But soon my nerves eased up. Abhimanyu's style of fighting was nowhere less than his father Arjuna. I saw grandfather getting cornered. That sense of relief followed me as I drove ahead. Bhima's roar was audible now. He must have been overcoming the eldest Kaurava.

Surges of dust swirled in the air, blocking my vision at times. Yells of dying soldiers and animals were too deafening to ignore. I did not see who was where. Bunches of broad-headed sharp arrows were showered from all directions, blurring my vision. I had to duck several times to save my head. My heart thudded loud as I saw my golden crown falling off.

It was a close call! The arrow could have found my neck instead!

I saw a couple of half-moon shaped darts beheading my wheel-protectors. Then, the ones protecting their backs lost their heads too. Those blood-drenched heads fell on the mud as if a violent storm was making ripe coconuts fall from the trees.

Who was doing this? I ordered Indrasena to drive towards the noise, my heart pounding beneath my chest. Such speed and far sight could not be any ordinary archer's. The only person who could have done this was...

Gangaputra Bhishma! There was his chariot! The palm-tree banner waved proudly atop it.

Wasn't he engaged in a duel with Abhimanyu just a while ago? When did that end? Was Abhimanyu alright?

I could not think much. The next thing I saw was the soldiers of my cavalry getting struck in a row. A volley of arrows claiming their lives. The horses and their riders' lifeless bodies heaped up in front of me. Smell of flesh and blood made it difficult to breathe. My chariot wheels drenched in the blood of my own warriors! A pang of grief hit my sense as I saw the elephants thumping those fallen bodies, and the foot soldiers and messengers rushing over them to make ways.

What an undeserving end for the warriors of Dharma!

It broke my heart when I found even myself doing the same. My chariot was also driving ahead over those bodies of the ones who gave up their lives for me. But even that was not easy. The bloodied corpses, broken arms, chopped heads lay scattered around us. Finding ways to run the chariot in a desired speed was difficult even for a skilled charioteer like Indrasena.

Within a while, that entire place turned into a crematory.

The Kaurava Senapati was in no mood to stop. He seemed to have been enjoying the taste of slaughtering the Pandava army. After routing the horse riders, he had now targeted the foot soldiers. His arrows showered on my army like fire catching the grass. Within a few blinks of eyes, more corpses piled up in my way.

My soldier's deafening screams were the only thing that I could hear.

*This has to be stopped!*

Where was Arjuna? I looked around in search of him. My eyes found Satyaki, just returning victorious from a battle against Kritavarma.

"Satyaki, ask Arjuna to stop Pitamaha." I ordered. "Don't let him finish our army."

I would have driven towards grandfather but the Madra king had again come for me by then. As I involved myself in the duel with him, twang of Gandiva assured me.

Arjuna had come!

The Kuru patriarch countered his favourite grandson. In between my own battle, I could see nothing except bunches of arrows being shot from both sides, covering each other. Krishna's Panchajanya's notes were assuring. I felt relieved to concentrate on my own battle.

King Shalya gave me a harder duel this time. I lost my chariot and bow twice. Thanks to Indrasena's skill, I persisted. When I could finally defeat my opponent, I found that Arjuna was still fighting against grandfather.

I glanced at the sky. It was almost midday. Still there was no result in their duel except that grandfather could not continue killing our army.

Why was this duel dragging so long?

I observed my brother for a while. His style of fighting surprised me. Not just because Arjuna was not using the divyastras he had achieved with so much hardship. But he was not fighting to the best of his efforts. He was just defending grandfather's arrows with equal strength, despite of having the ability to turn fiercer.

As if he was not himself today! Some spirit had overpowered him to stay so low!

I saw Krishna turning back and talking to Arjuna. His motivation seemed to have worked. Arjuna returned to his real form soon enough. His sharpest arrows ran to grandfather in brunches.

Grandfather's armour broke. Blood flowed from his chest and arms. The Kaurava commander chose not to answer back. Instead he went back to crushing my army. His arrows and darts now kept showering like rains on my ordinary soldiers.

As if he was answering Arjuna's arrows by killing his army!

If this continued, we would lose one akshouhini of our army today itself! Perhaps even more!

I looked around for help. The eldest Matsya prince Shankha fought well against uncle Bhurishrava. Abhimanyu was overpowering Brihadvala, the king of Kosala. Arjuna had been involved in fighting against Avanti princes. Deciding in a while, I ordered Indrasena to drive towards grandfather.

I stopped in front of grandfather and blew my conch to give him warning. He turned to me; his face showed wrath mixed with annoyance. It was clear that he did not want to fight me or my brothers. He just wanted to kill the soldiers who seemed to him as invaders to Hastinapura. But I could not allow him to do that.

I pierced grandfather with two arrows quickly to engage him in duel. He replied back with three arrows, each piercing through my armour. Blood gushed down my arms and shoulders. I killed his horses and the protectors of his chariot wheels. He changed the chariot even before I could think. The next moment I found my chariot sinking down to the ground with a loud yell of my horses. I picked up a sword and jumped down my chariot. Grandfather too did the same. After that I heard nothing except frequent clanging of swords. He retaliated my each blow. Surge of blood erupted in the air, mixing with the dust that flew. I persisted despite the severe wounds on my shoulders and arms. Blood flowed from my both palms, threatening my grip over the sword to slip. I invested all my strength in my grip and launched the best blow I could. Grandfather's sword slipped from his hand. He held it before falling on ground. I steadied myself for the next attack from him but to my surprise, he drove away with a reluctant gesture.

His weird withdrawal caught me unawares until I heard the familiar twang of Gandiva. Grandfather again started his duel with

Arjuna. Uncle Shalya rushed to me again. Indrasena quickly brought me a new chariot. As I boarded it, Shalya hurled a dart at me, the weapon carrying all desperation to avenge his previous loses. I picked an arrow and cut his spear midway. His arrow cut my bow and felled my crown.

"Samrat!" I heard a cry. The next moment, young Bhuminjaya jumped in between us and guarding me, faced king Shalya. His frame looked radiant in determination. His fast-moving arrows spoke of Arjuna's teachings. King Shalya looked annoyed at this sudden interference. He tried to remove Bhuminjaya but the boy persisted, making his opponent bleed through a broken armour. Shalya's brother saw this and came running to help his elder. I hurried and blocked his way.

King Shalya's brother cut my flagpost. I broke his bow in reply. He picked up a sword. I took mine and came down my chariot. Our swords clang against each other, generating sparks. I increased my force on his sword. He quickly withdrew and stepped back. I launched a quick blow on him. Blood flowed from his armour. He stumbled a little. But he recovered soon and hurled his sword at me. It hit my left arm. I ignored the heavy flow of blood and countered the attack. His sword fell off his grip. Almost immediately, Bhuminjaya rode on my chariot. Uncle Shalya had killed his charioteer. Bhuminjaya fought bravely but lost the horses again.

Indrasena sprung up to get new horses. But Bhuminjaya could hardly wait. I saw him jumping on a large elephant he found close. He guarded me from both the Madra warriors and faced them alone. He seemed to be at the peak of his enthusiasm. I did not feel right. He was too inexperienced for this kind of general combats. I faced Shalya's brother to make him fight me instead the boy. He did accept. I could not follow with Bhuminjaya next, focusing on the task at hand. By the time my opponent fainted, I heard a loud roar of elephant, followed by a familiar scream.

The first thing I saw was Bhuminjaya's elephant lying on a pool of blood. My breath raced as I looked for the boy. There he was, tossing about on the ground in pain. King Shalya's spear had pierced

Bhuminjaya's armour and emerged from his back. His youthful and energetic body still struggled to fight that killer blow, refusing to give up. Lump formed in my throat. The boy was still clasping his bow tight, as if he could not just accept his death nearing him. But his strength gave up. In front of my blurred vision, the young body of king Virata's brave boy stopped moving. His head rolled to one side.

The setting sun's last rays mirrored Bhuminjaya's blood-drenched body.

# CHAPTER FOURTEEN

The entire camp felt lifeless. Light from thousands flambeau could not remove the darkness inside hearts. Our soldiers seemed to have lost half of their initial enthusiasm on the first day itself.

I could not meet king Virata's eyes. It was dreadful for me even to imagine how it might feel to light your own son's pyre yourself! Somewhere deep down in my heart I felt guilty for his irreplaceable loss. Bhuminjaya was of our sons' age. The boy trusted us. He dedicated himself for us till his last breath. What could I do to protect him, being the leader?

*How will that emperor brighten Bharata's future who could not even save the future generation from dying?*

"Twenty-three hundreds of foot-soldiers died today." I heard Dhrishtadyumna breaking the cold silence of my tent. "And seven hundreds of..."

"I am aware of the number of casualties." I raised my hand to cut him off, and slowly walked away from the meeting, without bothering the surprised faces.

I came out of the tent. The stars and moon looked pale in front of the light that came from hundreds of pyres. I closed my eyes, only to sense that these dead soldiers' widows and children lamenting and cursing upon me. Young Bhuminjaya's smiling face shone in my vision. His last words still rang in my ears.

*"You won't see me retreating from my battle anymore, Samrat!"*

I pursed my lips. He did keep his promise. He had paid the greatest Gurudakshina to Arjuna whom he considered his mentor. One day, Arjuna had encouraged Bhuminjaya to not give up and fight. The boy did follow his lesson to his deathbed. He had given up his life to make Dharma win.

But Arjuna himself could not yet charge himself up. To prevent this huge number of casualties on the very first day. To stop grandfather. To end this war soon.

“Samrat!” a dark arm warmly held my shoulder. I knew who he was. The one I needed the most right now.

“I did not want this, Krishna!” I muttered. “It feels like I’m snatching away these innocent lives for my own selfish reason.” I pointed to the burning pyres.

“Neither did I want this, Jyeshtha. But I told you, some price has to be paid for the sake of a greater cause.” Krishna gently squeezed my shoulder. “We are just doing that.”

I slowly nodded. “I know. I had agreed to pay this cost when I decided war. But shouldn’t we at least try our best to minimize the deaths, Krishna? If we cannot, what benefit are we going to bring in this country where only widows and orphans will survive to lament forever?”

Krishna nodded subtly. “We should have been more careful when Gangaputra Bhishma is our opponent Senapati. Maybe we are taking him too lightly.”

“We are not taking him lightly. It’s us who are being light in front of him. Our Sarvasenapati Arjuna himself is not giving his best whenever the Kuru elders counter him.” I voiced it. The entire day Arjuna had restrained himself as much as he could, especially in front of grandfather and Gurudeva.

“Arjuna could have easily stopped grandfather from this mass-killing. But he chose not to!” I groaned.

“Arjuna is seized within his own emotions, Jyeshtha.” Krishna softly said. “He simply cannot think of killing his beloved grandfather.”

“I know the depth of his love for Pitamaha. After all it was Arjuna who shared the closest bond with him since childhood. But this is a battlefield, Krishna. Not our home where we can afford to express love to a relative who fights against us. I know that my brother can kill an invincible grandfather tomorrow itself if he wants." I shook my head, sighing. "But he does not want to do that!"

"Your disappointment is justified, Jyeshtha." Krishna calmly replied. "As the king and leader of Pandavas, you have complete right to complain. Not just against Arjuna but also against me. You have given the responsibility to guide him in my hands. I could not do that despite of my best effort."

"I am not blaming you, Krishna. I have seen you talking to him several times whenever he seemed down."

"I have tried enough to charge him up." He nodded. "Arjuna was convinced, too. But only until he faced his revered elders." Krishna hid a sigh.

I shook my head. "This cannot continue. We have to do something."

"Bhrata Bhima is giving his best. All the Panchalas too. Even our Abhimanyu and his brothers are no less than Yama's messengers on battlefield." Krishna tried to assure me. "Keep faith on them."

"I do have faith on them. I know that none of them shares Arjuna's emotions towards grandfather. But still, it's Arjuna alone who knows all the divyastras, Krishna. Without them, someone like Parashurama-shishya Bhishma cannot be defeated." I looked at him. "Arjuna has to shoulder this responsibility by himself. None else can do this."

"That's correct." Krishna nodded. "Worry not. I shall try my best to bring his real form back. Just give me a little time."

***

*After fourth day of war:*

Forty thousand today.

Everyday the number of burning pyres kept on doubling the previous day's count. And still I could do nothing to stop this!

I walked restlessly around my camp. Countless wounded bodies were piled up at the respective tents for treatment. Some of the soldiers were too severely injured to survive till tomorrow's sunrise. I knew that the number of pyres would increase even more. As it did in the past three days too.

And tomorrow night, it would be even more than this!

There was a single person, a noble one, solely responsible for these innocents' lives deserting their bodies. Our venerable grandfather, the eldest Kuru patriarch Bhishma. He had become unstoppable now. He seemed like a fire standing in the battlefield who was always ready to swallow whoever would come in front of him.

The noble grandfather who was still affectionate to us, had turned into Yama himself for our own soldiers. He had taken this way to prove his loyalty to the Kuru throne. Or maybe, to Duryodhana who seemed to have been complaining everyday to him for not killing us.

*When will this stop?*

A sharp cry made me turn round. Two soldiers walked ahead, carrying a bed where lay a young body that had just lost the life-breath. At a distance, other soldiers were arranging woods for another pyre.

*One more for the day!*

Something churned in me. I hurried to pay my last homage to the martyr who had given his life for me.

*Whoever you are, warrior of Dharma, Samrat Yudhishthira will forever be in debt to you!*

They took the body to the pile of woods. The white cover from his face flew in wind. And I froze there.

Maitravarma! Satyaki's youngest son!

I felt a stabbing pain within my heart. Satyaki's nine sons had died today during battle. Only this last one was still alive, struggling with Yama. Now he too had given up.

Guilt replaced my every other feeling. Satyaki was always ready to jump in to support us whenever needed in battlefield. But we could do nothing for his sons when uncle Bhurishrava attacked them together. Our true friend, who defended us even at the cost of breaking away from most of the Yadavas, we caused the loss of his progeny too!

The yells of injured soldiers were dying down one by one. I watched more corpses being carried to the pyres. A part of me felt restless. I wished this war to end soon. But that did not seem to happen, thanks to my own brother who still could not reveal his fierce form in front of Kaurava Senapati. Arjuna's mild fight against grandfather still kept allowing the Kuru patriarch to turn more violent everyday.

Arjuna would not kill his grandfather. The eldest Kuru would not stop destroying my army behind his vow of not killing us five. How long we would sit quiet and let this continue? *How many more lives we need to give away before this stops?*

Satyaki sat at a corner of the tent. He had fallen completely quiet since Maitravarma had left his last breath. All my efforts of consoling went in vain. That wordless pain in his eyes made my heart ache.

My eyes met Arjuna's vacant gaze. He too sat numb, without a word. I knew that Satyaki's pain had affected him too. I dearly hoped that he would come out of his shell at least after this. That he would fight with his full might at least now, to stop grandfather who had become a killing machine for our army just in four days.

"Such unstoppable form of Pitamaha was beyond my imagination." I heard a disappointed Bhima. "What has happened to him out of sudden?"

"He is trying to compensate for his vow of not killing you five." Shikhandi commented, frowning. "After all, he has to do something to prove his loyalty to the Kurus!"

"I am shocked to see that the great pillar of morality is continuously breaking the rules of war that he himself has made before war began." Bhima groaned, his fist hit his thigh. "He decided that a Ratha can fight only against another Ratha. Now he is killing hundreds of foot soldiers in a day!"

"The matter is serious, brothers." Dhrishtadyumna pressed his temple. "We already are with lesser army than theirs. Losing such a huge number of soldiers everyday is making it worse. Mahadeva forbid, if only we are alive with all our armies dead, we have to lose."

"Maybe that's what Pitamaha wants, Dhrishtadyumna." I softly said. "Our loss."

Arjuna turned his head to me.

"Maybe we shall never know how he himself is bleeding everyday to cause our loss. To cause their loss whom he wanted to win. We shall never know what an unkind pressure he is going through, to prove his loyalty to Kuru throne." He muttered. Pain and sympathy sparkled in his eyes. "We shall not know how badly Duryodhana might be misbehaving and pressing him for this!"

His chocked voice churned a spark of emotion in me as well. I knew Arjuna was correct. The Kuru Yuvaraj must have been squeezing his grandfather's blood and sweat for his own interest. A part of me felt bad for the helpless old man who had to stand on battlefield at this age, just to pay his debt to the Kurus.

"You are not wrong to sympathize with him, Arjuna." I admitted. "But we have to keep that sympathy outside the battlefield. Because the Kaurava commander will never sympathize with us."

"The Kaurava commander did promise to not kill his main opponents." Arjuna softly reminded. "Maybe even at the cost of his own insult from the Kurus."

"That is his guilt, not sympathy." I was grave. "And his promise is only for us five. Not for our friends. Not for the ordinary soldiers. We cannot let them die in his hands just because he won't kill us."

"We are doing our best to protect them." Arjuna calmly stared at me. "Aren't we?"

"Then how come every day the number of deaths is exceeding the previous ones?" I patiently stared back at him. "Why can't we get rid of the Kaurava Senapati?"

"Pitamaha is disciple of Parashurama, Samrat." Arjuna grimaced. "Defeating him would require more effort."

"Pitamaha's so-called invincibility is just a myth, Arjuna. He stood defeated in front of you in Matsya war. He had no reply to your Aindra weapon just yesterday. He will meet his defeat for sure. All you need to do is keeping your emotions at bay while fighting him." I looked straight to his eyes. "That's the only 'effort' we still lack."

Arjuna's gaze dropped to the ground. I heard his sigh.

"I know it hurts even to think of killing the grandfather whose love is so precious to us. But now he is no more the same. We never wanted to fight him, brother. It's he who chose to stand in our opposite. If that is his Dharma, removing him from our path of victory is ours too. Dharma cannot win unless his death. He has to die."

Arjuna looked up to meet my gaze. His eyes did not hide the pain within.

"I did not want to sound so harsh, Arjuna." I was calm. "But I had to. I am the king. I am bound with duty to every single person who has come to fight for me. Those piling up bodies of nameless foot soldiers might be normal to others but not to me."

No one spoke.

"This war is for a greater mission, Sarvasenapati Arjuna. We have to remove every hinderance blocking that aim even if it's our grandfather Bhishma. Otherwise there is no meaning of wasting everyone's blood and sweat thus.""

"Your mission won't fail, Samrat!" Krishna came forward. "Dharma will win. If Arjuna is unwilling to kill Bhishma, I shall do that!"

"Not happening, Vaasudeva." I shook my head. "Whatever might come to us, we cannot and shall not let you break your vow for our reason."

"Jyeshtha, my vow is never greater than Dharma's victory." Krishna's jaw tightened. "I have to fight if I must."

"Hold on, Krishna. You don't have to break your vow." Arjuna spoke after long. My gaze returned on him. He now looked different. Determination has replaced that deep pain and guilt in his eyes.

"My emotions won't follow me tomorrow to the battlefield." He added, looking at us. "I promise."

# CHAPTER FIFTEEN

*The eighth day:*

Today my morning had begun with four arrows hitting my four horses together.

Indrasena was always skilled enough to help me change chariots fast. Boarding the new vehicle I looked for my first guest on battlefield today. It was king Shrutayu.

He shot a bunch of arrows at me. Each stung on my chest, beneath the armour. I replied back, shooting both at him and the protector of his chariot wheels. His next arrows drew more blood from my both arms. Fury replaced my physical pain.

This was just waste of time!

I shot a boar-ear shaped arrow at Shrutayu's chest, causing him vomit blood. Bow slipped from his grip. I shot another half-moon-shaped arrow. He ducked just in time. My arrow found his flagpost, throwing his banner off.

Shrutayu did not take much time to recover. He steadied himself soon and attacked me with more rage. I cut off his bow and without giving him time, killed his charioteer. Even before he could understand, another bunch of arrows from my bow pierced his four horses. Shrutayu then jumped down his motionless chariot and fled away as fast as he could.

After Shrutayu escaped, I drove towards grandfather whose full attention was in killing the foot soldiers. Uncle Shalya came in between to stop me. Realising that I needed to reach the Kaurava Senapati soon, I threw four darts at the Lord of Madra. King Shalya lost all his horses. I quickly turned to proceed.

I moved forward, slashing the opponents whoever came to stop me. A messenger came with news that Iravan had won over Shakuni's five brothers. Four of them lost their lives to the valiant son of Arjuna, while the fifth one fled with his life. I exhaled with a smile. But then the next messenger came to inform me that Duryodhana had sent his friend Rakshasa Alambusha to avenge his dead uncles.

"Where is Arjuna?" I asked the second messenger.

"He is busy at the other side, fighting Duryodhana and his brothers."

"Ask Ghatotkacha to go for Iravan's help." I ordered and proceeded further.

Grandfather did not seem to have expected me. But he faced me with full might. I pierced him with sharpest of my arrows. Blood gushed down his body but he did not seem to be affected much. My next arrow knocked down his palm tree banner. He replied back with more arrows that hit me everywhere on my body. I sliced the throat of his wheel protector of left side and shot a dart at him. He cut it off in the midway. His arrows then made my four horses collapse on the mud.

"Jyeshtha! Here!" Nakula quickly offered his chariot to me. I rode on it and found Bhima and Sahadeva too had come to my help by then. Grandfather pierced Bhima on his chest and beheaded Sahadeva's charioteer. Nakula tried to kill grandfather's horses but failed.

The news of Kaurava Senapati being attacked by Pandavas might have spread everywhere. Duryodhana himself came to join grandfather with Jayadratha, Guru Kripacharya and his brother Chitrasena. A general battle began between us. Arrows launched on us from all directions and we too answered with equal numbers. Surroundings went almost dark with the shower of arrows. Dust flowed to my eyes repeatedly. My chariot kept stumbling over chopped off limbs, broken flagposts and chariot wheels that were scattered everywhere.

Bhima had managed to injure Duryodhana enough to make him withdraw. Nakula had overpowered Jayadratha in sword-fighting. Sahadeva fought well with Chitrasena while I fought against Guru Kripacharya. Seeing his warriors on the verge of defeat, Grandfather went more violent than before. He shot multiple arrows at us one after another. Nakula lost his charioteer and Sahadeva, his new steeds. Grandfather then focused on Bhima and me.

He pierced both of us together with a good number of arrows. I continued as much as I could, but sensed that my strength gradually slowed down with continuous bleeding from my chest and shoulders. To my and everyone's surprise, grandfather stood unaffected even after so many deep wounds all over his body.

He was now in his most rare, most violent form. Even mighty Bhima could not stand long in front of him.

As Bhima gave up, Grandfather turned to me and cut my bowstring. I changed my bow and shot as many arrows as I could at once.

He held his chest to hold himself. The next moment his arrow sliced my flagpost and two more arrows took my crown off. Warm blood tickled down my forehead. For a while, I saw darkness.

I could not know how long I took to recover. The first thing I heard was a familiar loud scream.

Ghatotkacha! I remembered that I had sent him to Iravan's help.

"Samrat, Alambusha had slain Aarjuni Iravan. Ghatotkacha is fighting Alambusha to avenge his dead cousin." Someone spoke to me in low voice.

I felt like receiving another fresh injury straight to my heart.

Iravan was no more!

For a while, I could not even speak. The messenger kept narrating his final battle with Alambusha.

"The Rakshasa deceived Iravan with his illusive strategies. But the son of Arjuna overcame everything." He informed. "Alambusha killed Iravan's maternal grandfather, Naga chief Kauravya, in front of his very eyes and then beheaded him with a sword while he was grieving."

My fists curled. That was the real deceit to take opportunity of someone's weakness.

"Inform Arjuna soon. And take Iravan's body to our camp with respect." I said, and turned around. Battlefield was not a place of emotions for sure. Neither was there time to mourn. Yet I knew that the loss of my Naga nephew was never going to leave me soon.

The Naga boy had given himself up silently in the making of an empire of Dharma. And I knew that he had earned my lifelong respect and debt already.

*History must recognize the ones who build ways for its glory with their blood!*

Uncle Shalya had come back to me. I distracted myself, concentrating on my opponent and my weapons. Ghatotkacha's roar was audible even from here. I saw Kaurava army fleeing in fear of the violent Rakshasa king. A part of me felt avenged and proud.

They must have experienced what Bhima's son can do!

Ghatotkacha's spirit was influencing. I hurled a spear at uncle Shalya. He sank down on his chariot, pressing his chest. Within that short while, I called the nearest messenger available and asked him to send Bhima and Abhimanyu for Ghatotkacha's help.

The king of Madra recovered soon and attacked me with more spirit than ever. I slashed his horses. While he was busy changing his chariot, I found Arjuna driving close. A look at his face told me that he had heard the news of Iravan. I saw Krishna consoling and encouraging him to fight back.

Shalya was back on his new chariot. I heard frequent noise as I fought him. My soldiers were yelling in pain and fear. They were running to save their lives. Grandfather had already killed more than he did yesterday.

"Arjuna!" I called out to him. "Go and stop Pitamaha!"

He looked at me and picked up Gandiva with a quick nod. Meanwhile, uncle Shalya picked up a spear and jumped down his chariot. With my weapon, I followed.

The frequent clanging of my spear against my opponent's detached me from other noises for a while. By the time I managed to disarm him, I heard Gandiva's twang.

My brother had been back to his real form! I exhaled.

I left uncle Shalya and drove towards Arjuna. Perhaps spurred by Iravan's loss, Arjuna was at his best now. But Grandfather chose not to respond. He just ignored Arjuna's shower of arrows and drove towards our elephant riders. Within a while, it was all the same again. Hundreds of Panchalas, Chedis and Magadhas fell lifeless around me.

My fists curled. It seemed like only we five would stand unharmed with all our friends dead, thanks to grandfather's weird vow not to kill us!

*Lord Rudra! Pray, show me a way!*

I did not drive towards grandfather this time. The violent Kaurava Senapati would not fight against Arjuna or me for long. Even if we tried to face him, he would withdraw after some time. Someone else had to face him now. Preferably a Panchala whom grandfather would not refuse to fight.

I looked around. My eyes caught Shikhandi showering arrows at Ashwatthama. My breath eased. There was the way! Shikhandi had a weird kind of anger on grandfather. I had to use it in our favour.

"Bhrata Shikhandi!" I called out. "Need I remind you that you have vowed to kill the son of Shantanu?"

It worked. Shikhandi slashed Ashwatthama's last horse and turned round. His eyes met mine.

"Your enemy is shattering your fellow Panchalas." I said again to charge him up. "Would you stay quiet, eldest Prince of Panchala?"

"Drive towards Bhishma!" Shikhandi ordered his charioteer. His face had turned crimson. His eyes spat wrath. Within a few blinks, his steeds led him to grandfather. The twang of Shikhandi's bow made grandfather turn to him.

"What will you get from this mass-killing, Bhishma?" Shikhandi screamed. "Come, fight me!"

Grandfather did not even bother. He turned away, shifting his focus to the fleeing army.

"I challenge you, son of Shantanu! Fight me!" Shikhandi cried again. "Today I shall avenge the late Kashi princess Amba who had to die because of you. Her soul will rest in peace after decades." He uncovered his long sword.

Grandfather left the soldiers and turned to him. Fury shook his frame. Princess Amba's mention must have triggered him. He placed a half-moon arrow on his bow. The rage in his eyes made me regret. I could only pray for Shikhandi's life.

He released the arrow. I held my breath. To my relief, it did not land on Shikhandi but on the wheel-protector at his left. The broad-headed arrow knocked his head down to ground. The Panchala prince shot a bunch of arrows at grandfather. The Kaurava commander killed the guard at Shikhandi's right now. Next, Shikhandi's charioteer lost his head. My raged brother-in-law shot more, drawing blood from grandfather's arms. In reply, grandfather's arrows hit every other Panchala warrior surrounding Shikhandi. But none of them touched the prince. Not even once. Shikhandi stood unhurt without a single fresh wound on his body.

Something felt odd. Though it was common to target an opponent's protectors to cut off his help and resource, it was not normal to do that without striking the main opponent himself. Neither could a warrior like grandfather Bhishma miss his target every single time thus. He must have been sparing Shikhandi willingly. I was sure after observing for a while.

Grandfather was not directing his arrows at Shikhandi at all. Every time Shikhandi hit him, he targeted his weapons at somewhere else, carefully avoiding his opponent. Something he had not done even for us, despite of vowing not to kill us five.

Had he taken another vow of not hitting Shikhandi? Not possible!

I regrated my decision. I wanted Shikhandi to stall grandfather. But the outcome backfired us. Panchala army suffered the most. Grandfather's arrows showered on them without any break, taking hundreds of lives at once.

As if grandfather was pouring all his anger over the commoners of Panchala which he could not do on their prince! The more Shikhandi threw his challenge and arrows at him, more aggressive grandfather was turning on the army. None of the Panchala Maharathas could stand in front of his wrath.

Only I knew how deeply I exhaled when sun went down the horizon, stopping the violent series of killing at least till he rises again!

# CHAPTER SIXTEEN

*After the ninth day:*

The outer battle had stopped for the day. But my inner battle had not.

I could not still shake away the violent form of grandfather that had shown up on the battlefield today. That was not something I could have afforded to forget and retire to my tent for rest. Even in this cool breeze of moonlit clear night, sweat broke on my face. I wondered what awaited us tomorrow.

What made grandfather turn so fierce out of sudden? Duryodhana's nagging? His own sense of loyalty to Hastinapura? Or mockery from Karna who was unable to join the war unless grandfather was defeated? Knowing him, I could sense that it had to be any of the three to hurt his ego enough. Now he won't stop unless either he died, or we.

I walked around the camp. Piles of lifeless bodies lay around me, as always. I knew today's count. One thousand of foot soldiers had died today itself, along with four hundreds of horsemen and seventy-five Rathas. Each day, grandfather was exceeding his own previous day's record. And our camp was becoming shorter. Had the sun not set at that moment, even more corpses would have surely been there.

*Will this never stop?*

I felt an intolerable heat on my whole body. Fire had been set on the pyres. The dancing flames rose to the sky, making the whole camp feel like under midday sun even in this night.

*May all your souls attain heaven, friends!* I whispered.

Something soft touched my feet as I turned around. I looked down to find another pile of corpses lying near my feet. Some of them had died just a while ago. Fresh blood was still flowing from their limbs.

"We have to bury these remaining bodies within ground, Samrat." I heard someone speaking to me. "We are already run out of woods and ghee to burn so many pyres."

"What?" I turned to him, frowning. "How can our stock exhaust so soon? Why didn't you inform me or Dhrishtadyumna earlier?"

"Pardon me, Samrat." He lowered his head. "But we could never imagine that the requirement will be so high just in nine days. Everyday the number is exceeding our estimation. Yesterday it was seven hundreds. And today, more than double. If this keeps increasing in this rate..."

I could not listen anymore. Heated arrows seemed to have been piercing my ears. Such a worthless king I was, who could not even provide the rights of proper *agnisanskara* to his own soldiers! What sin they had done to have fought for me, for Dharma, that they had to stay deprived even from the last rites?

"Bhrata!" Dhrishtadyumna called. "Come inside. We need to discuss tomorrow's..."

"Enough, Dhri!" I snapped, cutting him off. "Enough of playing with formations and failed strategies! Now it has to be either us or the son of Shantanu!"

Dhrishtadyumna looked shocked. He had never seen me this angry.

"I want this pile of bodies to reduce tomorrow, Senapati Dhrishtadyumna!" I firmly declared. "We *have* to save these lives! Come what may!"

Without waiting for his reply, I turned and walked in my tent, Dhrishtadyumna silently following me. All other chiefs of our army were present there for deciding tomorrow's formation.

"But how are we going to achieve that?" Dhrishtadyumna came closer to me as he came over his initial shock. "Arjuna is still not fully convinced. We all have tried our best at times. Vaasudeva himself was almost going to break his vow for encouraging him. But," he shrugged. "You know the result."

"I do." I nodded. "But Arjuna cannot and won't remain thus forever. He alone has the power to vanquish this entire Kuru army along with its Senapati. The day he will take his own form will be the last day for Pitamaha in this battlefield!" I looked at the others. "We just have to ensure that his last day is tomorrow itself!"

There was a silence. I saw Arjuna's brow arched.

"If Arjuna still hesitates, I will do this, Samrat!" Shikhandi's eyes shone in determination. "I cannot stay quiet anymore to let Bhishma finish our whole army. I cannot shy away from fulfilling my vow."

I did not feel surprised. Shikhandi was always raged whenever it came to grandfather. The reason, as we had heard, was his deep sympathy for Devi Amba who was a relative of Panchala family. Being the eldest prince of Panchala, he had grown up listening to Amba's tragic story from his grandfather. Those childhood emotions were strong in him even in this age. He used to consider that unfortunate Kashi princess as someone very close to him. Her pain of betrayal had lived in him with a desire of revenge.

"It's my bad that Bhishma is still breathing!" Shikhandi continued in same tone. "I'm feeling guilty, Yudhishthira. Princess Amba is seeking her revenge through me. She comes in my dreams every single night, asking me to fulfill her wish. Her wounded soul won't find peace unless Bhishma dies."

So I had guessed it correct. It was not about the Panchala soldiers dying, but it was about his own vow and his weird emotions for a princess who had died decades ago. Sometimes it felt to me as if Shikhandi himself had been Amba in one of his past births. Or if it was Amba's spirit that was affecting him from time to time.

But whatever the reason might be, we needed this fury of Shikhandi to let grandfather down sooner.

"I have complete trust on your prowess, Bhrata." I encouraged Shikhandi. "I have trust on all of you. But this task is not possible without Arjuna's active participation."

Shikhandi frowned but managed to give a brief nod. Curves deepened on Arjuna's brow. His finger ran in and out through the fire of a night lamp.

"Time has come that he has to be himself on the battlefield now. The main task of killing the Kaurava Senapati will be his, with we all providing necessary help to him." I added, looking at Arjuna.

Arjuna's fingers stopped caressing the fire.

"So the onus of killing a venerable elder falls on my shoulder alone!" He almost whispered. His eyes betrayed pain.

"It's not like how you might be feeling, Arjuna. Killing someone who stands there to kill you is not a sin." Krishna calmly said. "Rather it's your Dharma now to defend yourself and your co-warriors as the chief commander of your army."

"I do understand my duty, Krishna." Arjuna said keeping his gaze fixed on the lamp. "Still, a part of me cannot help but feel sorry for the grandfather on whose lap I have played once. The ill-fated man has made sacrifices throughout his whole life but received nothing except this anguish from his own family!" He heaved a long sigh. "That noble soul did not deserve this!"

His radiant face darkened. I could sense what might have been going on inside him. Arjuna had always been the most sensitive and most compassionate of us five. And he had the most intense bonding with grandfather since childhood. It was normal for him to feel thus today.

"Pitamaha had done everything for the welfare of Hastinapura, Krishna." Arjuna continued in same gloomy tone. "And now when he should get all his grandchildren to serve him with love, all he gets is mental injuries from one side of them and physical injuries from the other."

Pain dripped from every word that he uttered. For a while, I also felt a pang of guilt. True it was that grandfather had his debt on us. We could not deny that. Neither could we escape without returning it to him.

Could I do something that would relieve the pain of both?

“I feel you, dear friend.” Krishna softly said as he patted Arjuna’s arm. “But do you think that he wants to live anymore to see his grandchildren fighting each other? Know that even he himself must be praying for his own death now.”

“I’m not against his death, Krishna. I only wish I could give him the death he wishes for. A respectful farewell from earth. A couple of peaceful final moments that he deserves.”

I had decided by then. I had to do this for my brother’s sake. Otherwise Arjuna would never be able to forgive himself. I could not let him live with such a lifelong regret.

*I would ensure that my brother feels no guilt for fulfilling his duty. And grandfather’s honour prevails, too.*

“Let that only happen, Arjuna.” I voiced my decision.

Bhima looked up to me, his brow arched.

“Jyeshtha?” Dhrishtadyumna looked at me with question.

“Arjuna is correct.” I calmly continued. “Grandfather Bhishma must depart with peace and respect. If his other grandsons cannot give him that, we shall do. We, the sons of Pandu, owe this to the Kuru patriarch.”

***

The entire Kaurava camp was sleeping. Only except the white tent that looked isolated at its center, bearing palm-tree banner on the top of it. There was no light inside the tent.

*Just like the heart of its owner!*

“Who’s there?” the old man in his white robes sat straight on his bed, trying to adjust his eyes in the darkness.

“It’s us, Pitamaha.” I softly said, lighting up a flambeau. My brothers too had entered by then.

“You?” Grandfather’s eyes widened for a while. The next moment he looked away.

“Why have you come here at this time?” his tone was displeased.

“According to the rules set by you, there is no restriction for anyone to go to opposite camp after sunset.” I calmly reminded.

He raised his right palm. “I’m not interested to hear war rules from you! Tell me what you want.”

"Pitamaha, on the first day of war, you have blessed me to achieve victory. You have promised to give me anything I want only except your participation in my side."

"My memory has not yet been so fragile that I would forget it within nine days, Yudhishthira." He sounded annoyed. "Tell me directly what you have come to ask."

"Will you give me whatever I ask for, Pitamaha?"

"You are doubting Shantanuputra Bhishma's words?" his eyes shone in that darkness. "Do you even know, ignorant child, it's just a couple of words for whose honour I had given away my entire birthright?"

I joined my palms. "We know, Pitamaha, that your words are never in vain. Hence, we have come today to seek your advice and help to win this war."

"What help do you need when you have these valorous brothers by your side, along with Krishna Vaasudeva?" he pointed to the brothers standing behind me.

"Pitamaha, everyday my uncountable soldiers are dying in your hands. As their king, it's my duty to save their lives. And I cannot save them as long as you are standing on Kurukshetra." I spoke in a slow, measured tone. "Hence, I pray to you, Pitamaha, show us a way that we can remove you from our path of victory!"

He smiled now. A smile of satisfaction that I saw on his lips after more than a decade.

"Don't you already have the way, Yudhishthira?"

"I do, Pitamaha." I slowly nodded. "But I cannot execute the same without your permission."

I knelt down at his feet. His weary eyes rested on my face.

"They say you are Ichchhamrityu, the one who does not die unless he wants to. We cannot cause your death unless you yourself wish for the same. Otherwise that will be disrespecting you, our beloved Pitamaha, who has been the father for these five fatherless orphans." I softly said. "We do not have the audacity to let you down thus."

He laughed now. Laughter shook his old frame as he leaned back, a relief spreading over his face.

*As if he too waited for this moment!*

"Wise you are, my son! And noble too, that you have given me this honour to ask me my way of death, despite of having Arjuna by your side. No one else could have lowered his ego to this level just to save his grandfather's honour who stands as enemy Senapati now." His smile now turned softer and loving, his palm reached my head. "You have proven again why you deserve to rule my Hastinapura. I bless you with all my heart, child, become the Chakravarti once again!"

I bowed to him. "Your blessing is our victory, Pitamaha!"

"Listen, Yudhishthira. I want to leave this world, free from every debt that I have not yet paid, knowingly or unknowingly. If you want to kill me, then free me from the guilt that chases me even after decades."

Silence followed as he paused a little, searching on my face whether I had understood his hint or not. A couple of night owls' sharp cry shattered the silence.

"You are wise. This much should be enough for you." He said. "I hope you have understood."

"As you wish, Pitamaha!" I touched his feet. "Forgive us for everything that we are going to do!"

Grandfather shook his white head, gently patting my head. "You are doing no wrong, children. You are doing your duty. Just like I'm doing mine!" he heaved a sigh, glancing at a sleeping Kaurava camp through his window.

"Now my duty has been over!" a satisfied smile played on his lips. "I gladly give you permission to kill me."

My brothers bent down to touch his feet now.

"Pray, do not take our offence, Pitamaha!" Arjuna's eyes were moist.

"You have never done anything offensive in your whole life. How can I take your offence, Arjuna?" Grandfather raised him with a smile and smelt his head. Then he looked at us.

"Be blessed, sons of Pandu! End my life to restore a rule of justice in my Hastinapura once again! My blessings will always be showered upon you from whichever loka my soul goes to."

# CHAPTER SEVENTEEN

"Free from guilt?" Dhrishtadyumna's brow arched as he walked within the tent from one corner to the other.

"That's what he has asked for. We have to fulfill Pitamaha's last wish no matter what." Arjuna was determined.

"Fine. But I'm not getting what exactly he has meant." Dhrishtadyumna paused and looked at us. "What can be his guilt? Is it..." he turned to me. "...his silence in Krishnaa's insult?"

"Not just that." I shook my head. "Because that can be paid by his death itself. He wants to tell us something more than that. He wants some specific means of his end that would release him from his decades long pain."

"Grandfather's decades long guilt can be only one incident." Arjuna's eyes shone like something had just struck him. "A mistake he had done in his young years."

"Correct. Princess Amba's abduction." I said.

Everyone straightened themselves.

"Amba is Pitamaha's only deep guilt that has remained as a wound in his heart even after decades. He could never have forgiven himself for causing misfortune to that young maiden who had to lose her love and happiness, finally succumbing to a helpless death." I explained. "This is the only debt he wants to clear now."

"But this is impossible." Bhima said. "How can that dead princess come here now to fulfill Pitamaha's last wish?"

"Princess Amba cannot come. But he can who is a descendant of her maternal family. He who still has sympathy for her. Such a deep sympathy that he wants to avenge Amba's insult of decades ago." I paused a little and then turned to the Panchalas. "Bhrata

Shikhandi!"

All the eyes moved to the eldest Panchala prince. Shikhandi's facial muscles relaxed. His sparkling eyes spoke of deep satisfaction.

"He is son of that Panchala family that had been Amba's mother's natal home. He represents Amba's pain even after so many years like it's his own pain. No doubt that he alone can fulfill Pitamaha's last wish." I added.

"But Jyeshtha, it's only us who are aware of Bhrata Shikhandi's soul connection to Amba." Arjuna expressed his doubt. "How will Pitamaha connect her to him?"

I smiled. "He already connects Shikhandi to Amba. I have noticed that Shikhandi's challenge triggers grandfather in a weird way."

A look at their faces told me that they were not yet convinced.

"I said it right, brothers. Today grandfather shuttered Shikhandi's protectors without hitting him even once. He crushed the entire Panchala army but did not even directly respond to the Panchala prince's challenge." I voiced my observation. "Now I realise why he did that."

"You mean," Dhrishtadyumna thought aloud. "He won't shoot at Shikhandi?"

"Precisely." I nodded. "Shikhandi's very sight will trigger Amba's memory in him. And his heavy guilt will never allow him to aim at someone who represents his past. Within his heart he will know that he is dying after paying Amba's debt. This will please his guilty soul and also will fulfill our mission."

I paused for breath. Everyone was listening attentively.

"We have to keep Shikhandi standing in front of Pitamaha." I finished.

Bhima shook his head. "But Shikhandi alone cannot..."

"I know. Arjuna has to be there. But he will be behind Shikhandi." I explained. "Arjuna has to finish the task that Shikhandi will begin."

There was a little silence.

"I get it, Jyeshtha." Arjuna slowly nodded. "If this gives Pitamaha peace, I shall do it. I shall be with Bhrata Shikhandi tomorrow, as his wheel-protector."

***

*The tenth day:*

We had lost five hundred foot soldiers and one hundred elephant riders already since morning.

Grandfather was in his best form, as if the sun shining the brightest before setting. Maybe he wanted to pay his debt to Hastinapura as much as he could before leaving the earth.

As per our plan, Shikhandi was leading us today. Bhima and Arjuna protected his both chariot wheels. Our sons protected their back along with Satyaki and Dhrishtadyumna. I was at their back with Nakula and Sahadeva.

Today Arjuna was in his form from the beginning itself. He kept answering to grandfather's mass killing by showering infallible arrows at Kaurava soldiers. I hoped that grandfather would shift his attention to Arjuna. But he was not doing so.

We could not afford to waste more time.

"Rajkumar Shikhandi! Face the Kaurava commander. We are with you." I sent my message to him.

Shikhandi confronted grandfather and blew his conch.

"Get ready, Gangaputra! Your time has come." His loud scream overpowered the yells of dying Pandava soldiers.

Grandfather turned to him. Shikhandi launched the first attack. His arrow hit grandfather on his chest. Smirking, he picked it up with ease. He then targeted Shikhandi's both wheel protectors Bhima and Arjuna.

"Fight *me*, not my protectors, son of Shantanu!" Shikhandi cried. He shot more arrows at grandfather, probably to provoke him to attack him. But grandfather did not shoot even a single arrow on Shikhandi. As I had presumed, Duryodhana rushed to grandfather's help along with Guru Drona and all his brothers.

I played Anantavijaya to alert my major warriors. Dhrishtadyumna came running to me.

"Now unite everyone, Senapati." I ordered. "It's time for the decisive action!"

The other Maharathas of my army had come by then. They steadied themselves to counter the Rathas of other side.

King Shalya faced me. I knew I had to keep him from helping grandfather. I pierced him on his chest. He replied back with a sharp dart. I cut it in the middle. He cut down my banner and targeted my bow. I sensed it and killed his charioteer. As he went to take another, I drove to Dronacharya who came for grandfather's help. But he ignored me and confronted Arjuna.

Duryodhana and Bhagadutta with other Kaurava warriors blocked Shikhandi from reaching grandfather. Arjuna was in action. He kept all of them away from Shikhandi, clearing his path. Thanks to his swiftness, everyone helping grandfather got defeated and left his side one by one. Now it was only Shikhandi standing against grandfather, with Arjuna by his side. And behind him stood we all for guarding both from others' attack.

Shikhandi kept shooting arrows at grandfather who did not even respond to him. He just shifted his attention to Arjuna. My brother replied back with twenty-five arrows at once. Grandfather was at his best, probably knowing that it was the final battle of his life. He fought like a young man of twenties. Arjuna did not stop. Scores of arrows rushed from his Gandiva, targeting all the parts of Kuru patriarch's old body. The Panchala prince still stood at the lead, doing his part. But I noticed that Shikhandi's arrows were not even having any effect on his body unlike Arjuna's.

Arjuna cut down grandfather's bow and the palm-tree banner. Grandfather took a new bow and shot arrows at Arjuna. The wielder of Gandiva cut down this one too, and shot arrows all over grandfather's chariot. Without changing his chariot, grandfather hurled a spear. Arjuna cut it into three pieces in the midway itself. Grandfather now picked up sword and shield in his both hands. But before he could jump down his chariot, Arjuna cut his shield into pieces. His arrows pierced grandfather on his chest, arms, and legs. Grandfather pressed his chest, vomiting blood. But he still managed to shoot. My brother kept shooting more. Grandfather now lost his grip over the bow. With blood gushing down all over his aged body, he finally lost his balance and fell down from his chariot.

His bleeding white robed body mirrored the sky with setting sun.

Guru Dronacharya rushed to him, followed by Duryodhana and Duhshasana. Despite of their joint effort, grandfather could not make himself seat straight anymore. We heard Duryodhana crying out, hurling curses at us.

"Cowards!" he screamed. "You shot him hiding behind Shikhandi! What made you deceive that grandfather who loved you even more than us?"

I went down from my chariot and moved closer to grandfather.

"Don't even dare to touch his pious body!" Duryodhana shouted at me as I knelt down to touch grandfather's feet. "You have killed him!"

"Duryodhana, don't blame them, son." Grandfather managed to utter through his pain. "I wanted this ."

"Pitamaha!" Duryodhana cried. "How can you..."

"I am Pitamaha to you both, Duryodhana." He said. "You both are equal to me. I have fulfilled my promise to you, and now, giving up my life to their hands. I didn't act partial, Vatsa." He half-lifted his head to look at me. "Come, Yudhishthira."

I clasped his feet, placing my forehead on them. "Forgive us, Pitamaha!"

"I have already forgiven you, child. Now let me die in peace."

"No!" Duryodhana sprung to his feet. "I won't let you leave me thus! Duhshasana!" he turned to his ever-obedient younger brother. "Summon the royal physician. Quick!"

"That's not required anymore." Grandfather waved his hand. "I have already cut all my bonds with worldly desires. Do not bind me now with medicines and treatments. Just take me to some peaceful corner where I can see river Ganga and die by her bank. That's all I want from you."

"As you wish!" They wept, and took his body respectfully to an isolated tent at a corner of Kurukshetra. With my brothers and Krishna, I followed. They made his wounded body rest on a bed of Kusha grass. With all those arrows pierced into his body, it appeared as if he was lying on a bed of arrows .

"Too much blood is lost." The royal physician commented, worry large writ on his eyes. "It's surprising that he is still breathing."

"Pray, cure my grandfather, RajaVaidya!" Duryodhana pleaded in joined palms. "I'll do everything for his treatment."

*You should have cared for him much earlier, Duryodhana! It has been too late now.*

"I fear his condition is beyond healing, Yuvaraj." The physician shook his head slowly, applying medicinal paste on grandfather's wounds. "He might be alive a little longer owing to his yogic powers. But he won't be able even to sit anymore, let alone stand and fight. He has to spend the rest of his life by lying on this bed itself."

Grandfather looked at Duryodhana now and indicated him to come closer to him.

"Duryodhana, son, you have seen that even I too could not stand in front of Arjuna. Take my words at least now, Vatsa, and reconcile with your cousins. Let my death be the last death on this battlefield."

"That I cannot do, Pitamaha." Duryodhana denied. "Reconciling with them at this point of time will be insulting your sacrifice." He glared at me. "Battle has started, Pitamaha. And I won't leave this battle unless I win or die."

"Your stubbornness will cause destruction of Kurus." grandfather shook his head in despair. "May Yama take away my life before seeing that!"

"Pitamaha, I just..."

Grandfather raised his palm. "Not anymore, son. I need some peaceful solace. Go back to your battlefield if you must. Just leave me alone with my last moments."

"We won't disturb you anymore, Pitamaha." I joined my palms. "But before everyday's battle begins, I shall come to take your blessings."

He smiled a weak smile, moving his head slowly into a nod. Bowing down to him, I came out of his tent as he closed his weary eyes in deep sleep.

# CHAPTER EIGHTEEN

This night was very different from the past nine.

Raindrops dripped down the dark clouds that covered Moon God's pale face, resembling the drops of blood that dripped down grandfather's body. Moonlight had been in oblivion of those clouds, as if grieving for the Chandravanshi who lay injured, waiting for obvious death. Continuous rainfall had extinguished all pyres of both the camps.

As if every light had gone dim in front of grandfather's glory.

*How does it feel to sacrifice your own desires for a single wish of your father, only to breathe through such an intolerable pain before dying?*

Arjuna had gone to meet grandfather. He had not yet been free from his guilt.

My entire camp was silent in unnamed emotions tonight. Almost none could express any joy of achieving victory over the opponent Senapati. Even Bhima and Shikhandi, who were the happiest initially, could not celebrate the success. Entire Kurukshetra had been under a weird gloom that could not help but affect even Panchalas who had no personal attachment to grandfather.

It was not that I felt no sting in my own heart. But at the same time, I knew that I had no other way to stop this mass killing. A battle ground is a place of anything but soft human emotions.

*Sometimes, you have to let go, for something bigger!*

"Bhrata!"

I turned my head. It was Dhrishtadyumna.

"I know what you all might be feeling right now." He softly uttered, patting my arm. "But we cannot afford to waste time over the past. There will be no break from the war due to this."

"Pitamaha's fall has marked the end of one phase, Dhrishtadyumna." I mused. "Not only of our life but also of this war. Tomorrow a new phase will begin. A new start. A new series of hardships."

"And also a new Senapati from their side. I feel it will be..."

"Guru Dronacharya." I finished his sentence. "I already have got the news."

"That means the struggle will be no less than these ten days." He said. "Adding to that, Angaraja Karna will enter the battlefield from tomorrow."

"I remember." I slowly nodded. "He has vowed not to fight till grandfather is fighting. Now his time of joining the war has come."

"We need to be more careful with the planning now, Bhrata."

He was correct. The very name of Karna used to trigger two different emotions in me. One was sheer anger. And the other was worry. I was sure that he would target my brother from the very first day of his joining the war. And Gurudeva was not like grandfather who vowed not to kill any Pandava. Maybe even the rules set by grandfather would not be there anymore from tomorrow.

"Has Arjuna returned, Dhri?"

Dhrishtadyumna nodded. "He has, just now."

"Come. Let's assemble the others for a discussion." I said, and walked towards my tent. My brothers, Krishna and all the chiefs were already there, awaiting us.

"Spies have just returned." King Drupada informed. "Drona's coronation as Senapati has been done in the Kaurava camp."

"Still better that Duryodhana remembered to give this respect to Gurudeva." Bhima smirked. "I was almost sure that he would choose his best friend Karna as a Senapati now."

"He might have done that , Bhima, had it not been for Drona's promise to him." King Drupada said.

"Again promise?" Bhima rolled his eyes. "What else now?"

"Duryodhana has taken promise from Drona that..." king Drupada paused for a while and looked at me. "...that he will capture Yudhishthira alive to end this battle."

I straightened myself. This was new to me. It must be king Drupada's personal spies who brought him this news.

"Because that coward knows that killing Jyeshtha won't be possible for him." Bhima groaned.

"This is alarming, Bhima." Dhrishtadyumna's tone was alert and concerned. "A king's capture causes his army to surrender to enemies and thus, accept defeat."

"Duryodhana is doing this very wisely, Dhri." I slowly uttered. "He knows that killing me would result in his own killing in Bhima's hand. Rather it's easier for him to seize me and create pressure on you all to surrender."

"Duryodhana's own version is little different, Yudhishthira." King Drupada looked at me. "He wants to seize you alive to manipulate *you*, not *us*."

Manipulate me? What more manipulation could be done to me at this stage of war, other than uncle Dhritarashtra's honey-coated words? Knowing my cousin well, I could not even visualize Duryodhana using that way. Rather it had to be something trickier. Something I had guessed thirteen years ago. And thankfully, I did!

"He wants to force you to play another game of dice with him." King Drupada added. "So that you leave the war and retire to forest once again."

I smiled to myself. I knew this. Thanks to my own intuition years ago that I was prepared even for this now.

"That is never going to happen again, Janaka." I said with confidence. "Now I am well-versed in the game, thanks to Rishi Vrihadashwa who taught me aksha-hridaya during exile. And the present Yudhishthira is not the one who existed thirteen years' ago that he would give up to any pressure to gamble." I looked at others who looked tensed. "Duryodhana does not know that the Yudhishthira he knew does not exist anymore."

"We do not need to even think to that extent, Jyeshtha." Arjuna spoke after long. "Whether you can win in dice game or not is not a question at all. The enemy leader wants to seize you alive and we have to stop them anyhow from doing that. The situation of you being forced to play again should never ever come."

"Agreed, Arjuna." Dhrishtadyumna nodded. "But it's easier said than done. Dronacharya is teacher of almost all the major warriors of our side, including me and my brothers. There is no doubt that his knowledge and experience is beyond all of us. His vyuha formation and weapons can be too unpredictable at times."

"Let it be. We too shall surprise him by showing what his students can do." Satyaki said. "We need to divide ourselves in two segments from tomorrow. One will be majority of Maharathas led by Dhrishtadyumna. Their task will be to keep Guru Dronacharya involved in fighting with them."

"And the other segment's task will be to guard Bhrata Yudhishthira." Dhrishtadyumna added.

"Let this responsibility be mine." Arjuna volunteered.

"Alright." Dhrishtadyumna agreed. "But see to it that we don't end up taking another ten days to get rid of Gurudeva. We don't have that much time and army left now."

Arjuna stared at him, realising what he meant.

"Worry not, brother." He calmly replied. "Yes, it's true that I cannot bring myself to take that teacher's life who has been like a father to me. But it's also true that I won't let him seize my king as long as I am present beside him." His jaws tightened. "I know and shall fulfill my duty. Mark my words."

***

*The eleventh day:*

The formation of Kaurava soldiers advanced towards us from three sides open.

"*Shakata* vyuha." Arjuna muttered. "The most popular formation that can grab a target with certainty."

"Shall I give order for *Vajra* formation then?" Dhrishtadyumna looked at him and me. "Samrat can be at the centre."

"No. *Krauncha* vyuha will be the best for defense." Arjuna suggested. "Let Satyaki with his army be at the bird's neck. Make strong defense at the wings. Samrat will be at the centre. Let the Panchala warriors protect his both sides and back."

Dhrishtadyumna nodded as he picked up his conch. Following the code of his specific note, the seven generals ordered their soldiers to take positions. Arjuna led the army. Panchala prince Kumara became my wheel protector while Shikhandi and other Panchalas protected my back. The Shakata formation of Kauravas advanced towards us. Guru Drona himself was leading the vyuha.

Our Krauncha collided with their formation, leading to separate battles. Sahadeva confronted Shakuni while Bhima targeted Vivinshati. Abhimanyu fought with Paurava who was backed by Jayadratha.

Arjuna had begun the day as my guard. But he could not stay with me for long. The Kaurava Maharathas came to counter him one by one and as a result of frequent duels, Arjuna gradually went far away from me.

This had to be Dronacharya's plan to separate me from him!

As every Maharatha of my side got engaged somewhere else, I expected the Kaurava Senapati to come for me. But to my annoyance, he started killing Panchala army with his divyastras. The same cry as I had been hearing since past ten days came from everywhere.

"Gurudeva forgot that we too have divyastras." A raged Dhrishtadyumna remarked, ordering his charioteer to drive ahead.

"Alert our Maharathas to protect the army." I ordered. "We need stronger defense."

Dhrishtadyumna agreed and gave his command. My brothers and Satyaki along with our sons rushed to Guru Drona and surrounded him. Dhrishtadyumna himself joined them. But Dronacharya was too terrible to handle even by almost entire Pandava power. My eyes eagerly searched for Arjuna. He was not nearby. Kaurava Maharathas must have blocked his way. Dronacharya defeated almost everyone who countered him. Bhima and Satyaki still persisted but he ignored them and drove closer to me.

I picked an arrow, my grip tightened on the bow. But the Panchalas would not let him face me so soon. I saw king Drupada blocking Gurudeva's way. He could not persist for long in front of him. Dhrishtadyumna came to fight Dronacharya. He persisted longer before Dronacharya's arrows killed his charioteer and made him fall unconscious. I steadied myself, knowing what would follow next.

Aacharya faced me in his aggressive mode of fighting. I pierced him with as many arrows as I could, causing him deep wounds all over the body. But he recovered quickly and cut my bow. I took a stronger bow and shot more arrows at him. He replied back with half-moon-shaped arrows that killed my horses. I jumped down my motionless chariot. As I tuned to board another, a shadow seemed coming close. The next moment, it backed away with another shadow colliding with it. I turned round. My wheel protector Kumara was fighting Guru Drona. My heart caught in my chest.

*I would have almost got seized had Kumara not jumped to my front and guarded me.*

The young Panchala prince held the Kaurava commander in check for quite long. He shot arrows at Dronacharya and wounded him heavily on his chest. But Guru Drona was unstoppable today. He took a dart and hurled it to the Panchala boy who failed to cut it in the midway. The dart pierced Kumara's chest. He cried out in pain, fresh blood erupted from his mouth. His lifeless body fell on the ground, beside my chariot.

Heaving a sigh, I faced my opponent again. Shikhandi and other Panchala princes who were protecting my back, came forward to help me. Dronacharya pierced all of them with multiple arrows. He shot twelve arrows at my chest that penetrated my armour. I sank on my chariot, holding the flagpost. Satyaki and our five sons rushed to my help. But none of them could defeat Aacharya.

When I recovered, I saw Panchala princes Yugandhara, Vyaghradutta and Simhasena had surrounded Dronacharya and pierced him with almost fifty arrows together. But Gurudeva still stood unaffected. His arrow hit Yugandhara. He fell lifeless from his horseback. The scared horse fled away with a loud neigh. Vyaghradutta persisted much longer but only to get beheaded at the end. Simhasena followed his fate soon after.

Dronacharya finally turned to me. His first arrow sliced my bow. Before I could pick another, I lost my crown. Within a blink my horses sank down, neighing sharply. I picked a dart but he slashed it in the midway. His next arrow made Indrasena faint.

A loud cry arose from my army. From their tone it was clear that they had assumed me either dead or seized. A loud cheer from Kauravas followed. They were sure about their success now.

I stood on a motionless chariot, without a crown, without anybody at my rear to provide help. The armour I wore was already broken. My charioteer had fainted. With Dronacharya standing just a few fingers away from me, I could only think of the worst.

"Samrat Yudhishthira seems to be no more!" I heard someone cry out loud. I felt like I was rooted at my place.

*Is everything going to end here?*

"Samrat is alive and safe! Don't panic, soldiers!" A louder declaration came along with the twang of Gandiva. A loud note of Devadatta followed it.

I exhaled. Arjuna had reached just in time.

"I won't allow you to seize my king, Gurudeva." He calmly said. "Fight me!"

"As you wish!" Gurudeva said and faced Arjuna. The Kaurava Maharathas, who had been certain about winning the war today, made noises of frustration. On the other hand, Arjuna's timely arrival had filled the Panchalas and other Maharathas of our side with much needed relief and confidence that they were about to lose. They involved themselves in countering the Kaurava warriors with more energy than before.

Both Guru and shishya were at their best. Arjuna covered his teacher with arrows and Aacharya replied back with equal strength. The battle continued for long. Arrows from both their bows seemed to cover even the light of setting sun.

Dust flowing from their chariot wheels and horses covered them frequently and I could see nothing. Gandiva's frequent twang was the only thing that kept assuring me.

Neither of the teacher and student could defeat the other. Their battle ended without result as the sun set soon, with Arjuna still having an upper hand.

# CHAPTER NINETEEN

*The twelfth day:*

"Samshaptakas?" Dhrishtadyumna's nostril flared.

"They are a group that vows either to kill their specific target or to die in his hands." Arjuna explained. "They won't leave the battle unless they can kill me."

"Like a group of insects vow to jump in fire." Bhima retorted. "But I'm not getting why king Susharma suddenly formed a Samshaptaka squad today."

"Simple." Arjuna's jaw clenched. "To keep me away from Jyeshtha. Yesterday Gurudeva could not seize him due to my intervention. Today Kauravas have not taken any risk."

"What if you don't go?" Satyaki looked at Arjuna.

"That's not possible." Arjuna shook his head. "It's a challenge and I have no way other than accepting." He turned to the Panchalas. "Dhrishtadyumna, Satyajit, Bhrata Shikhandi! I'm giving the responsibility of protecting Jyeshtha in your hands. Take care of our king till I come back."

The three princes nodded, exchanging a quick glance.

I rose. "Take care of yourself, Arjuna. Trigarta king Susharma will be desperate to avenge his defeat at Matsya. Be careful."

"I shall be. Worry not." He nodded. "Jyeshtha, stay with the Panchalas today. If they also get weak in front of Gurudeva, especially Dhrishtadyumna and Satyajit, do not stay on the battlefield anymore."

I hesitated for a while. He was asking me to flee from battlefield? How would that affect an ordinary soldier's mind who was fighting for me?

"Pray, don't act otherwise, Samrat." Arjuna requested again. "Remember, your capture will cause the entire Pandava army's defeat. All our labour of eleven days will be wasted."

I shifted my gaze, only to find that even Dhrishtadyumna and Satyaki were nodding with emphasis. I looked back at Arjuna, assuring him with a nod.

Arjuna exhaled and asked Krishna to drive to the samshaptakas.

The Kaurava commander had formed Garuda vyuha. He himself was at the mouth of it while Duryodhana was at its head along with his brothers. Karna was in one of the wings. I saw Dhrishtadyumna look with narrowed eyes at the formation for a while, possibly thinking.

"Ardhachandravyuha." I suggested. "Make everyone form a semi-circle that will spread wider and eat this Garuda."

Dhrishtadyumna looked at me, nodding. Within a short while, our army was positioned in a half-moon shape. Bhima moved ahead to counter Duryodhana. Abhimanyu faced Karna with his full might. Realising that someone needed to stop the commander, I turned to my Senapati.

"Lead the front, Dhri." I ordered. "Stop Dronacharya by any means!"

Dhrishtadyumna led the half-circle and confronted Guru Drona. Duryodhana's brother, Durmukha, rushed to his commander's help and blocked Dhrishtadyumna's way. Dronacharya took the opportunity to drive towards me.

My teacher welcomed me with a shower of arrows. I welcomed him back with a similar way, showing him that he had taught me well. I cut down his bow and beheaded his wheel protector. He did not take more than a blink of eye to change his chariot and bow. Aacharya then cut off my horses. I quickly changed my chariot and shot five arrows at him. He replied with double the arrows. Before I could even understand, my bowstring went loose.

I took a new bow and readied myself to answer back. Panchala prince Satyajit, my brother-in-law and my wheel protector for the day, came between me and the Kaurava commander.

Satyajit fought not just bravely but it looked like he had given his entire self into pushing Dronacharya away from me. He pierced Gurudeva with powerful arrows. With five arrows he made Dronacharya's charioteer fall unconscious and then with more arrows, he killed his opponent's horses. Satyajit cut off Dronacharya's golden kamandalu banner. My army cheered Satyajit. Guru Drona stood perplexed for a while, rage large writ on his face.

The teacher cut off Satyajit's bow and shot ten arrows at him. The Panchala prince changed his bow and shot more arrows. He persisted with all his willpower, despite blood gushing down all over his body. Another Panchala prince Vrika came to Satyajit's help. Both of them were at their best. Their joint resistance made Dronacharya fall unconscious.

I moved forward and congratulated both Satyajit and Vrika. My brothers and Dhrishtadyumna too came and congratulated them.

But the victory was not meant to persist. Before long, we heard a familiar twang.

Dronacharya had recovered.

Both the Panchalas steadied themselves and rushed to counter him. Gurudeva cut down both their bows. He killed Vrika's charioteer and horses. Before Vrika could change his chariot, Dronacharya's arrows claimed his life. Vrika fell lifeless on his motionless chariot. The horses ran in fear carrying his body to the opposite direction.

Satyajit flared up and began fighting with much more energy than before. He again cut off Dronacharya's banner and horses. The Kaurava commander made Satyajit bowless again. He shot a half-moon shaped arrow on Satyajit's neck and within a blink I saw his head fall down on the ground in front of my chariot.

A pang of grief struck me. He was my youngest brother-in-law. Just like my Sahadeva was to me!

Panchala warriors around me cried out. Dronacharya advanced me once again. This time, king Virata and Satyaki too joined the Panchalas. But no one could persist for long in front of Guru

Drona's violent form. I saw Shikhandi's son Kshatradeva falling dead, followed by Dridhasena, Kshema and Vasudhana, sons of my brothers-in-law. My chest throbbed in pain. They all were of our children's age!

A grief-struck Shikhandi rushed to Drona. But he got heavily injured along with Dhrishtadyumna. Even the mighty Satyaki could not stop Gurudeva. Removing everyone whoever came to block his way, the Kaurava commander finally faced me.

I fought with my all might to stop him. He cut down my flagpost and my horses. Every time I took a new bow, I lost it. I left the bows and picked up a spear. But Dronacharya cut it into half before it could reach him. Shikhandi and Satyaki tried to cover me once again but Guru Drona cut down bows of both at once.

"Escape, Yudhishthira!" Shikhandi cried. "Don't let Dronacharya capture you!"

I still continued fighting, refusing to give up. Aacharya cut down my golden moon banner and pierced my charioteer Indrasena with four arrows in both his arms. The reins of my horses were soaked with my loyal charioteer's blood. Still he outdid himself to keep me safe. His condition pushed me to fight harder. I picked up another bow but Drona sliced this one too. Indrasena cried out leaving the reins as Dronacharya's arrows hit hard on his chest. The next arrows hit just above my stomach. Blood flowed profusely. I gritted my teeth and picked a shield in front. He slashed it into three pieces.

Heart thumped against my chest. There was no hope around. And worse, today Arjuna had been far away, engaged in countering a larger group.

Dhrishtadyumna came running and faced Gurudeva, guarding me.

"Escape, Samrat!" he pleaded, offering me a speedy brown horse. "Arjuna won't forgive us if you fall in Dronacharya's hands. Leave!"

I remembered Arjuna's warning in the morning. He had taken promise from me.

I got down my chariot and rode on the horse. It led me to the opposite corner of battlefield. The first man I met there was a messenger from Arjuna. He had come to check with me. I assured him about my wellbeing and asked about Arjuna.

"Sarvasenapati Arjuna is destroying the Trigartas just like Fire-God swallows insects rushing to him." He proudly informed.

I realised that the Samshaptakas were a huge number for Arjuna alone. It would take time. He could not come back to my help now. And till he returned, I had to be on my own guard.

The bodies of Panchala martyrs had been taken to our camp. The remaining Panchalas looked broken and unconfident. Dhrishtadyumna's messenger came to me to inform that he could not hold Dronacharya back for long. The veteran Kaurava commander had gone back to his mass killing as he did not get to seize me. My army stayed somehow low and focused more on defense. The Panchalas and Matsyas feared to launch open attack until Arjuna was back.

It felt shameful to avoid the main battlefield despite of hearing such news. My dying soldiers' cries kept ringing in my ears. Seemed like no one from my side could stop this slaughter.

I decided to return.

By the time I reached the main battlefield, Bhima had launched attack on Dronacharya. I exhaled to see that at least someone was there to encourage the whole army that had lost confidence.

"Fear not, friends!" I shouted. "We shall make it!"

My voice seemed to have worked. Most of the Maharathas came back and joined me. Satyaki and the twins rushed to Bhima for offering help. I joined them along with Shikhandi and Dhrishtadyumna. Duryodhana and Karna came running to Dronacharya's help. Other Kaurava Maharathas too joined them.

Another general battle began. Uncle Shalya faced me. Yuyutsu countered Subahu. Duryodhana rode on an elephant and attacked Bhima.

The king of Madra was desperate to protect his commander now. He did not waste much time with shooting arrows at me. After I cut his bow, he came down the chariot with a spear. I took my weapon as well.

He launched the first attack. I responded with the trickiest blow I knew. His quick footwork saved him but he stepped closer even faster and resisted my next blow. It did not take me long to realise that he was planning to disarm me. I stepped back and hurled my spear on his chest. His armour broke, letting blood gush down his body. He picked up another spear and shot it at me. Before it could hit me, I held it and shot it back to the Madra king. His crown fell down. Without thinking much, he quickly rode on his chariot and ordered the charioteer to drive away.

My Maharathas had successfully cut all help from the Kaurava commander. Abhimanyu had made Karna faint. Bhima had won over Duryodhana. But that did not make much difference for us. Dronacharya was alone yet fiercer than ever. The Panchalas, Matsyas and Chedis were fleeing in fear. Dronacharya's rage continued. No one could dare to stop him. My army seemed to have lost all hope by now. Except Abhimanyu defeating Karna, no remarkable feat happened in the whole day.

Panchalas kept me guarded till the end of the day, still hoping that Arjuna would enter at the right time just like yesterday and everything would instantly turn into our favour. But that was going to take time as my brother was engaged in a life-threatening duel against king Bhagadutta of Pragjyotisha. Message came that Bhagadutta had turned so fierce that even Krishna had to station himself in front of him to guard Arjuna. I worried for both of them.

However, Arjuna was never to ignore the loud yells of his soldiers who were fleeing in fear. He did return after killing Bhagadutta. His arrival at the final hours before sunset did make a difference for us. But it had been too late. We had lost many of our friends from Panchala along with nearly thousands of common soldiers.

The twelfth day of war did not favour us at all.

***

*The thirteenth day:*

"Not anymore!" Shikhandi frowned. "Yesterday we had almost lost."

His frustration was on expected levels. The Panchala family had not yet done with mourning late Satyajit and their sons. And today even before the war began; Samshaptakas had come to challenge Arjuna again. This time towards the southern side of Kurukshetra, much away from the main battle.

Everyone in our camp was unwilling to let Arjuna go. But my brother had his own vow to fulfill.

“Pray, don’t go at least today, Arjuna.” Dhrishtadyumna pleaded. “Spies brought news that Dronacharya has promised Duryodhana to make a great damage to Pandava side today. I’m not feeling good.”

“I have no other choice, Dhri.” Arjuna’s tone was helpless. “I have to answer their challenge. Let our Atimaharathas take care just for today. I shall ensure that I don’t have to leave thus anymore.”

“Duryodhana has played really wise.” I was grave. “He knows well about Arjuna’s vow that he would never deny any challenge of fighting a battle. He is using this to keep Arjuna away from us.”

“You don’t worry, Jyeshtha.” Arjuna assured. “I’m not going without strengthening your guard. Today father Drupada along with Satyaki and Dhrishtadyumna will be with you. Bhrata Bhima and twins also will be there.”

No one spoke. Dhrishtadyumna and Shikhandi’s frown told me that they were not convinced. That was normal. We all had seen Gurudeva fighting yesterday. He was simply unstoppable.

We needed Arjuna to stop Dronacharya from vanquishing us.

“I shall try to return as soon as I can, Jyeshtha.” Arjuna said again. “Till then, take care of this side, all of you.”

“You go without a worry, Janaka. I shall take your responsibility today.” Abhimanyu came forward, his young eyes sparkled in excitement and enthusiasm. His yesterday’s feat against Karna had added to his burst of confidence that shone on his radiant face.

“Leave it to me for a day, Janaka. I won’t disappoint you.” The young boy smiled, assuring his father.

Arjuna smiled and patted his beloved son’s head.

“Vijayi Bhava, child!” He uttered, kissing Abhimanyu’s head. “Be with your uncle Yudhishthira till I return. Do not let any danger befall him."

Seeing Abhimanyu nod, Arjuna exhaled and touched my feet. I raised him, my heart had begun racing for some unknown reason. A weird sense of foreboding was creeping over me.

*Something repeatedly cried to me that I should not let Arjuna go!*

I knew well that this worry was completely redundant. My invincible brother who was conqueror of grandfather Bhishma, what could that Lord of Trigarta do to him? Killing the Samshaptakas was just a matter of a while for Arjuna.

I pushed myself to brush away the suffocating thought. All was going to be well. *It had to be!*

"Vijayi Bhava!" I uttered blessing to my brother.

# CHAPTER TWENTY

None of us was prepared for this.

Since past two days we had been used to with the unpredictability of Guru Dronacharya's ever-changing war strategies. Everyday we had to be ready for some unique vyuha formation or his choice of weapons that would require us to modify our own planning in a short while. But what he did today was totally beyond our guesses.

"This is called chakravyuha," Dhrishtadyumna pointed at the round shaped spiral arrangement of Kaurava army. "It advances like a moving discus and engulfs the enemy."

"So this is their new way to capture me." I muttered.

Dhrishtadyumna's jaw gritted. "We need to stop this before it can proceed further." He was about to blow his conch. I held his hand.

"Chakravyuha cannot be stopped like other formations, Senapati. It needs us to break the opening and get inside the layers one by one. But we cannot do that."

Dhrishtadyumna looked at me with question in his eyes.

"None of us knows how to break this vyuha, Dhrishtadyumna." I had to confess our weakness. "Gurudeva has not taught this to anyone except Arjuna."

Dhrishtadyumna turned his head to Bhima and the twins, concern large writ in his eyes. "None of you know? Not even Satyaki?"

"No, Dhrishtadyumna." Satyaki shook his head in despair. "This is the most difficult formation to break. Even none from Yadavas knows this only except Krishna and his son Pradyumna."

"Then what is the way out now?" Dhrishtadyumna sounded helpless. His unanswered question echoed in the entire Pandava army.

The Kaurava army was not to wait for us. We watched the Chakravyuha advancing faster than we could have thought. Our soldiers panicked and began to run away in fear. My fingers curled around the flagpost of my chariot, my breath racing.

Now I knew why I smelled something ominous when Arjuna left.

I observed the Chakravyuha again. Duryodhana and his thirty brothers were inside the circle. Guru Drona himself was leading the army, securing the opening of the circular formation. Besides him stood Jayadratha, the king of Sindhu, along with Ashwatthama who was protecting the commander.

*We have to get over this to enter within!*

I instructed Dhrishtadyumna to order all seven commanders to launch attack on the opening of the vyuha. I myself got ready to join them. But our teacher stood there like an impenetrable mountain. His arrows rushed to all of us as soon as we moved ahead.

Satyaki lost his charioteer. King Virata lost his horses. My brothers got injured. Dronacharya kept repelling whoever dared to face him. None of us could even counter his destructive attacks, let alone making a way to proceed further in his army.

The circle appeared just like the mouth of Kaala himself, approaching towards us while showering arrows from all directions. And being the king, all I could do was watching my army getting destroyed.

*Will everything finish so soon?*

My army was in danger. My valourous Maharathas were helpless in their inability to solve this problem. The only two people who knew how to break Chakravyuha were far away from here. Our defeat seemed confirmed unless some miracle occurred.

*This cannot happen!* A part of me protested. Something inside me denied believing that today was the last day of this war, resulting in victory of Duryodhana.

*We cannot give up till we had weapons in hand, and strength in our arms!*

I looked around, desperate to find a way. My gaze hovered over all my commanders and soldiers. Then it fell on Abhimanyu who advanced towards Kaurava Rathas, leading his brothers. My breath evened. That was the only way left!

"Abhi, now it's you alone who can save the Pandava army." I drove closer to him. "Only you are aware of Chakravyuha."

"I can, Uncle." He nodded, picking up his Raudra bow with complete enthusiasm. "But..." he hesitated a little. My brow arched again. He had never hesitated thus in the past twelve days, even for a while.

And then, I remembered.

Abhimanyu indeed knew how to enter Chakravyuha. But he did not know how to exit. He had told me once.

"Something bothers you, Abhimanyu." Dhrishtadyumna observed him closely.

"I don't know how to come out if needed, Uncle." He admitted, his voice turned softer. The next moment he lifted his eyes with double enthusiasm. "But you don't worry! As long as I have this bow in my hand, making my own way of exit will never be a problem. I shall ensure so that no one inside the vyuha stays alive to stop me from coming out." He smiled.

I sensed a little relief, seeing his young eyes sparkling in excitement. He was now our only hope.

A part of me regretted to send an inexperienced boy to counter the toughest vyuha. But rest of me knew that there was no other way. Given the way Kaurava army was shattering ours, we had no time to waste pondering over this. All we needed was immediate action. And if Abhimanyu knew how to initiate that action, I had to give him this responsibility.

"We have complete trust on your valour, son. But after knowing your weakness, we cannot let you go alone in this risk." I softly said, holding his shoulder. "We too shall be there with you."

"You just help us in entering the first layer." Bhima seconded me. "We shall get inside along with you. We shall make the way for you to come out."

"Alright, Uncle." Abhimanyu nodded. "I shall be leading you all to the inner layers. Janaka has given responsibility of protecting you on me today. I shall not let him down. The Kauravas won't feel the absence of my father even for a while."

"You will make your father proud today, son." I beamed. "Let Kurukshetra witness the combination of Arjuna and Krishna in you!"

He came down from his chariot now.

"Even my father and uncles never begin any work without taking your blessings." He smiled and fell at my feet. "Bless me, Uncle!"

Something churned within me as I placed my right palm on his bowed head. Was I doing this right?

All major Kaurava Atimaharathas were there at the centre of the vyuha, including Guru Dronacharya, Kripacharya, Ashwatthama and Karna. The Kaurava Senapati was in his unstoppable form which even we could not counter. Wasn't I putting this young, inexperienced boy's life at risk?

*So what else would you do, Yudhishthira? Let danger befall your army? On those friends and relatives and all unnamed common soldiers? Can you let all these people get killed just for guarding your beloved nephew?*

I made up my mind. Now I was not just the head of my family on this battlefield. I was the king.

"Go, Abhimanyu!" I said. "Bring victory to us!"

## CHAPTER TWENTY-ONE

Today was not going to be normal by any means.

Abhimanyu did perform what he had said. We too followed him with all our Maharathas, as planned. But more surprise awaited us as we had just tasted the first victory.

Abhimanyu had created terror within Kauravas. His arrows fell on everyone who were at the outermost circle, leaving their chopped off limbs scattered around everywhere. The very twang of his Raudra bow made Kaurava soldiers flee. Guru Drona himself had to get back to the inner circles. To protect Duryodhana, I guessed. The defense had been much less in his absence.

But still, we could not enter the chakravyuha yet. As soon as Abhimanyu had crashed the first layer, Jayadratha rushed to the gap he had created. He challenged Dhrishtadyumna who was leading us.

Initially I did not bother much. My entire attention was on the entrance of first circle. I had noticed exactly how Abhimanyu had made the gap so fast. Killing the opponents on your left and right was the way, it seemed. I searched for a way to break through in the same manner. Abhimanyu's golden peacock banner was visible. He was on a rampage in the second circle.

But soon I had to shift my attention. The king of Sindhu was fighting my Maharathas, not letting them follow Abhimanyu. I was alarmed when Dhrishtadyumna's charioteer fell lifeless and king Drupada fainted. Giving them the time to recover, king Virata and Dhristaketu took the lead. But as they were about to enter, Jayadratha came back again to challenge them. The path Abhimanyu had made for us was blocked.

I frowned. It was just waste of time while we needed to penetrate inside as soon as possible. This king of Sindhu had to be removed from our path.

I shot arrows at Jayadratha in a hurry to follow my valiant nephew. Jayadratha replied back with ten arrows at me. I lost my crown and banner. Jayadratha shot three more arrows at me, making me taste my own blood. Before I could reply back, Bhima moved to Jayadratha and attacked him with a shower of arrows. Bhima cut down his bow. He shot arrows at Jayadratha's silver-boar banner and his horses. Even after that, the Sindhu king remained steady. He boarded a new chariot driven by four horses of the most fast-paced Sindhu breed. Jayadratha then picked up another bow and shot a bunch of arrows at Bhima. My brother lost his horses. He had to ride on Satyaki's chariot.

As Satyaki readied himself to counter Jayadratha, I looked at the first layer again. I could not see the way I had found earlier. The positions of soldiers changed every moment. Everything moved so fast that shifting my attention from it even for a while would make a huge difference. Now I did realise why that king of Sindhu was coming back again and again with his super annoying challenges to each of us.

Getting diverted would cause us lose our way to reach Abhimanyu. And that was what Jayadratha wanted.

*This has to be stopped!*

Abhimanyu had gone inside the circle trusting my promise. He was fighting inside trusting that we would come soon to help him. I could not fail him thus!

I faced Jayadratha again and hurled a spear at him. The spear hit his bow, cutting it into halves. He changed his bow before I could even think. He shot arrows after arrows at me. My armour got pierced. I did not stop and kept on shooting more arrows at him. Jayadratha replied back with equal strength and cut down my bow.

*By the name of Mahadeva, I had never seen such a skill and speed in him!*

Satyaki came forward and faced Jayadratha. To my surprise, even the valiant Satyaki could not defeat the Lord of Sindhu. Jayadratha pushed Satyaki away with his arrows. Dhrishtadyumna tried once again to overcome him. In vain. Jayadratha stood like unmovable mountain in front of our joint front.

A part of me denied believing. Where was that coward Jayadratha who once fled away in fear of the five of us? Was it the same person whom I was failing to defeat?

It was just a couple of years ago that the same Jayadratha lay half-dead near my feet, beaten to unconsciousness. I could not match him with this valiant warrior in front of me. That day only we five brothers vanquished him along with his army. Today our entire group of Maharathas was helpless in front of him alone. The same Bhima, who did not kill Jayadratha few years ago just to obey me and Draupadi, seemed weaker before him now.

How did this become possible?

Vengeance? Any special training? Or any divine power suddenly took over him?

I had no time for guessing around Jayadratha's sudden invincibility. I could hear Kaurava soldiers' cry along with Guru Drona's conch playing warning note. Abhimanyu must be in his most furious form. His peacock banner had gone beyond my vision by now. I felt tensed. The more he would torture the Kauravas, more would they make it difficult for him. The young boy was completely alone among the Kaurava Maharathas now.

I had to do something.

Deciding in a while, I jumped down my chariot with a spear in my hand. Jayadratha came down with a sword. I hurled my weapon at his armour. Blood flowed and he stepped back for a while. But he came closer soon and charged a couple of swords at me. I felt a burning sensation all over my body. Partly for his sharp blow, partly for the frequent noise that came from inner layers of chakravyuha. It was hard to conclude whether the noise was of fear or cheer.

What exactly was happening there? Had Abhimanyu reached the seventh circle? How would he counter Guru Drona with his

Maharathas alone? Situation was so dire that I could not even send a spy inside to check with him. All I could hear from my nephew was his Raudra's twang along with the joint noise.

Jayadratha's sword launched again at my right arm. I pushed it away with my spear but could not disarm him. Blood tickled down my face and arms. That coppery taste mixing with salty sweat drops made my tongue turn bitter. Soon I felt a sharp piercing on my chest. I saw darkness for a while before Indrasena held me from falling down.

Satyaki came running to guard me. But Jayadratha wounded him severely. Satyaki stepped back for holding himself, letting others take over. He, the student of both Krishna and Arjuna, could not win over an ordinary Ratha despite his best efforts.

The Kauravas' noise was more audible now. It clearly expressed cheer. The circles were moving faster, blurring my vision. My heart skipped a beat.

*What has happened?*

The noise became louder. But I could not hear Raudra's twang anymore along with it. My heart thudded louder as I heard Kauravas blowing their conchs.

*This is the note of victory!*

I sank where I was. Sun God was descending down the horizon along with the cheer from Kaurava side. His last rays spread over the west sky like fresh blood on a dying warrior's body. I heard the Kauravas hailing the son of Duhshasana aloud as I watched the sun fall down beyond my vision.

Light of the day had disappeared, making way for darkness.

Abhimanyu was no more!

# CHAPTER TWENTY-TWO

*"Abhimanyu! What are you doing here, child?"*

*I called out to the five-year-old boy who walked into my room with measured steps, holding an arrow on his tiny bow, his alert eyes glancing around the surroundings.*

*"I'm protecting our kingdom, uncle." He proudly stated. "The citizens' safety is my responsibility when Father is away for Digvijaya."*

*"Who gave you this responsibility, Abhi?" Amused, I drew him close. This brave boy was always super active with his bow and arrows, too eager to fight battles like his father. Just a couple of days ago, he craved for accompanying Arjuna in his Digvijaya mission. This protective form of his was new to me.*

*"I understand, Uncle. Father didn't take me with him. I know he wants me to do his part here in his absence." He gave an assuring beam. "You stay without a worry, Uncle. No harm can befall Indraprastha as long as ArjunaPutra Abhimanyu is alive!"*

My heart squeezed in guilt and pain until tears blurred my vision.

How was I to believe that my brave and lively boy was now just a mutilated corpse, awaiting his father's arrival for the agnisanskara?

Abhimanyu's childhood memories suddenly hit my senses all together, making it even more unbearable. I felt his invisible presence everywhere in the camp. His voice, his laughter felt like being echoed from every corner of my tent. More tears rolled down my face. I could not forgive myself.

He was still a boy. This was the very first war of his life. How could I even think of pressing such a huge burden on his young shoulders? How could I become so selfish to let him take the lead instead of keeping him in our safe shelter?

We elders are responsible to protect the future generation, not the other way round! What a shame it is that we had let our young child die in order to save ourselves?

"Rajkumar Abhimanyu has fought till his last breath, Samrat." The messenger informed with downcast eyes. "The Kaurava Maharathas have done huge adharma in Dronacharya's guidance. They surrounded him from all sides and attacked from behind also..."

I kept listening, staring at the empty seat where Abhimanyu used to sit. The messenger narrated how my young nephew had killed Duryodhana's son, how he had made Karna and Guru Drona lose all hope of winning. I heard how they had to break every rule of war for getting rid of a boy they together could not handle.

*Glorious death indeed!*

He had said that Kauravas would not feel Arjuna's absence today. He had kept his promise. It was I who had failed to keep mine! I had no escape from this lifelong regret.

Messenger had left to bring the women from Upaplavya. I did not know how I was going to console Draupadi, the one who loved Abhimanyu more than her five sons. She would never forgive me for being this careless about her dear kid's life. Never!

How would I face a heartbroken Subhadra? Would she not ask me why did I let her son go into that trap of death instead of going there myself? What would I reply to her? How would I tell Uttara that the unborn fetus in her womb would never see its father?

I felt a stab into my heart. Uttara's smiling face flashed in my memory. Why did we even bring that fifteen-years old pampered princess to our family while we had no kingdom for ourselves? Why did we let her life get entangled with our misfortunes? Neither could we give her a marital home, nor a prolonged marital bliss. Poor child had to loss her three brothers and her husband just within six months! All delight of her life had ended even before a proper beginning.

"Samrat!"

A familiar yet cold voice addressed me. I turned to the door. It was Arjuna. My gaze lowered before I knew. I turned away, avoiding his gaze.

"Where is Abhimanyu, Samrat?" His voice sounded as if he did not belong to this world. As if some supernatural spirit had possessed him.

My heart raced. Had no one told him yet?

"Everyday when I return, Abhiamnyu comes to greet me first." Arjuna continued in the same tone. "Why don't I see him today? Where is my child?"

Lump formed in my throat.

"Forgive me, Arjuna!" I managed to utter, still back facing him. But I could hear his footsteps. Arjuna came closer.

"What has happened, Jyeshtha?" His voice was shivering now.

"Today I could not concentrate fully on my battle against Samshaptakas. My mind was diverted. All the time it felt like something unwanted has happened." He sank on the nearest seat, seemingly exhausted. "And now I don't see my son anywhere in the camp. None is responding to my question. What is it, Jyeshtha? What you all are hiding from me?"

I slowly turned to him and caressed his back, hoping to calm him down a little. Still no word came out of my mouth.

Arjuna lifted his head, as if remembering something. "Dhrishtadyumna told me that Gurudeva had formed Chakravyuha today? Is this true?"

I subtly nodded, looking away.

"But none of you know how to break that formation!" he gasped. "How could then..." his racing breath was audible now. "Did you...did you send Abhimanyu to break it?"

I pursed my lips, my chin dropped to my chest.

"I had to, Arjuna!"

He stared at me with disbelief in his eyes. I had not seen him looking at me thus even when I lost him in the dice game.

"I am your guilty, brother. Punish me if you want, but at that situation, I had no other option left." I softly spoke. "It was either this or our defeat."

His chin dropped. I heard his sigh.

"Your brave son has saved all of us from losing this war, Arjuna." I gently squeezed his shoulders. "He has set an eternal debt on us. Without him, I would have been under Duryodhana's grip by now. Abhimanyu has entered the vyuha in my order, to protect me and my army." I paused a little and brought my both palms close to join them. "I am responsible for his untimely death, brother. Forgive me, if you can!"

"But how?" he asked very softly, as if he was asking himself.

"I have not taught Abhi how to come out of Chakravyuha." He continued in same whispering tone. "But Krishna's teaching has made him an invincible warrior even at this age. How could he not handle this challenge then? What happened to him?"

"He has handled everything well, Arjuna." I said, hiding a sigh. "He has defeated all the six Kaurava Maharathas. They had no way left other than killing him. They cut down his bow from behind. They surrounded him from all sides and pierced him with their arrows."

Arjuna did not comment. His eyes were shining in pride now.

"Your son has not given up till his last breath, Arjuna. He has shown everyone what Arjuna's son and Krishna's nephew can do. They have not felt your absence even for a while today."

Arjuna rose. His sharp gaze pierced my soul. I looked away.

"My son has fulfilled the responsibility I have given to him. But what about *you*, Samrat?" His question whipped my conscience.

"I have left my young boy in your hands. All of you are Rathas and Maharathas, valorous, powerful with weapons in hands. Could you not protect my child when he was in danger only for your sake?" The last sentence sounded like a sharp cry emerging from his empty heart. I felt a pain on my left chest. I did deserve to hear this from him.

"Are your bows and spears only for show, Samrat Yudhishthira? Is Bhima's mace just his useless ornament? Have the weapons of illustrious Panchalas lost their powers? Has Yuyudhana Satyaki forgotten everything that I taught him? How could my child die in presence of all of you then?" His eyes blazed in grief and anger.

"Answer me, King Yudhishthira! What were you all doing after sending my Abhi alone in this risk?"

"Would you believe me if I tell you, Arjuna?" I softly said. "We were not to send him alone. We knew that he cannot come out of Chakravyuha. We all have followed him to the first layer. But..."

"But what?"

"Jayadratha guarded the opening that Abhimanyu had made for us. We could not go further due to his strong opposition. He alone had stopped all of us till Abhimanyu died inside thc vyuha."

I muttered, swallowing hard. It felt like an excuse to my own ears. Though in my heart I knew what I said was true, something in me kept screaming at me that I did not try enough to save the boy.

A part of me was still unable to believe the Jayadratha I countered today!

"Jayadratha? King of Sindhu?" Arjuna repeated in shock. "A warrior as ordinary as him has stopped the four Pandavas along with Panchalas and Matsyas? Is this ever possible?"

"I know it is not. But sometimes such unexpected things happen in a battlefield, Arjuna. Sometimes even a Maharatha falls weak, and even a coward can achieve unbelievable victories." I did not know whether I was trying to console him or myself.

"Death is too unpredictable, brother. And so is a battlefield! Today was Jayadratha's day, whatever the reason might be. Maybe Mahakala himself was with him today and not with us!"

Arjuna's frame fell back to his seat. A deep sigh escaped him.

"We had spared his life out of mercy one day, Jyeshtha!" His voice reflected his emptiness within.

I did not know what to say. The same thing came in my mind umpteenth times.

I had stood against Bhima that day to spare Jayadratha's life. I had made Bhima and king Virata spare Trigarta king Susharma alive. Both of them had caused Abhimanyu's death today. Susharma by taking Arjuna away. And Jayadratha by stopping us.

There was no way that I could free myself from this liability of my dear nephew's untimely death!

"It was I who did not let Bhrata Bhima take his life that day!" Tears rolled down Arjuna's eyes.

I patted his shoulders. A few moments passed in silence. Then I saw his fists curling. His racing breath felt hot against my arm. His tears dried in that heat of anger. He sprung to his feet, his eyes now glowing in vengeance.

"Let this entire Kurukshetra listen! Let all the Gods in high heaven listen! I vow in the name of Mahadeva and my illustrious ancestors. I will jump into fire if Jayadratha breathes after tomorrow's sunset!" His determined declaration was so loud that Krishna and Bhima rushed into my tent, followed by the twins and Satyaki.

"I vow in my Abhimanyu's name, no one can save that wretch from me tomorrow! Not even my respected Gurudeva if he comes to protect Jayadratha from me!" Arjuna repeated, this time even louder. He picked up his conch, Devdutta, and blew it. The twang of his illustrious Gandiva followed.

As if he was giving the declaration along with open challenge to the Kaurava camp today itself.

I saw my brothers' eyes shining in satisfaction as they heard Arjuna's vow. I saw Krishna blowing his Panchajanya in support of this. A part of me felt relived. The real Arjuna had been back to his form! I knew from tomorrow this war was going to be in our favour. Each of our warriors were going to be charged to give their best, led by their Sarvasenapati. I knew that my victory was confirmed now.

Yet, the burning in my heart had not fully soothed. For I could not agree with Arjuna's selection of target.

Why Jayadratha? Why not Karna or Duryodhana who actively participated? Why not Guru Drona himself who allowed them to attack a boy from all sides thus? Weren't they much more responsible than the king of Sindhu who had done nothing except blocking our way?

Did Arjuna still have respectful attachment to his teacher even after losing his beloved son?

*I shall avenge you, Abhimanyu! I shall ensure death of that Kaurava Senapati who caused this! The battlefield of Kurukshetra will see a different Yudhishthira from tomorrow! I promise you!*

# CHAPTER TWENTY-THREE

The moonlight was so bright today. Silvery aura descended down everything around me. The top of tents, the leaves of trees sparkled as if glitters had been sprinkled over them. This overflowing natural beauty was too weird in this mourning camp.

Why did Chandra Deva have to look so happy on this day of bereavement in his clan!

I heaved a sigh. Maybe that is the rule of life. Death of an individual cannot affect the greater flow of creation. No matter how humans might feel, everything would go normal just like another day. The Moon God would retire at right time. Sun will arrive at the dawn again. But Abhimanyu won't return anymore!

The entire Pandava camp had stayed awake even at this last prahar of night. The Goddess of sleep could not come here tonight to soothe all these grieving souls. Even the soldiers were mourning their beloved prince.

No heart here would know solace until Jayadratha was killed.

I walked through the camp aimlessly. Arjuna was sitting in deep meditation in front of Shiva Linga. Maybe praying for tomorrow's success.

Why didn't Arjuna take a similar vow after Iravan had died? A part of me cried for that young Naga boy who gave up his life so silently. Had his father turned this violent then itself, maybe Abhimanyu would not have to leave us so soon!

Subhadra was still weeping uncontrollably. Young Uttara was still numb in shock, sitting without taking even a drop of water. I worried for her and her unborn baby's health. The only one who could have coaxed her to eat and sleep, was herself lost in her own silence. Draupadi had not spoken a single word since she had seen Abhimanyu's lifeless body.

I knew that her very life had been lost. The son she had loved more than her own five sons, on whom she had kept more faith, had left her.

I saw a grief stuck Prativindhya sitting quiet, while Shrutakarma and Sutasoma were fuming. The eldest Ghatotkacha sat outside looking at flames of pyres, his eyes betraying guilt. I was familiar with this guilt that was probably the fate of every eldest son of our clan. His curled fist repeatedly hit against a rock, as if pouring out his frustration on it.

Sighing, I was about to enter my tent. And then I heard a familiar voice.

"Everything is ready, Vaasudeva. Let me know if any more weapons are required." The tone whispered, but it was clearly audible in this drop-dead silence around us.

Daruka! Krishna's charioteer! What was he doing here now?

"Whatever you brought will be fine. Thank you for finishing this so soon, Daruka!" I heard Krishna whispering now. "Shall send you a message whenever I'll need my chariot."

Chariot? What was Krishna planning to do?

I turned and stepped forward, following their voice. By when I reached Krishna's tent, Daruka had left the place.

"Krishna!" I called.

"Jyeshtha?" He turned back, surprised as he did not expect to see me. "You haven't slept yet?"

"What is this, Krishna? You are preparing your chariot and weapons for what?"

He looked away, sighing. "I have no way other than this. If Arjuna somehow fails to fulfill his oath tomorrow, I have to kill Jayadratha on his behalf."

"You won't! Arjuna himself won't let you do this. How could you think we would let you break your vow for our victory, Krishna? How can we become so selfish to let you raise weapon against your own Yadavas?"

Krishna shook his head. "It's nothing to do with you but myself. I cannot let Arjuna die, Jyeshtha!" His voice suddenly gave way to his suppressed emotions. "I cannot even think of living in a world where Arjuna won't live." He paused a little. This side of Krishna was too rare. But I knew how normal it was, given his immense love for my brother.

"Arjuna has vowed to die if his vow breaks. I shall save his life by breaking my own vow." He continued after collecting himself.

"Arjuna won't fail." I held his shoulder to assure him. "You know your friend, don't you?"

"I do." Krishna nodded. "But tomorrow it's not just about his valour but time. I'm sure Kauravas would take every possible measure to protect Jayadratha and distract Arjuna." He paused and looked at me. "I won't lift weapons as long as everything goes fine. But if it does not, I have to prevent the worst."

The suppressed guilt within me raised its head. I looked away.

"I am responsible for all these, Krishna! I have caused Abhi's death. This insecurity hanging on my brother's life is solely for my reason. And now if you too have to break your vow,..." I closed my eyes, shaking my head. "My single decision of a while has caused misery in everyone's lives once again!"

He understood and shook his head. "Don't compare, Jyeshtha. Dice game was your fault but not this. You have done the right thing as a king, preferring your army's good over your nephew's. Fault would have been there had you done the opposite."

"But I have failed as an uncle, Krishna." I muttered. "I have failed as the head of my family. What victory are we going achieve at this price?"

"Who said *you* are going to achieve victory?" Krishna threw a sharp gaze at me. "It's not you, the sons of Pandu, who need to win this war. It's Dharma that must win. And all our efforts are only to ensure this. We cannot afford to make any compromise in our ultimate mission."

It sounded too harsh to my grieving ears. But in the deepest of my heart I knew how true it was. Maybe today my love for

Abhimanyu had blurred my vision. But in greater realty I was aware of my need of paying the price of deaths to Lord Dharma.

*You need to make equally huge sacrifice to manifest a huge aim!*

Krishna stared at the fading moon. The east sky was gradually getting clear.

"You have done your duty, Samrat Yudhishthira. Your prince Abhimanyu has done his. Now Arjuna will do his duty, and I too shall follow mine." He softly mused. "Even if not for my own personal bonding with Arjuna, I have to save your brother's life. Because without Arjuna, our mission of Dharma sansthaapana will never come true."

I slowly nodded, letting out the sigh I had held for long.

"Alright. I won't stop you. I have given the responsibility of guiding my brother to you. Now it's upto you how you will make your Rathi achieve his aim tomorrow, *ParthaSarathi*!"

***

*The fourteenth day:*

I was mentally prepared to see a unique formation today. And here it was, in front of us.

Kauravas created three different vyuhas merged into one. In the outer layer it was a Shakata. In second layer it was Padma vyuha. And in the innermost, a needle-pointed Suchivyuha seemed to be the greatest challenge.

Guru Drona had left no stone unturned to protect Jayadratha.

Arjuna observed everything for a while. And then his brow evened.

"Satyaki! Today you have to protect our king." He ordered. "Don't let Gurudeva utilise this opportunity to seize Jyeshtha while I am away."

"You go without a worry." Satyaki picked up his bow. "No harm can touch Yudhishthira as long as I am here."

Arjuna exhaled and nodded. He then turned to me and bowed.

"Vijayi bhava!" I went down my chariot and embraced him. "Fulfill your oath soon and return safely!" My eyes then fell on Krishna who sat with his natural calm smile, holding the reins of Arjuna's white steeds. As our eyes met, he nodded in assuring gesture.

"Take care, both of you!" I uttered.

Arjuna drove ahead towards the outermost Shakata formation. His Gandiva's twang tuned well with Devadatta's notes. I looked at his monkey banner that went into the first layer of Shakata.

*Mahakala! Pray, reside in my brother's arrows today!*

Dhrishtadyumna took the lead and went to counter Guru Drona who was already on his way to our army. He challenged the Kaurava commander. The way Dhrishtadyumna checked Gurudeva for long and slaughtered his rear protectors told me how much charged my entire army was today.

To avenge the injustice against Abhimanyu!

Guru Drona was no less. He shot deadliest arrows at Dhrishtadyumna. My commander was drenched in his own blood but did not show any sign of tiredness. He was getting cornered, yet fought back with all his might, unwilling to give up. He needed immediate help.

"Satyaki!" I cried. "Save the Senapati!"

Dronacharya had killed Dhrishtadyumna's charioteer by then along with the horses. Dhrishtadyumna did not get time to change his chariot. Guru Drona's dart rushed to him, almost claiming his life. But before the dart reached my brother-in-law, Satyaki's arrow cut it down.

I exhaled to see Satyaki intervening at the right moment. But he too seemed having a hard time against the Kaurava Senapati. Sensing Satyaki in trouble, I urged Bhima and Dhrishtadyumna to help him.

Kaurava Rathas led by Duhshasana came running in Dronacharya's help. I joined Satyaki along with Nakula and Sahadeva. They faced Duryodhana's brothers while I countered uncle Shalya.

I had been familiar with the Madra king's style of fight. He liked being aggressive but lacked calculative strategies. Defense was his weakest point. Today I countered him there . My arrows did not give him time to guard himself. He looked puzzled but still persisted. Our battles continued longer than I expected. When uncle Shalya rode on Sudakshina's chariot and ran away, the sun had already begun his journey to the west.

I went to check with the others. Bhima had succeeded to rescue Satyaki from Dronacharya. Nakula had defeated Duhshasana and Sahadeva was having upper hand over Sudakshina. I breathed easy. But it was not long before Guru Dronacharya came to me.

I got no time to prepare myself. The Kaurava commander's arrows covered me. My umbrella broke. He hurled a mace at me. I replied back with another that collided with his weapon at the midway and both fell on ground. Dronacharya frowned and picked up his bow again. His arrows pierced me harder on my chest. My armour broke. I ignored the bleeding and kept shooting more at him, pouring all my wrath into my arrows.

*I have promised my valiant nephew that I shall avenge him!*

I slashed Gurudeva's banner. He shot an arrow that broke my bow. I picked up a spear and hurled it at him. My expertise at that weapon did not disappoint. The spear approached its target as if poisonous snake advancing its prey. Even Gurudeva looked perplexed for a moment. Kaurava army cried out in fear.

Guru Drona quickly picked up a new arrow, whispered something and shot it to me. It cut down my spear in the midway and rushed to me. The unearthly spark on its head was visible from a distance.

*Brahmastra!*

Deciding in a moment, I chanted the code that would manifest Brahmastra on my arrow too. I set the target on Dronacharya's weapon and set it free. My weapon burnt his arrow down. Without giving him time, I picked up another arrow and sliced his bow. Gurudeva took another and killed my horses. Indrasena brought me new horses but I lost them too. Aacharya's dart slashed my wheel protector's neck and his next arrow cut my bow into three pieces. I sensed trouble despite my strong will to vanquish him. If this worsens further, Arjuna would come running to save me. I could not let him get distracted from today's target and lose his time.

My dealing with Dronacharya can wait till my brother fulfils his vow!

I looked around. Sahadeva was driving close. I boarded his chariot. His charioteer drove me away from the Kaurava commander. My warriors exhaled at my safe retreat.

And then, a familiar note of conch reached me. A warning note that made my stomach knot.

*Panchajanya! Krishna!*

*What has happened to Arjuna?*

# CHAPTER TWENTY-FOUR

My ears were on alert, eagerly awaiting Arjuna's Gandiva's twang to follow Krishna's conch. But it did not come.

My breath almost stopped as Krishna's words of last night echoed in my ear. He said he won't break his vow as long as everything was fine. What could have happened now that he had to blow his conch?

Was my brother no more? Or was he in any crisis? Was Krishna summoning his charioteer or sending message asking for our help?

I could not think anymore. If the latter was right, I needed to send help fast. I looked around. My eyes fell on Satyaki first who had just returned from a life-threatening duel with Dronacharya. I found none else free from their duels yet and decided on Satyaki .

"Satyaki, go fast and check with Arjuna! Quick!"

"Arjuna?" he turned to me.

"Didn't you hear Panchajanya?" My breath raced. "Krishna won't play this warning note unnecessarily. Go, Satyaki! Help them!"

"Relax, Yudhishthira!" Satyaki assured. "Nothing bad can happen to Arjuna. He alone can kill the entire Kuru army in a while. Don't you know that..."

"I know, I know." I impatiently cut him off. "Arjuna has Pashupatastra that can stop this war in a blink. But I also know that my brother is never going to use that weapon in this war. He has promised not to do that even if his own life stands at risk."

Now Satyaki's brow too had a curve.

"Go, my friend! He needs your help! Don't delay anymore!"

"But Arjuna has given the responsibility to guard you on me today." Satyaki seemed to be in a dilemma. "How can I leave you thus?"

"You don't have to think of me. I shall manage Gurudeva if he comes. You go. That side needs you more." I urged again.

Satyaki nodded. "Going. But I cannot leave you alone in this risk. Your defeat means end of all our efforts. Arjuna himself will scold me if I rush to him without arranging an alternative for you." He looked around quickly and then added. "I'm keeping Bhima for your guard."

He played his conch to signal my brother. Bhima heard him and came close. After he agreed to stay with me, Satyaki prepared his chariot with extra quivers and bows. As he drove ahead, I asked Bhima and Dhrishtadyumna to follow him in the rear. I followed the three from a distance. Satyaki entered into the Kaurava army with ease. His very arrival made Kaurava soldiers fall lifeless on ground. The battlefield looked like crematory with chopped off limbs and crushed chariots spread everywhere. I could not see Dronacharya's banner. He must have been inside the vyuha, fighting against Arjuna.

I could not follow Satyaki for long. Duryodhana suddenly came to the rear and attacked our wheel protectors. He hurled his mace at the horse-riders protecting my left side. A bunch of arrows followed soon. The riders fell off their horses. Their last cries mixing with the neighs of dying horses made a deafening noise. Corpses of humans and animals blocked the path of my chariot.

Concerned, I sent Dhrishtadyumna to stop him. But to my surprise, my Senapati could not overcome Duryodhana. His arrows fell off Duryodhana's armour, without leaving any mark.

The Panchalas and Matsyas accompanying me shot arrows at him but Duryodhana stood unaffected. Dhrishtaketu threw his sword and Sahadeva from Magadha hurled his spear at him. But nothing could even break his armour, let alone injuring him.

Something seemed odd. How could Duryodhana turn so invincible today? Urge for protecting his brother-in-law? Or had he managed something new from Gurudeva? Perhaps a specially constructed armour?

I had no time to think. Our soldiers began to flee in fear, assuming Duryodhana to have a body made of iron. I straightened myself.

"Return, friends!" I called out. "Do not fear Duryodhana!" I said aloud and faced Duryodhana myself.

The Kuru Yuvaraj was as aggressive as he could be. Now I was sure that his armour was not an ordinary one. It had some different metal that reflected almost everything falling on it. This advantage had added to his confidence.

I countered Duryodhana with full might. He hurled a mace at me. I replied back with another that made his mace fall down. He then picked up a bow. I picked up mine and cut his bow into three pieces. Duryodhana took another bow and cut down my banner. I replied back by cutting his umbrella and crown. Blood flowed through his face. I shot another arrow at his neck. He looked puzzled for a while. I slashed the head of his charioteer. Duryodhana hurried and retreated inside the vyuha.

"Hail Dharmaraj Yudhishthira!" my army cheered. But soon their noise changed into fearful cries as Duryodhana's retreat had forced Guru Drona to come out of the vyuha. He faced and cornered Dhrishtaketu. The Chedi king's charioteer lost his life. His opponent did not give him the time to change his chariot. Dhrishtaketu fought from the motionless chariot till Dronacharya's arrow claimed his life.

Sahadeva from Magadha quickly replaced Dhrishtaketu. But he too could not stand for long. After he fell lifeless, Dronacharya again attacked Dhrishtadyumna. His young son Kshatradharma rushed to guard his father. The young boy gave Guru Drona quite a hard time before losing his life.

The Kaurava commander stood unstoppable, preventing our entry into his vyuha. I could not see Satyaki's banner anymore. He had entered into the third layer as I guessed. I waited to hear an assuring signal from Satyaki but instead I heard Panchajanya. This time even louder.

I held my breath. What happened there?

*Was Satyaki alright?*

I felt a surge of guilt passing through me. Satyaki was already severely wounded after his duel with Dronacharya. He might have needed some rest.

Did I just repeat yesterday's mistake once again by sending him alone inside the vyuha? For the sake of my brother, I did not even care for our ever-loyal friend?

*Mahadeva! Pray, prove my fear wrong!*

The Kaurava commander still guarded the opening of his vyuha. I needed to send someone for Satyaki's help. But who? Who would break that strong defense of Dronacharya?

I turned to my brother who stood alert with his bow and mace.

"Bhima! Go and see whether Arjuna and Satyaki are alright." I ordered.

"What happened again now?" Bhima looked at me with surprise.

"Something's not right. Krishna seems to be asking for help." I could hardly hide my worries in my tone. "Go there. Maybe they are unable to send messengers to us."

Bhima looked in front at the Shakata, and then at me. I knew he was in the same dilemma that Satyaki had.

"Go, Bhima! Don't waste more time!" I urged.

Bhima sighed, shaking his head. "You will invite some obvious trouble on yourself today as it seems." He clasped his Vaayavya bow and readied his mace. "Fine. I'm going. Let Dhrishtadyumna be here with you."

As soon as Bhima went inside the, Kaurava Maharathas led by uncle Shalya came for me. I fought with half attention. My mind was with Arjuna and the people who went inside the vyuha for his help. King Shalya had upper hand over me this time. His arrows made me bleed all over my body. I clasped my bow tighter and shot arrows at him. He threw a dart at me that made me lose my bow.

Seeing my condition, Dhrishtadyumna came and guarded me. He was in his full might today. His arrows covered king Shalya and killed his charioteer. The Madra king finally retreated, riding on his brother's chariot. And at the same time, I heard Bhima's roar along with his conch. Arjuna and Krishna's joint roar followed.

I exhaled. *Bless Bhima for relieving me from my worries!*

I steadied myself as I picked a new bow. Bhima's signal had increased my strength. The Madras who had surrounded me had to taste my new form. I shot arrows at them without stopping for a while. Those sharp-edged shafts claimed their lives. Many of the Madras fell unconscious, while the others fell dead. The remaining ones began to flee.

Kaurava warriors' noise inside the vyuha was getting louder. Soon, Satyaki's conch followed it. Note of victory.

Something seemed to have happened in our favour.

"Yuyudhana Satyaki has killed an armless Bhurishrava." A messenger informed. The first messenger who had managed to come out of the Kaurava vyuha.

"Armless?"

"Bhurishrava was going to shoot at an unconscious Satyaki. Prince Arjuna saved his friend by chopping his arms." He said. "Satyaki killed Bhurishrava in that condition ."

I felt relieved to hear that Arjuna indeed did that to uncle Bhurishrava. Thanks to all Gods that his excessive respect towards the Kuru elders did not stop him from saving Satyaki.

"Kauravas are raged to avenge this, Samrat." I heard the messenger again. I had guessed the same from their loud noise already. But I had no worries now. As long as Arjuna was alright and Bhima was near him, nothing could risk Satyaki's life. Right now I was not worried for him but for my brother.

There was not much time left for sunset. The fear I had kept suppressed since dawn was surfacing now.

It was not about his ability to kill Jayadratha. I did not have the slightest doubt about that. But time is never going to wait for anyone. If Arjuna somehow missed it today, the disaster that would follow would be irreversible.

*Arjuna should not have taken such a vow!*

"Bring me Arjuna's news as fast as you can." I ordered the messenger.

He bowed to me briefly before driving ahead. I looked in front. Dronacharya's banner was visible. He was in his full might now. His wrath was rising with time, as if replacing the radiance of setting sun.

My heart raced as I repeatedly glanced at the sun. If the Kaurava commander got to counter Arjuna now, my brother would lose more time to reach Jayadratha. I had to hold him engaged somehow to buy Arjuna time.

"Stop Dronacharya!" I ordered Shikhandi who was close to me.

The Panchala prince nodded and drove forward. He had a hard time against the Kaurava commander. I sent king Virata for his help. Duryodhana and Duhshasana came to assist their Senapati. I sensed trouble. Both my warriors felt weaker in front of Dronacharya's vigour and Duryodhana's armour.

They needed more assistance.

I looked around. Prativindhya was leading Shatanika and Sutasoma.

"Prati, join the commanders!" I ordered.

He obeyed. The three brothers countered the joint Kaurava front together. Abhimanyu's valour and wrath seemed to have possessed them too. Those young warriors gave their best. I exhaled seeing them getting upper hand. Prativindhya made Duryodhana faint soon. Shatanika wounded Duhshasana severely. The Kuru prince finally escaped on his brother's chariot. A raged Dronacharya countered Prativindhya. My son was drenched in blood but persisted. My gaze alternated between their battle and the sun.

I wished I could have held the sun back until Arjuna returned victorious!

Prativindhya had fainted on his chariot. I could not see Dronacharya. The sun was about to set. My heart was in my mouth until the most awaited note of Devadutta reached me. I made my senses alert. It was indeed the note of victory. I heard Kaurava warriors crying out in shock. And my warriors hailing Arjuna loud at the same time. There could be no more doubt.

It was finally over! My brother had won over all their strategies!

"Prince Arjuna has fulfilled his oath, Samrat." The messenger's excited voice reported. "Jayadratha's chopped head has fallen far away. So far that none has found it yet."

I smiled, breathing easy after the entire day. My brother's skill it was that amazed them. My army's loud cheer overpowered the Kaurava army's noise. I fixed my gaze at the east sky. Sun God was slowly sinking down the horizon, after listening to the news of Arjuna's victory.

As if he too was waiting to behold this remarkable feat!

"Hail Rajkumar Arjuna!" Senapati Dhrishtadyumna cried. All our commanders blew their conchs. A sense of deep relieve washed over me. All my tired and tensed nerves relaxed. The sun had set when Arjuna returned to me, bathed in sweat and blood, and also with praises from the entire Pandava army that could not stop hailing the victor of the day.

I hoped that Abhimanyu's soul was delighted, too!

# CHAPTER TWENTY-FIVE

Continuing after sunset was never easy. Both due to reduced light and exhaustion of warriors.

It had been a kshatriya norm since ages to call off every battle post sunset. Grandfather Bhishma had specifically declared this as a rule before war began. But Guru Dronacharya did not follow it today.

I could understand why Kauravas had decided to continue. Rakshasa Alambusha. This friend of Duryodhana had taken the charge along with his fellow Rakshasas. People of Rakshasa tribe were well-skilled to hunt at nights. This practice since childhood used to make their eyesight and physical strength more powerful than ordinary people. Now Duryodhana wanted to use that special skill of Alambusha to defeat a tired Pandava army.

"Uncle!"

I looked beside me. It was Ghatotkacha.

"Let me take the, Uncle." He volunteered. "You all are tired enough now. Leave this to me."

"You too are equally tired, child." I softly said. "Especially today has been extremely draining for all of us."

Ghatotkacha beamed. "We Rakshasas are trained to be active at nights even after an eventful day, Uncle. I won't have problem. Besides, I know Alambusha's strength and weakness which can come to our help."

True that was. Only a Rakshasa could understand and counter his own tribe's war strategies. I nodded and let Ghatotkacha take control of our side.

Ghatotkacha went ahead with his Rakshasas to face Alambusha. Guru Drona was engaged in crushing the Panchalas as always. He and Ashwatthama fell on my army as if a violent storm had come on them.

"Stall Dronacharya!" I instructed Ghatotkacha.

He obeyed and leaving Alambusha, drove to the Kaurava commander. The Rakshasas of Ghatotkacha countered the Kaurava Maharathas who came to help Dronacharya. Ghatotkacha's young son, Anjanaparva, fought bravely against Ashwatthama. Bhima went to counter Duryodhana. Arjuna faced Karna. I drove to the Bahlikas and Shivis who blocked my way.

The warriors of north-west were experts in sword fight that I had experienced earlier also. They surrounded me with swords and shields in hands. I rode on a horse and faced them. The Bahlika Rathas hurled their swords at me. I put a strong shield in front to resist their blow. Our swords clashed, the metallic clangs kept ringing in my ear. I whirled my sword as fast as I could. The sharp blade sliced through the enemies' limbs with ease. Frequent streams of fresh blood erupted in the air. My horse cooperated much in raising my speed, its hot breath blew against my neck. A small pool of blood formed around me that floated the chopped heads and arms. The remaining ones fled away as fast as they could. After the neighs of those fleeing horses died down, I saw the familiar figure of one of my messengers.

"Rakshasa Anjanaparva has died in the hands of Ashwatthama." He informed. Those words held me in a pause.

We had just lost our only living grandson. Poor Ghatotkacha had to witness his child's death in front of his eyes.

Who knew how much more we were still going to lose in this fatal war?

But I hardly had time to mourn Anjanaparva. The rest of the Shivis had again come for me. My grandnephew's death kept me charged against them. I whirled two swords in my both arms together. Death-cries rose from my opponents. The soil I stood over was so drenched in blood that even dust was not flowing from my horse's feet. I did not wait to see how many of them fell dead. Those who survived, fled as soon as they could. I breathed out before a spear hurled a surge of wind towards me. A violent yet focused storm that would engulf the target.

Vaayavyaastra! The weapon of winds!

Without a second thought I picked up my bow and chanted the hymn of Lord Pavana. The code for Vaayavya weapon. It was activated as soon as I finished chanting. My arrow left my bow and countered my opponent's arrow in the midway. Both weapons collided leaving a spark before falling down.

As the surge of dust settled, I saw my opponent. My preceptor Drona.

Expected!

Guru Drona gritted his jaw and invoked Varuna weapon. I hurled my Raudrastra to counter it. Excess heat was generated on my arrow that dried up his stream of water. He then shot Agneyastra and I nullified that with Varuna weapon. His frame shook in disgust. He picked up a dart and threw it to me. Black fumes covered the whole area. My charioteer and horses suffocated.

Yamya! The deadly weapon named after Lord Yama!

I immediately uttered the hymn to activate Vaayavyastra on my arrow and shot it on Gurudeva's dart. Surge of fresh wind from my Vaayavya overpowered Yamya's toxic air. The poisonous fumes disappeared.

Dronacharya fumed more. He shot Savitraastra at me that carried radiance of sun. Knowing that it could burn me down with my chariot, I shot Parjanyastra. Heaps of dark clouds shielded the sunlight. My knowledge of divyastras did not fail me. Gurudeva's weapon lost its power and fell on ground.

The Kaurava commander did not stop. He kept hurling more divyastras at me. I countered his Twastra and Aindrastra too. His wrath rose with each failure. I laughed to myself.

He must see that his disciple had not forgotten the weapons he had taught him one day!

"You think you can defeat me, Yudhishthira?" he snapped.

I briefly joined my palms. "I may or may not, Gurudeva. But I shall make you proud today." I picked up another arrow, waiting for his next move.

Gurudeva looked more disappointed. He launched Brahmastra again towards me. I invoked my own Brahmastra to counter it. As both the darts fell inactive, he reluctantly withdrew and turned to the Panchalas. I ordered Dhrishtadyumna to guard his army.

News kept coming from Ghatotkacha. The Rakshasa king wreaked havoc on the Kaurava army to avenge his son's death. He had killed Alambusha by then along with more Rakshasas from Kaurava side. Deafening noise was heard from both sides of Rakshasas. While the Pandava side cheered Ghatotkacha, the other side fled in his fear.

The son of Bhima looked like Kaala himself standing on the battle ground.

"Samrat, Angaraja Karna has faced Lord Ghatotkacha." A messenger informed.

*Good!* My valiant nephew would avenge his cousin Abhimanyu today!

"Where is Dronacharya?" I enquired.

"He is slaughtering the Panchala soldiers." He said with downcast eyes.

My jaws gritted. "And Arjuna?"

"The group of surviving Samshaptakas took him towards the south."

"Ask Senapati Dhrishtadyumna to stop Drona." I ordered and turned to look around for Ghatotkacha. He was bravely gaining upper hand against Karna. I saw Ghatotkacha killing Karna's horses. Karna took a new chariot but Ghatotkacha destroyed this one too, simultaneously crushing the army that backed Karna. Fearful noises rose from the Kaurava warriors that made me feel proud of my nephew.

*He will make his father's name shine!*

I turned to the other side. Dhrishtadyumna had checked Guru Drona for long. They both wounded each other and both were bleeding heavily. My Senapati needed assistance. I sent Bhima for his help. As he drove ahead, I heard Duryodhana and his brothers cheering Karna aloud. My heart pounded when Bhima's scream mixed with it.

"Ghatotkacha! Son!"

I turned to my left, my eyes searching for Ghatotkacha's vulture banner. There it was. Fallen on the bloodied mud. Along with its owner who also lay on the ground. Karna's dart had penetrated his broad chest.

A part within me went numb for a while.

Bhima jumped down his chariot and rushed to Ghatotkacha's fallen body. I followed along with Arjuna. The young Rakshasa chief lay breathless, his heart had stopped beating.

He who had never lived with his family, whose mother had never entered her marital home, that selfless son had given up his life while fighting for the sake of the family. The very family that had done nothing for him except taking his help. Even on the last day of his life.

A shattered Bhima could not hold back his emotions. Neither did I have any strength left within to console my brother.

Ghatotkacha was my dearest child among all our sons. Even dearer than my own son, Prativindhya. My inability of giving him the place he deserved had always remained like a thorn in my heart. His ever-loyal services for us in our hardships of exile were never to be forgotten. I would never be able to forget that without his active help, Draupadi would have ended up dying long ago in our journey through Himalayas.

How were we going to be free from this burden of guilt?

A loud noise reached my ear. Kauravas were celebrating. They hailed Angaraja Karna who had saved them from the misery named Rakshasa Ghatotkacha.

Karna! The humiliator of my wife! The perpetrator in my Abhiamanyu's slaughter! And now, the killer of Ghatotkacha!

*Why didn't Arjuna vow to kill him instead of Jayadratha today?*

Uncontrollable anger rushed through my veins, making my hands shiver. I felt my own breath sounding like storm blowing in Kurukshetra.

*I shall avenge you, dear Ghatotkacha!*

"Samrat! Where are you going?" someone sounded concerned, seeing me riding my chariot. I did not even bother to see who it was.

"Jyeshtha! Listen! What are you going to do?" cried someone else.

"Drive towards Karna, Indrasena!" I ordered my charioteer, my grip tightened on my bow.

"No, Jyeshtha, wait! Don't take this risk!" it was Bhima now. Concern replaced the fresh grief in his tone.

"This Karna has no more right to survive, Bhima!" I replied. "I'll kill him right now!"

"I can understand your anger, Jyeshtha. But pray, calm down. Karna's death is written in Arjuna's hand." Krishna reminded.

"I know that, Krishna. But I regret that my brother did not do that today. Karna and Dronacharya are responsible for our loss of two sons in two successive days. Had Arjuna taken the vow of killing them today," I paused and glanced at the massive body of my Rakshasa nephew. "Then we would not have to lose Ghatotkacha thus!"

Krishna came down to me and squeezed my shoulder.

"I cannot forgive myself, Krishna!" I vented it out to him. "For Abhimanyu we had at least tried our best to reach him. But Ghatotkacha received no help from any of us! Shame on our valour, that we have let this son die who has done a lot for us whenever we needed him!"

My voice chocked near the end. I let Krishna embrace me and caress my back.

"Don't mourn a true warrior's valorous death, Samrat." He softly said. "Ghatotkacha has given up his life to make you the emperor again. If you want to pay him true homage, do focus on winning strategies."

"We shall win when that Lord of Anga will die!" I gritted my jaw. "And I won't delay anymore in that!"

"No, Jyeshtha. Dronacharya is waiting for such a mistake from your side. Don't let him get you thus." Krishna warned. "Pray, don't do anything in haste that might not be in our favour."

I ignored him and drove forward.

"Samrat, even Ghatotkacha and Abhimanyu won't want you to do this and lose."

This held me in a pause. I turned back. My eyes rested on Ghatotkacha's lifeless body. His both large arms were still grabbing the throats of two Kaurava soldiers. My warrior nephew had killed his father's enemies even while letting out his last breath. The least I could do was to insult his sacrifice!

I sensed my eyes getting moist, washing away the anger within.

"Karna will die, Jyeshtha." Arjuna consoled me. "Wait a little more! I promise you; you will become the ruler of Bharatavarsha in just a few more days and satisfy the souls of our late children. Keep trust on me."

# CHAPTER TWENTY-SIX

*The fifteenth day:*

Guru Dronacharya was unstoppable today.

It seemed like some unnatural, evil power had possessed him out of sudden. The teacher who himself had taught us never to misuse divyastras on the ones who did not have it, was hurling his divyastras on the common soldiers. The same person who once refused Brahmastra to Karna due his lack of self-control, had himself lost his control today.

*If this cannot be stopped, our defeat is confirmed!*

I instructed Dhrishtadyumna to focus on defense till we could kill the Kaurava commander. He went ahead to lead the army. King Drupada stayed on his right and king Virata on his left. Three of them advanced Dronacharya. Bhima went ahead to target the remaining brothers of Duryodhana, and Arjuna to Karna.

I remained at the rear of our vyuha, at the secure guard of my twins and Panchalas. Messengers kept bringing me the news. Guru Drona was having a tough duel against my father-in-law, who had once been his childhood friend. Though Dhrishtadyumna and Matsya Rathas were there to protect his back and wheels, something bothered me seeing Gurudeva's extreme violent form. Frequent twangs from his bow along with loud cheer from Kaurava Maharrathas did not feel good at all.

"Dronacharya has slayed Maharaja Drupada." Someone uttered beside me.

It took me a while to take the news in. Memories from the past flashed in my mind's eye, starting from our battle against king Drupada to pay Gurudakshina to our teacher.

That vengeance had completed its circle today! What an unkind ending of an age-old friendship!

King Drupada's lifeless body sank in his chariot. We did not even get time to mourn him. Dronacharya's arrows pierced king Virata almost simultaneously, snatching away his life.

We had lost not just our supportive father-in-law but the best friend in need too.

Dhrishtadyumna was inconsolable while Shikhandi fumed in wrath. The Panchala Yuvaraj regretted not fulfilling his lifelong vow of killing Drona earlier. And then, his grief turned into fury.

"Either Dronacharya will survive today, or I will!" Dhrishtadyumna screamed. A twang in his bow followed. The other Panchala warriors joined him, blowing their respective conchs in a warning note.

They pounced on Guru Drona. While one kept him on the check, others guarded him. But even this much collective effort went in vain. The Kaurava commander made Dhrishtadyumna faint, cut down Shikhandi's banner and horses. Whoever else came in front of him lost his life. The raged Kaurava Senapati started his game of mass killing. His sharp arrows kept showering over my helpless soldiers like thunderbolt descending on grass. Each of his divyastras claimed huge number of lives.

*Even grandfather Bhishma had not become so inhuman!*

Panic-stricken soldiers began running away. A concerned Krishna left the reins and came down to me.

"Situation is getting out of our hands now, Samrat." His facial muscles could not hide worry. "If Dronacharya continues fighting like this even half a day more, we all are doomed."

The same thought had struck me as well. But I was much calmer today. Getting restless won't solve this problem. I had to think with patience.

Dronacharya's support had always been with us irrespective of his physical participation. I knew all these aggressions from his side were not to make Duryodhana win, but it was solely for Panchalas whom he still considered his enemies. He still wished us well.

Won't he then show us a way to achieve victory like grandfather did?

And then, I remembered something.

*You cannot defeat me as long as I have weapons in my hand, Yudhishthira!* He had said. Now I knew it was a clear hint.

"He won't continue." I said with confidence. "We shall not let him anymore."

"But how?" Bhima sounded impatient.

"The only way to stop this disaster is doing something that would make him put down his weapons." I evenly stated, looking at the others.

"You mean we have to make Gurudeva weaponless?" Arjuna looked at me.

"Correct. When I went to seek his blessings in the beginning of war, he had hinted me that we have to make him unarmed to defeat him. Now we need to apply his own advice on him ."

"Well, but how shall we do that?" Arjuna wondered aloud. "We can try countering all his weapons so that they get exhausted. But that will take longer, causing more loss to our own side."

I shook my head. "We cannot afford that much time, Arjuna. We have to use wise strategy to make him do this willingly."

I said, knowing well that the task was difficult as well as risky. Someone like Dronacharya was certainly not going to leave his weapons on battlefield out of sudden. My gaze moved around the dying and running Panchala soldiers, searching for a way that would work.

"Dronacharya won't leave his weapons unless he wants to leave his life." Krishna said. "We have to make him want his death."

Arjuna's face turned pale. His eyes betrayed pain. But Krishna did not stop.

"Samrat, now we have only one way left to make Drona unarmed. We have to make something happen that would cause immense grief in him. Such a grief that he won't want to live anymore."

"Sounds logical, Krishna." Bhima nodded. "What can be that?"

"Guruputra Ashwatthama's death." I muttered. All the faces around me lit up. But Arjuna looked aghast.

"Ashwatthama, Gurudeva's only son, is dearer to him than his life." I continued in the same tone. "For his sake alone, he had once left his Brahmin lifestyle and chose Kshatriya's job. He won't be able to tolerate the pain of losing Ashwatthama."

Arjuna frowned. "I cannot agree with this!"

"I too would not have agreed, had there been another way left for me to save my army." I calmly replied. "We have to kill Ashwatthama soon."

"Our Guruputra Ashwatthama is not an ordinary warrior, Samrat." Dhrishtadyumna reminded. "He has almost all divyastras including the most destructive Brahmashira in his arsenal. Killing him won't be as fast as we need it."

"I know. But Arjuna has even more divyastras in his arsenal that can do the job much quicker." I lifted my gaze to Arjuna. He understood and shook his head firmly.

"Leave me out of this." His frown deepened. "I cannot commit this sin."

"What sin is it to kill someone from the enemies?" Bhima turned to Arjuna.

"Killing someone is not. But using a son's death for defeating a grieving father is." Arjuna was grave. "I can't do this deceit with my revered Guru."

Krishna did not remark. His silent gaze now moved towards me. I understood what could be the alternative to this, and what I needed to do. It was only me other than Arjuna who could have done this successfully.

But at what cost?

It took me a while to battle my own emotions. My eyes rested on the battlefield. One after another divyastras were hurled on my soldiers. It seemed like Gurudeva would kill even more of my army than what grandfather did in ten days.

My jaws tightened. This was not the time to uplift my personal ideals.

*My vow, however noble it might be, can never be greater than saving these lives!*

"If Arjuna cannot, then I shall do this, Krishna." I firmly uttered. All the eyes turned to me.

"I may not have the ability to kill Ashwatthama right now. But I'm taking the responsibility to inform and convince Gurudeva that his son has died."

Krishna just smiled with a subtle nod. The others looked so shocked that they could not even speak. Arjuna looked at me as if he could not believe that it was indeed me.

"You have a lifelong vow of speaking truth , Jyeshtha." Nakula voiced the surprise on behalf of all. "The vow that you have never broken even during our incognito!"

"I have to break it today. Gurudeva knows that I never speak lie. He will trust my words more than the others'. Anybody will." I was determined and much calm. There was no trace of dilemma within me now.

"We have to make haste, brothers." I said, looking at all the shocked faces. "Ashwatthama is fighting somewhere else now. We have to do this before he returns."

"You don't have to utter a complete lie, Jyeshtha." Bhima sounded softer. "Today morning I have killed an elephant whose name was also Ashwatthama."

I faked a smile, nodding at him. Bhima won't understand. But I knew that deception cannot be done to one's own conscience. A lie is always a lie, whatever disguise of truth you might make it wear!

Bhima had driven towards Guru Drona by then. We heard him celebrating Ashwatthama's death.. Within a while, Gurudeva's chariot came closer to me. I noticed signs of worry on his wrinkled jaw lines. This time he was no more the Kaurava Senapati trying to capture the enemy king. Now he was a loving father worrying for his son.

"Yudhishthira, is this true?" His voice echoed the emptiness of his heart. "My son, my Ashwatthama...he is... no more?"

His old eyes pleaded to me for assurance. I knew a single word of truth from my lips could have saved this eighty-five years old man's life. For a moment, I went weak. Truth came to my throat, ignoring all my determination. But hundreds of dying Pandava soldiers' yell pierced my senses at the same time. Abhimanyu and Ghatotkacha's lifeless bodies appeared in my vision.

I swallowed the truth.

"You heard it right, Gurudeva." I uttered in an unperturbed voice. "Ashwatthama is dead now." My voice did not shiver. Only the word "elephant" subtly slipped off my tongue, ignoring all conscious resistance.

*Habit of four decades!*

I pursed my lips tight as soon as I heard myself, hoping that Gurudeva had not heard me mutter that word. His reaction told me that he indeed did not.

I saw Gurudeva sinking on his chariot. His bow had loosened from his grip.

"You heard what Samrat has said, didn't you?" Bhima addressed him. "I hope you don't have anymore confusion?"

Bhima was as harsh as he could be.

"For whom did you kill so many soldiers, Gurudeva? For your debt to Hastinapura? For wealth? Did you even think that these people also have come here just for the sake of money like you?"

Guru Drona did not reply.

"You have bound yourself to the debt of Kurus for the sake of your son. That very debt made you accept all their wrongs without a protest. Even today, you are killing the common soldiers with those weapons that are prohibited for them, for the same reason." Bhima spoke almost like conscience. I was glad that he had voiced the unpleasant truth that I could not.

Dronacharya lowered his head.

"The son for whom you have done all these is no more. For the sake of Mahadeva, stop fighting now!" Bhima continued in same tone. "Enough of injustice you have done by hurling divyastras on weaker warriors. You have violated the ideals of both Brahmin and a true Kshatriya. Still there is time. If you have any trace of guilt for this, retire from this war!"

"You are right, Bhima." Gurudeva softly said. "I have violated the lessons given by Guru Parashurama. I could not uphold my Dharma." He sighed. "Maybe the Gods themselves are reprimanding me in your voice now. Maybe it's my own Karma due to which I had to lose my son thus."

Keeping his bow aside, he came down his chariot and sat on the ground in meditating posture.

"I discard my weapons, sons of Pandu! Now you have no more fear from me. I bless you to win this war. Vijayi bhava!" He said before closing his eyes.

I took a deep breath, bowing to him within my mind.

After grandfather Bhishma, another chapter of our life had ended. Another step towards the victory.

"You may discard your weapons, son of Bharadwaja, I didn't!" Dhrishtadyumna shouted.

I shifted my gaze to him. The commander-in-chief of my army had come down his chariot, with unsheathed sword in his right hand that shone in the rays of midday sun.

"Dhrishtadyumna!" I called out. "This is no more required. Our intention has been fulfilled. Gurudeva won't fight anymore."

"But my intention has not yet been fulfilled, Samrat!" He cried. "This Brahmin is the killer of my father! I won't spare him!"

"Calm down, Dhrishtadyumna!" Arjuna objected. "He is your Guru too. Don't commit this sin."

"What sin? It's my vow to kill him since childhood. Don't you all know?" He fumed and rushed towards Gurudeva who sat unmovable in meditation.

"Dhrishtadyumna! Stop! I say stop right now!" Arjuna jumped down his chariot and rushed to hold him back. But it had been too late. By when Arjuna reached, Guru Drona's chopped head fell off his meditating body. Dhrishtadyumna's blood-smeared sword flashed in the sunlight. Fresh blood spilled over his face, making him look even crueler.

"Vengeful Prince of Panchala! You stooped so low to kill your own Guru?" Arjuna cried out, his eyes had turned copper-hued.

"Is this your valour to kill an unarmed warrior who was sitting in meditation?" Arjuna almost jumped on Dhrishtadyumna. "You lost all senses of fairness for your own revenge, Senapati?"

"As if you have never done the same?" Dhrishtadyumna glared at Arjuna. "Which fair way did you take while killing your own grandfather?"

"You are accusing Arjuna for that, fool?" Satyaki intervened in Arjuna's defense. "It was your own brother who did the deception to Bhishma, not Arjuna."

"Better you keep quiet, grandson of Shini!" Dhrishtadyumna turned to Satyaki, fuming. "Don't even come to teach us fairness after killing an armless Bhurishrava!"

I sensed trouble. The greatest strength of my side was our unity and dedicated groupwork. This internal clash between our major warriors would do even more harm to us, if not stopped immediately. I exchanged glance with Krishna and found him sharing my concern. But the Maharathas in front of me showed no sign to realise this and stop.

"Stupid Senapati, I do fight like a warrior, not like a coward who can only cut heads of meditating people." Satyaki screamed. "Don't you even feel ashamed to defend yourself after having committed an unpardonable sin of Guru hatya? Shame on your so called 'divine' birth that gave you a demon's character instead of God's!"

"Oh you see only my fault, right?" Dhrishtadyumna raised his tone even louder. "What justice these Kauravas have shown from the first day itself? What fair fight did they do with young Abhimanyu? Why should I alone show morality in this battlefield?"

"Wonderful, Commander!" Satyaki retorted. "You are using one wrong to justify the other?"

"I'm not here to hear your lectures, Yuyudhana." Dhrishtadyumna waved his hand. "If you are so proud of your valour and Kshatriya Dharma, better stop blaming me and fight. That's what we are supposed to do here."

"Better I shall die rather than fighting under someone like you!" Satyaki jumped down his chariot with sword in his hand. "You have killed my Guru's Guru, shameless Panchala! Either I'll avenge this, or die."

"Satyaki! No! Control yourself!" I rushed and pulled him back. The Yadava still gasped in rage, casting crimson eyes on Dhrishtadyumna.

"Leave me, Yudhishthira! This wretch thinks that I'm a meditating Dronacharya whom he can easily behead. His death is in my hand!" He screamed.

"Satyaki, dear friend, pray, calm down." Krishna put an arm on his shoulder. "Dhrishtadyumna is our Senapati. Do not let today's victory turn into a greater defeat for Pandavas. Pray, at least for their sake, forgive Dhrishtadyumna."

"Leave him to me, Vaasudeva!" Dhrishtadyumna cried. "I'll show him that I am no armless Bhurishrava."

"You are not in your senses, Senapati Dhrishtadyumna!" I chided him. "Your enemy is dead now. Come out of your vengeful mood! You are the commander-in-chief of this army. Would you kill a Maharatha under your own leadership? Do you think that's' right for you?"

Dhrishtadyumna stared at me for a while, and then looked away, curling his fist.

"Dhrishtadyumna! Satyaki! Pray, stop this now, both of you!" I looked at both. "Don't let Kauravas laugh at us!"

Satyaki groaned. "I don't understand how you five and Krishna are tolerating this, sons of Pandu! Shouldn't this sinner be killed right now for his heinous offence?"

"We too have not liked what he did, Satyaki. Neither do we support that." I came closer to him. "But fighting within ourselves is not going to undo this anymore." I firmly stated. "That would do nothing except causing more loss to ourselves . Should we allow that, my friend?"

All my brothers came down their respective chariots and surrounded Satyaki and Drishtadyumna.

"We have no friend dearer than you and Krishna, Satyaki." Sahadeva said, holding his hands. "And we equally depend on the Panchalas too. If two of our greatest well-wishers fight among themselves thus, we'll have no more hope left for winning."

His placating words seemed to have pacified Satyaki a little. But his frame was still shivering in anger.

"Forget not, friends, losing unity means losing this battle for us." I said. "We are still on the battlefield and I'm sure Ashwatthama won't spare us when he will hear this. We must stay together now."

I saw Satyaki exchanging a reluctant glance with Dhrishtadyumna, before going back to his chariot. Looking away with a sigh, our Senapati too did the same.

And then, we heard the twang of Guruputra Ashwatthama's bow.

# CHAPTER TWENTY-SEVEN

"Where are those cheaters? Where are sons of Pandu?" A familiar voice's sharp cry reached us overpowering all the noises of battle.

"Did you hear, Samrat? Guruputra Ashwatthama's voice that is." Arjuna's eyes, crimson in a mix of rage and grief, rested on me. "He is coming to avenge his father."

"Where is that wretched Dhrishtadyumna?" Ashwatthama yelled again. "Has that liar Yudhishthira hidden you now in the camp? Come, face me, coward!"

"I knew this would happen." I muttered. "Ashwatthama won't spare us now."

"He would not, given the way we killed his father." Arjuna breathed away, frowning more. "His anger is justified. No one can save prince Dhrishtadyumna today!"

I glanced at Arjuna once. He was still caught in sorrow. I could feel how much he had been wounded within his heart after losing the teacher who loved him more than his own son. But this was just not the time to give in to emotions. I had to pull him out of this grief before something unwanted happened.

"We cannot let that happen, brother." I shook my head. "I agree that Dhrishtadyumna's way of killing Gurudeva was wrong. But at the end of everything, he is our Senapati. We have to save his life."

"We can save him only if we are alive, Samrat." Arjuna evenly replied. "Ashwatthama possesses the deadliest of divyastras that can turn entire Kurukshetra into ashes just in a moment. We should be prepared to face the worst now."

I stared at him for a while. Seemed like he was not in his senses out of grief, and maybe, even anger.

"If this is true then you must take immediate action to save everyone, Sarvasenapati. Keep control on your emotions." I had to make my tone grave. "This is a battlefield."

"My emotions are well in control, Samrat. Your Senapati's is not." He flared up now. "I have asked your Senapati repeatedly not to commit this heinous crime. But he had no control over his vengeful instincts. And you, the king, did not care to stop him either." His eyes turned moist as he glanced fondly at Gurudeva's beheaded body.

"Dhrishtadyumna has not listened to me. Now we have to suffer the consequence of this sin." He sounded dry. "We all are going to be doomed."

How wonderful! The son of late Kaurava commander was about to destroy our army and our Sarvasenapati was not even willing to counter him. Were we supposed to sit idle now in this battlefield just because our so-called well-wisher Gurudeva had died after causing so much harm to our army? Were we supposed to let our Senapati, our brother-in-law, die in Ashwatthama's hand in the grief of such a Guru who always kept betraying us? The reply came to my throat but I decided against.

It was not the time to fight within ourselves. I could not afford to start another conflict between us after Satyaki and Dhrishtadyumna's. My army was in crisis. Ashwatthama was at his worst. My soldiers' corpses were falling around me like trees being uprooted in storm. Within a short while, the entire area around me was flooded with blood. Strong smell of burnt flesh made me cringe.

*Like father, like son!*

"Samrat!" Krishna stood up. "Ashwatthama has Narayanastra and he might..."

Even before he could finish, I saw a fiery dart rushing towards us. A vibrant discus adorned its head.

*Narayanastra! The deadly weapon that could destroy an entire locality within a few moments! The weapon that has no counter.*

*Death is confirmed!*

*I could not let all these people die!*

I picked up my conch Anantavijaya and played the note that hinted serious danger. Dhrishtadyumna and all the Maharathas turned to me.

"My fellow commanders, Rathas and Maharathas!" I cried as loud as I could. "Escape! Leave the battlefield as soon as you can!"

"Samrat?" Satyaki was shocked.

"Escape, Satyaki! Return to Dwaraka with Krishna. Dhrishtadyumna, run towards Panchala with all your warriors. Matsyas and Chedis, return to your respective kingdoms. There's no counter of this deadly dart. Run!"

I heard my soldiers' cry. The fiery dart had begun its work. The discus was moving faster with time. Multiple killer arrows were being showered from every edge of it. I did not have time.

"We are not here to leave you alone in this crisis, Samrat." Krishna strongly denied.

"No! This war is ours. Let only us five get perished. You escape!"

"Jyeshtha stop this and listen to me!" Krishna cried. "Ask all your warriors to discard their weapons and come down their chariots. Narayanastra would become ineffective then."

I looked at him, still not fully getting what he was telling me.

"Do what I say! Quick!" he cried again.

I was not in a condition to think. Almost in a trance mixed with disbelief, I ordered Dhrishtadyumna to discard his weapons and to make others follow him. I went down my chariot and removed my armour. Arjuna and the twins followed me. But Bhima did not.

"Bhima!" I cried. "Get down and drop your mace!"

"I won't!" he denied. "I have to destroy this dart." He held his weapon in one hand, ready to hurl it. My heart was in my mouth. The fiery dart did not target any of us and moved towards Bhima.

"Bhrata Bhima! Do what we say!" Krishna cried out. "Don't attract the weapon's rage upon yourself!"

"Let it come, Krishna." Bhima tightened his grip on his mace. "My mace is enough for..."

He could not finish. Krishna pushed him hard, making him fall from his chariot. Arjuna hurried and snatched the mace from his hand. I saw the fiery dart falling down immediately.

"What were you going to do?" Krishna scolded Bhima. "This could have ended your life right now."

I could not shift my gaze from the weapon that was now fallen on dust, powerless but still holding spark on its head that was dying down. My heart had not yet stopped pounding.

*It felt like we had just returned from the dark mouth of death!*

"What was so different in this?" I voiced my wonder.

"It has a special ability to target only those people who are in contact with iron." Krishna replied. "Once you stay away from weapons and chariots, you are safe." He pointed towards the discus. The fire had been put off now.

"Since all of you left weapons and chariots, it got deactivated." Krishna explained.

I listened to him, air slowly returning to my chest in aching breaths.

*What a huge crisis had just been over! What could have happened had Krishna not have this knowledge?*

"Danger is over, Samrat. Now get back to your chariot." I heard Krishna again. "Take your weapons back. Inform the others too." He added.

"Should we?" I doubted aloud. "Won't the dart begin its action again as soon as we take back weapons?"

"No. This weapon can be used only for a single time." Krishna assured. "Even the owner of it cannot reuse it. The code of activating Narayanastra expires after one use. Unless its constructer himself resets a new code, this weapon won't work anymore."

In a mix of surprise and relief, I exhaled, picking up my bow. My soldiers' loud cheer greeted my ear. Kaurava army's noise of frustration mixed with it.

They had lost their confirmed victory!

The daylight went dim as the noise started dying down. With the note of Dhrishtadyumna's conch, the sun sank beyond the horizon, marking the end of an eventful day.

## CHAPTER TWENTY-EIGHT

Dhrishtadyumna was inconsolable while king Drupada's last rites were performed with due rituals. The ever-angry, vengeful prince had such a hidden soft corner for his father and his siblings! I had seen him the same when Satyajit had left us.

The world might know him as a man of fire running in his veins, but his close ones knew that the fire always came from a deep sense of love and responsibility for his loved ones.

Draupadi had come from Upaplavya to attend her father's rites. She was much calmer, as always. I saw her consoling Dhrishtadyumna and Shikhandi, hiding her own tears. Leaving a mourning Uttara in her care, I went to attend king Virata's last rites. For I could not let that friend in need to leave us feeling so alone.

My father-in-law still had his children and sons-in-law for biding him the final farewell. Poor Lord of Matsya did not have anyone except his newly-widowed daughter!

*Will both our older and younger generations get perished in this war thus?*

None of my brothers spoke until the rituals were finished. News had already come that Karna had been coronated as the next Kaurava commander. I knew that my commander would have no ability to bring himself to make tomorrow's plan now. And the one who alone could handle Karna was equally numb. Partly for king Drupada, partly for Guru Drona.

I knew Arjuna had not forgiven Dhrishtadyumna yet. He just could not. Maybe he was equally angry with me as well but could not express it. The way he was avoiding me could have no other reason.

"Arjuna," I heard Krishna telling him. "Tomorrow, you have to take the main lead."

"Both of you need to be careful, Krishna." I added, turning to both. "Now Karna would be even more desperate to kill Arjuna."

"You leave that to me." Krishna assured.

Arjuna rose and slowly walked away towards his tent. I exchanged a meaningful glance with Krishna.

"Arjuna, wait!" Krishna called him.

Arjuna turned a little. "Let me be alone for tonight, Krishna."

I moved closer to Arjuna.

"I can understand your pain, brother." I squeezed his shoulders. "But pray, come out of this now. We still have Karna, Duryodhana and Duhshasana alive."

"I don't have that urge within me anymore, Samrat." He sighed, shaking his head. "After losing two of my greatest well-wisher elders, even Indra's Amaravati won't be able to attract me, leave alone Indraprastha!"

I hid a sigh. I had seen this detachment in him since the first day itself. Today's losses had only amplified it.

"I don't feel any attachment to the kingdom to keep on fighting." Arjuna added in the same tone.

"We all are feeling the same after losing our friends and relatives." I softly said. "But we cannot just stop it in the middle for this is our duty. We are duty-bound to persist till the end of the war, at least to honour them who have died for us. And we need you in this."

"Duty indeed!" he sounded dry now. "I know. It's our duty to win this war no matter how. It does not matter whatever sins are being committed every day to achieve victory."

So I knew it right!

"I know that you did not like what happened today, Arjuna. But do you think we were left with another option?" I looked straight into his eyes. "Gurudeva could have finished the war today itself. Was it not our responsibility to stop him?"

"We had option to defeat him in a fair fight." Arjuna groaned. "Instead of that we chose a lie to disarm him and got him beheaded. Did we do this right, Dharmaraj?"

I pursed my lips, choosing not to voice it to my grieving brother. Arjuna was the only person in our side who could have made the fair option work for us. We had to go with the other way only after he chose not to do it, even after losing Abhimanyu!

"How could you do this, Jyeshtha?" his voice grew a little louder from a whisper. "A well-wisher elder, that too an aged Brahmin, his death was so much preferable to you even more than your truth?"

"Who do you call our well-wisher, Arjuna?" I calmly stared at him. "That person who kept betraying us every time we needed his support? Who do you call a Brahmin? Being Brahmin needs one to have compassion and honesty, not just the blood inherited from his father."

Arjuna looked away.

"Ask your conscience, Arjuna. The person who can allow his own students to forget lessons of fair warfare, who can be so inhuman to hurl divyastras on weak foot soldiers, could he be a true Brahmin in character?"

"I don't want to go into that argument at all. He might not have followed the norms of his community. But he indeed was affectionate to us like his own sons." Arjuna continued in the same tone. "He loved you, Jyeshtha. He had the firm belief that his dear Yudhishthira would never lie even in the greed of heaven's throne! How could you break that trust of the old man, just in desire of winning a kingdom?"

For a while, I could not speak. His strong words had triggered the guilt I had forced to suppress within.

*Am I really greedy for getting Indraprastha back?*

Yes, I did want to defeat Gurudeva. I did want to win this war. But was that only for myself? Didn't I want my rights back for my family? For my brothers, for Draupadi, for our children? For the greater mission of Dharma?

“Call it my desire or greed if that pleases you. But I do not regret breaking my vow. It was my Dharma to save my army from dying.” I gravely uttered. Arjuna stared at me with weird look. Perhaps he had expected me to confess my guilt for lying.

“If I truly regret anything then it’s for not doing this earlier. Then maybe,” I paused to struggle my emotions. More words threatened to come out of my lips. But I decided against.

“Maybe Abhimanyu and Ghatotkacha did not have to die if I could. So many of our soldiers did not have to die.”

Arjuna did not reply now. His eyes had softened. Abhimanyu’s mention might have triggered him. The next moment, his gaze dropped to the ground. He heaved a sigh and sank on the nearest rock.

I believed that in the depths of his heart, he too knew that Guru Drona was responsible for Abhimanyu’s death. It was just his conscious self that denied accepting that.

Krishna moved closer to Arjuna and held his shoulder.

“Arjuna, if a lie saves hundreds of lives, it is much more precious than hundreds of truths. You are aware of this, aren’t you?”

Slowly, Arjuna lifted his gaze with a subtle nod.

“I don’t mean to accuse Jyeshtha alone, Krishna. I can feel what is going on in his heart. Do not mistake me.”

He then rose and joined his palms to me. “Don’t take my offence, Jyeshtha. I might have vented it out to you alone, but trust me, in my heart I do not hold you the sole responsible for all these. We all have equal share in the events that are taking place in Kurukshetra every day. It’s our collective desire, our Kshatriya ego of not compromising for peace caused this destruction.”

I drew him to my embrace. “I am aware of your thoughts, brother. Still, it’s better that you have not let it fester within.”

“Arjuna, don’t weaken yourself thus, dear friend.” Krishna softly said. “You are that warrior who never leaves battlefield in the middle. Losing yourself at this crucial moment of war doesn’t suit you. A new Kaurava Senapati awaits you tomorrow. You have to fulfill your remaining duties.”

Arjuna listened quietly, his gaze lowered.

"Your Guru has attained divine abode, Arjuna." Krishna said again. "Now stop mourning him. Know that he too won't like it if you fail to give your best tomorrow."

Arjuna looked up to meet his gaze.

"I won't disappoint him, Krishna. Karna's death is destined by my arrows." He assured.

***

The light of the burning pyres had been put off. Moonlight seemed brighter now, playing on the window of my tent.

I saw a familiar shadow moving closer. The guards of my tent bowed to the shadow with respect. Tinkle of anklets felt closer as the shadow moved towards me, along with a very familiar fragrance that I had loved since decades.

"It is already past midnight, Samrat." Draupadi reminded, her voice did not have any trace of weeping. Maybe she had not found time to cry at all while consoling her brothers and Uttara.

"Have a little sleep before the dawn." She softly said. I felt her soft palm caressing over the fresh wounds of my arm. *After so long!*

"Have your brothers slept?" I looked at her. "And our sons?" I added, knowing well how much our children were attached to their maternal grandfather. Perhaps today they would understand what we, their fathers had felt after our grandfather's fall.

She nodded slowly.

"Has Uttara eaten her meal?" I enquired. It was next to impossible to coax the girl to eat or sleep since Abhimanyu had left. We could not even take the risk to let her return to Upaplavya in this condition. Her body and mind were too weak to take the journey.

Draupadi sighed and shook her head. "She has fallen asleep after weeping till midnight. I did not feel like waking her up."

"She listens to you the most, Krishnaa." I said. "Your absence, I fear, is making it even worse for her.

She did not remark. Reflection of moonlight darkened on her face as a piece of cloud covered the moon.

"Would you mind staying here in the camp for few days? At least till Uttara recovers?"

"Not me, Samrat. She needs her mother the most right now." Draupadi remarked. "I must have told you earlier. We should ask Maharani Sudeshna to come and stay here."

"Alright. I shall send message to Upaplavya tomorrow itself, requesting her to come."

Draupadi nodded and looked at the sky. "I shall take your leave now. I have come here to make you sleep, not to talk the whole night which you would do if I stayed here." Her lips curved into a slight smile that was too affectionate. The same smile that I had seen on her face during our Indraprastha days.

She walked away, maybe assuming my silence as my agreement.

"Draupadi!"

She turned back. "You need something?"

I turned away to the window again. A part of me hesitated. But I needed to hear her opinion. My conscience would keep biting me forever if I did not share it with her.

"Do you also think that I did wrong today?" I managed to ask.

The tinkle of her anklets felt closer.

"No." She replied. "Rather I think this is the rightest thing you have ever done. I wish you had done this much earlier, thirteen years ago."

I slowly turned back, facing her.

"That day you could not rise above your personal preferences to protect your kingdom and family. Today you could. Even at the cost of something so dear to you." She came closer and placed her palm on mine. "You won my respect once again, Dharmaraj."

I exhaled, letting out the self-doubt that I had kept inside till now.

"It was not easy, Draupadi." I whispered. "But I could not repeat my mistake of getting stuck into the older conventions of Dharma. That would have left me with even more guilt."

"I am glad that you have realised, Aaryaputra." Her eyes shone in appreciation. "You have passed even the final test of Dharma. Now

I believe that our victory is no more far from us."

# CHAPTER TWENTY-NINE

The sixteenth day of war began with a clear mission of killing Karna as soon as we could.

The Kauravas had formed Makara vyuha today, with Senapati Karna at its mouth. We had replied with ArdhaChandra vyuha with Bhima and Dhrishtadyumna at the two free ends. I instructed Arjuna to stay at the middle to counter Karna. Nakula and Sahadeva guarded my wheels at the rear.

As I had always observed, Karna was a total disappointment whenever it came to take a role of saviour. Or perhaps, that is the reality of any self-centered person who cares only for himself. The new Senapati of Kauravas was unable to save his friends today. Bhima killed more brothers of Duryodhana than he did in the previous days. Still, the Senapati just kept hanging around Arjuna who was his personal target, ignoring the welfare of his army.

Arjuna defeated Karna in their first duel and went to counter the remaining Samshaptakas. Nakula went to counter Guru Kripacharya and Sahadeva, to Duhshasana. Dhrishtadyumna attacked Ashwatthama and Shikhandi cornered Kritavarma. Even our sons were equally charged to finish this war today itself. Prativindhya was gaining upper hand against Chitra and Shrutakarma bravely fought Chitrasena from Abhisara.

I ordered Indrasena to drive towards Duryodhana.

The Kuru Yuvaraja fumed as he saw me facing him. I did not give him time to start verbal duel. My first arrow killed his charioteer, the second one felled his flag, and next ones claimed the lives of his four horses. As soon as he realised it, I sliced the bow he was holding. Duryodhana quickly picked up a sword and jumped down his inactive chariot. I shot more arrows at him that chopped his sword into several pieces.

*Just like I wanted to slice his body into pieces beyond recognition!*

"Yuvaraj!" Karna rushed to his friend, followed by Kripacharya and Ashwatthama. I found that my twins were back as my wheel protectors. Dhrishtadyumna and Shikhandi too had come for my help.

I assured my warriors with a nod. They attacked the Kaurava Maharathas accompanying Duryodhana. The Kuru Yuvaraja had returned on a new chariot by now, with new vigour. I shot a dart at him. His arms bled. The next moment, I lost my bow.

I took another bow and cut down his banner again. He shot more arrows at me. I replied back with a couple of arrows that cut down his bow into pieces. Duryodhana again changed his bow. His frame shook in wrath. His arrows pierced me harder this time. I persisted despite the blood dripping down my chest. I hurled a dart at him with all my might, my raged breath racing like storm. My dart penetrated through his armour, drawing more blood. He sank on his chariot.

Loud cheers from my warriors greeted me. I did not miss the familiar note of Prativindhya's conch, informing me about his victory against Chitra. Pride filled me with newer energy to fight.

Those cheers seemed to have added to Duryodhana's ego. He quickly steadied himself, grabbing the flag post. Then he threw a lance at me. I cut it into half at the midway. Another loud cheer followed, this time accompanied by Panchajanya's notes of victory.

My next arrow shoved Duryodhana's crown. Blood tickled down his face. I kept shooting more arrows at him, letting them carry all my anger of thirteen years. They drank his heart-blood, quenching my thirst for revenge. Duryodhana leaned on his flag post for a while. But he recovered soon and raised a club. Before he could hurl it at me, I threw a spear at him. It pierced his armour, making him bleed from chest. The club slipped down from his grip. Blood splurred out his mouth and he fell unconscious on the chariot.

"Samrat!" Bhima cried. "His death is in my share. Spare him for me!"

I nodded, breathing out at my fainted opponent.

"Go, Duryodhana! Keep breathing till my brother fulfills his vow." I said and ordered my charioteer to drive ahead.

Bhima saw me sparing Duryodhana's life and went to attack Kritavarma who had come for Duryodhana's help. And then, I heard Devadutta's note.

Arjuna was back from killing Samshaptakas.

I exhaled. Arjuna wreaked havoc on Kaurava army. Ashwatthama rushed to stop him but failed. Duryodhana had regained consciousness by then. He too attacked Arjuna but could not stand him for long. My brother cut his horses and standard. Before Duryodhana could change his chariot, Arjuna pierced him with arrows that broke his armour. Duryodhana stood perplexed for a while and then retreated.

The Kaurava commander came to the fore and attacked Arjuna now. He pierced both Arjuna and Krishna with arrows. Krishna's injury seemed to have added to Arjuna's wrath. He killed Karna's wheel protectors and charioteer. Duryodhana again came to assist his friend but Arjuna drove him away.

Karna returned with a new chariot. Arjuna covered him with bunches of arrows like group of dark clouds cover sun's radiance. Karna bled heavily but kept answering back. Their duel continued longer than my expectation. I waited eagerly for the result. But to my despair, it had to be left without a conclusion.

The sun had set, as if saving Karna from my brother's wrath.

My fist curled as I watched the red ball sinking down the horizon. Had we got a little more time, it could have ended today itself!

Dhrishtadyumna played the note of calling off today's battle. The fellow Panchalas rejoiced our dominance over Kauravas till the end of the day. But I could not share their jubilation.

The person I wanted to see as dead was still alive!

***

*The seventeenth day*:

"Today should be the last day for the king of Anga!" I declared, glancing upon my commanders. Each of them nodded, clutching their weapons tighter. Their joint notes of conch followed.

The battle had begun for the day. Though I had strategized earlier regarding who would counter whom, it was not maintained in the heat of war. Satyaki fought Kritavarma and Dhrishtadyumna against Kripacharya. Arjuna countered Trigarta king Susharma who was leading the Samshapataka army. Bhima's target was the only remaining brother of Duryodhana and that was Duhshasana himself.

I straightened up as I saw Karna. He had taken a new charioteer today. And it was none other than uncle Shalya!

The promise I had taken from him surfaced in my mind. I hoped he would also remember, and fulfill my wish!

I approached Karna. But Ashwatthama came in between to counter me. From his aggressive mode of attack I understood that he was pouring out his wrath on me for causing his father's death.

He cut down my banner with two arrows and then my bow with two more. I replied back with a dart that killed his charioteer. He changed his chariot within a blink of eye and shot multiple arrows at me.

Satyaki rushed to my help. He cut down the lance Ashwatthama hurled at me. An annoyed Ashwatthama left me and started duel with Satyaki.

And then, I heard Bhima's roar.

"This is how you once grabbed my wife, remember?"

I turned round. Bhima had grabbed Duhshasana's hair. The Kuru prince was standing on ground, his armour broken, his crown fallen on earth. Behind him was his chariot, motionless as his charioteer and horses had lost their lives to my brother.

Bhima hit him at the chest with mace. Duhshasana staggered back, vomiting blood. Bhima hit him once more on the stomach and kicked him hard. Duhshasana fell on the ground. Bhima kicked him again. The Kuru prince's trembling body skidded across the mud.

Bhima's sword flashed in the air for a while. The next moment, Duhshasana yelled in pain.

Two streams of blood erupted in the air. The soil where the Kuru prince lay got drenched in blood and flesh coming out of his shoulders. His both arms lay on that pool of blood, separated from his body, unable to move anymore.

*They would never be able to assault another woman!*

I took a deep breath. Duhshasana's deafening yell coupled with the uncontrollable trembling of his blood-drenched body gave me a deep feeling of contentment. After years!

*I so wished Draupadi was here in the battlefield to see how her offender was getting his Karmaphala.*

Bhima did not stop. His sword slashed Duhshasana's broad chest, making blood flow like fountain. I saw my brother cupping his palms to hold it, and then he touched that blood with his lips.

"I tasted nectar today!" Bhima cried in delight. Duhshasana's blood rolled down his jaws. As he lifted his head, our eyes met for a while. His blood-stained jawlines mirrored my own satisfaction, or maybe even more.

*My brother has kept his vow! No matter how inhuman people might call him, he has proven himself again! As a husband. As a Yuvaraja of the empire of Dharma!*

Bhima continued taking blood within his mouth and spiting it out. Kaurava warriors who were close to that place saw Bhima in that condition and fled away, mistaking him to be a man-eater Rakshasa. Their scream made Senapati Karna rush to the spot. His very sight made my blood boil.

This inhuman also deserved a similar punishment as Duhshasana did!

I gathered all my might and faced Karna. He fumed equally as I blocked his way. I shot arrows at his flag post. His banner fell down. Karna gritted his teeth and cut down my bow. As I took a new one, my standard fell down, and at the next moment, my horses gave out a sharp cry. I realised it as my chariot sank down.

Indrasena took no time to shift me to another chariot. I replied to Karna with as many arrows as I could shoot together. He pressed his chest, sinking on his chariot. My next arrows hit uncle Shalya who held Karna's reins. Karna sprung to his feet, fuming. He shot a bunch of arrows at me that hit my hands and armour. His next arrow felled my crown. I shot at the warriors who protected Karna's wheels and back. He became more furious now. Arrows after arrows rained upon me. My armour got broken. Blood from my chest and arms had smeared my weapons. I tightened the grip on my bow, struggling to hold myself. I could sense that he was gaining upper hand over me.

I steadied myself again and hurled a spear at Karna. He sliced it in the midway. The next moment two sharp-edged arrows dug deep into my both shoulders. As I picked arrows to shoot at him, two more struck to my chest, drawing more blood. Karna's face held a deep satisfaction while his lips were curved in sheer contempt. He laughed in a weird pleasure as he saw my blood spill.

As if he was playing a game!

"Leave him, Karna. What will you get by killing Yudhishthira?" I heard uncle Shalya speaking. "Rather let me drive to Arjuna." He suggested Karna.

"You do your job, Sarathi!" Karna hissed, and shot an arrow at my head. I ducked just in time. His next arrows hit my neck and shoulder.

For a while I saw darkness. I clutched the flag post to hold myself. But Karna's arrows did not stop. They kept coming like showers of monsoon, drenching me in blood. My entire body felt like burning in pain. Blood gushed down from almost every pore. Through my blurred vision, I saw Karna laughing.

The same offensive laughter that he laughed in the dice hall!

"Retreat, Samrat! Or send a note to the Senapati." Indrasena's voice held concern.

He said it right. I should not risk my life and my freedom thus! While I vehemently hated withdrawing the duel with someone like Karna, I could sense that I had no other way.

"Drive away!" I ordered Indrasena. As soon as my chariot moved away, I heard Karna's laughter growing louder.

"Fleeing away in fear, Chakravarti Samrat Yudhishthira?"

It felt like hot iron being poured into my ears.

*Should I remind you how you fled in ghosha yatra battle, Angaraja? Or in the battle of Matsya?*

"Drive ahead!" I told Indrasena.

"I knew that you don't carry a kshatriya's blood, Yudhishthira! You must be a Brahmin by birth!" I heard again. "Go, hide in your camp with this fragile life. I don't kill a coward like you!"

My breath raced.

The cowardest man, who could stoop as low as disrobing enemy's wife, was calling that to me!

I would still have retreated, if not for Sahadeva's conch Manipushpaka crying out for help. Karna had now targeted him and Nakula together. His insulting remarks accompanied each arrow he shot at them.

I could not let the twins face what I did!

I turned back to guard my twins, wondering how long I could fight for them. My physical strength was failing me. But the protector in me still persisted. I began shooting arrows at Karna. His arrows kept pierced my chest, arms, and legs. At a moment I felt that I also would end up being permanently inactive like grandfather Bhishma.

I lost my horses and banner before I knew. Karna's next arrow hit close to my heart. My bow fell down from my grip. I could not lift my arm to pick it up.

The last thing I could sense was Indrasena calling out to me. Then, it was all dark.

# CHAPTER THIRTY

I woke up on a bed, royal physicians standing around me with worry on their faces. My eyes moved around and I was sure it was my tent. A worried Indrasena sat close to me, tying pieces of cloth on my wounds. He was instructing few servants who seemed busy in grounding something.

Why had they brought me here?

My gaze shifted to the window. Sun had not yet set, and here I was, in the camp instead of battlefield!

"Don't, Samrat!" Indrasena said as I tried to arise. "You need more rest."

I shook my head. "Battle is still going on, Indrasena. My soldiers might get discouraged if they don't see their king present."

"Your physical condition does not permit that, Samrat." Said the chief physician. "You have to take rest for the day to fully recover from these wounds. If you want to fight tomorrow, pray, forget about doing that today."

I looked around. Even my charioteer and servants nodded, agreeing to the physician.

"Still I need to visit the battlefield at least once, Vaidya." I tried to explain. "The news of my retiring to camp must have spread by now. My brothers and friends might feel worried."

"I'm seeing to it." Indrasena volunteered. "Let me send a message to Senapati Dhrishtadyumna that you are conscious now." He hurried and left the tent. The chief vaidya came beside me and checked all the wounds.

"Paining a lot, doesn't it?" he said with concern. I managed to nod a little. The bleeding had stopped by now but not the pain.

"There has been excessive bleeding. I myself have never seen any warrior injuring his enemy in this way." The vaidya remarked. "Better they would kill the enemy with fewer blows. But this looks more like playing with the enemy instead of trying to kill him."

I curled my fists, turning my head to the other side. Karna's actions and words kept piercing my memory. It seemed like he would have spared my life even if I did not retreat. It was my greatest pain that Karna had left me thus instead of killing me. No insult can be greater than this for a warrior!

But why? What had made him do so with the enemy king? Or did he do this willingly to leave me alive with an insult that was way worse than death?

"It will take longer to heal." The vaidya said. "And pray, have your evening meal on time today. You have lost too much of blood and fasting will worsen it further."

"I have informed Senapati's charioteer, Samrat." Indrasena entered in. "Now stay assured and relaxed."

"We shall take your leave now, Samrat." The chief physician said. "Your danger is over. All you need is a good sleep. Let only Indrasena and a few servants be here for calling us in any urgency."

He bowed to me and left with his group.

"Try to get some sleep, Samrat." Indrasena softly said. Now he was no more a charioteer. He had taken the role of my dear friend, as he always used to do in my need.

I closed my eyes only to please Indrasena. But sleep was not to come in this condition. The very thought that I was lying on bed without avenging Karna's insulting words made my heart burn. Each of his spiteful words kept piercing me even more than his physical arrows.

My entire being craved for rushing to battlefield and countering Karna again. But reality did not allow me to. The physical pain had become more intolerable now after the weapons had been uprooted from deeper flesh. Bitter medicinal herbs mixing with them had made it even worse. I could not even move my arms. It felt like arrows and darts were still piercing into all my limbs. I doubted whether I would be able to fight even tomorrow.

Only the news of Karna's death could heal me now! Would that happen today?

"Jyeshtha!"

I opened my eyes. It was Arjuna. His eyes and his voice could not hide worry.

My eyes immediately moved to the window. Sun had not yet set. Why had he come here then?

"I just heard it from Bhrata Bhima and could not just stop myself." Arjuna sat beside my bed as Indrasena had left the seat for him. "How are you now?" he took my hands within his. But even his affectionate gestures failed to soothe the burning pain in my heart. Rather it leapt up more.

I did not want a loving caress from my brother now. I wanted to see Karna's corpse!

"I'll be well only when I shall see Karna's chopped head, Arjuna." I struggled to raise myself to a sitting position. "Has that happened yet?"

Arjuna's expressions said that he had not expected me to ask that. He shook his head.

"Then what are you doing here, brother? You need to be there now."

"We had to come, Jyeshtha." Krishna entered. "The way the news of you retiring to camp spread that even we thought for a while that something worse has happened."

"You two should not have left battlefield at this crucial time, Krishna. At least not until Karna dies." I gravely said. "He is in his most aggressive form today. I don't want any more loss in our side."

"Bhrata Bhima is there to take care." Arjuna tried to assure me.

"Bhima has not taken the vow of killing Karna. You did. Bhima is fulfilling his vow and you must do yours." My voice was turning sharp. "Why did you escape from your duty before sunset?"

Arjuna frowned. He had not expected this tone from me. Even Indrasena looked at me in shock.

"I did not escape, Jyeshtha. I heard that you are seriously sick and hence came to check your wellbeing." He sounded grave now.

"For what? You are not a physician. You are a warrior. Your duty is to stay on battlefield, not in camp of injured warriors. We have enough vaidyas for this job."

"What has happened to you, Jyeshtha?" Arjuna's voice betrayed hurt. "Why are you talking thus to me?"

I knew my tone was gradually leaving my usual calmness, as did my mind. But a part of me felt satisfied to behave rudely with Arjuna. The rest of me wondered why.

Was I pouring out my anger with Karna on my brother?

"I am the king and I have right to tell you that you are not doing your duty." I continued in even more raised tone. "You have left my army to Karna's fury for nothing. What will happen if my army faces danger in your absence?"

Maybe I was not doing this right. But I could not just stop. My bleeding body and mind both craved to release the fire within. Arjuna's misfortune that he had to come in front of me at this moment.

"You want to say I'm not doing my duty to your army?" Arjuna's face darkened.

"From the very first day you are being mild on the Kaurava commanders out of love and respect. Do you even have an idea how many soldiers have given up their lives just because of your mildness with grandfather and Guru Drona? Do you remember how our friends, relatives, even our sons, died to pay for this?" I burst out now. My suppressed annoyance on him since seventeen days had finally found a channel to escape today.

"That Lord of Anga has insulted your brothers today in battlefield. And you came here without avenging that? Have you forgotten that this is the person who called your wife a ..... that day?" I sensed a couple of my wounds had opened owing to my restless movements and excessive stress. Fresh blood flowed again from my shoulder and chest.

Arjuna's jaws gritted. "I have not forgotten anything, Samrat."

"Then out of which sympathy are you setting him free to destroy our army in your absence? Or is it out of fear?" I lashed out the deadliest weapon, knowing well that it would become intolerable for him. "Shame on you that you feel scared of that suta even after having a bow like Gandiva and charioteer like Krishna! If you are so afraid to fight Karna, better handover the Gandiva to Krishna and hold the reins yourself!"

"Samrat!" he cried, anger leaping up in his eyes now.

"Before telling this to me, kindly turn your finger to yourself, Samrat Yudhishthira!" he fumed. "It's not me who is scared of Karna. *You* are! Do admit the truth now!"

"Arjuna!" Krishna came forward. "Jyeshtha is not himself today. Don't take his words to heart."

"He has no right to call me a coward, Krishna!" Arjuna breathed angrily. "How dare he accuse me of escaping the battle while he himself is lying in the camp? How just is it to blame us after depending solely on our prowess?"

"Arjuna, calm down, friend!" Krishna softly said, patting him.

"I cannot. This is grave insult on my valour, my very existence." Arjuna's hand moved to the sheath of his sword. Realising his intention, Krishna quickly snatched the sword from his waist.

"Have you gone insane, Arjuna?" Krishna snapped. "Whom are you going to kill? Your brother, your king, the one you revere as your Guru?"

"No, the one who has caused all the troubles in our lives." Arjuna vented out. "It has been my biggest folly to stay loyal to him. I have surrendered my valour, my life, even my first wife to him. I have silently watched him gambling away all my hard-earned wealth and yet followed him without a protest. And this is the reward for that?"

"This is not time to reminiscence our past ignoring the crisis at hand." I frowned. "If that's your regret why didn't you speak up when needed?"

"I could not, Samrat. For the sake of our unity." Arjuna fumed. "Can you even imagine my agony of seeing the princess I won, marrying you? But I stayed quiet because I had seen desire in your eyes for her. In all four of you." Pain replaced anger in his tone. "I didn't want to become a cause of division."

It felt like a stab in my heart. As if someone threw my dark past over me to extinguish the fire of my anger.

*He had kept that grudge suppressed for decades? And I could never even know!*

Yes, he saw it right that day. But my conscience knew that I would have suppressed my desire for the rest of my life had Arjuna agreed to marry Draupadi alone. I would even have pushed the other three brothers for the same. I was ready for that. But Arjuna did not cooperate with me then.

"Still I had swallowed that pain, accepting it as my destiny." Arjuna continued in a raised tone. "But you didn't stop even there, Dharmaraj! You have gambled me away along with my wife and brothers. Who gave you that right to play with our freedom that day?"

Arjuna's entire frame shook in anger. Krishna indicated him to stop but he did not.

"Can you explain me why I should stake my life for your sake today? What Dharma we are fighting for, Samrat Yudhishthira? To make someone sit on the imperial throne who can gamble it again?"

I bit my lips. The surroundings felt darkened even in this daylight.

Arjuna had always been my strongest support. Even at the most vulnerable moments when Bhima and the twins opposed me. I could never even know that he had this much anger, and maybe hatred, suppressed within against me!

Today's sudden outburst had cleared it all!

I rose. The pain within had replaced all the physical wounds now.

"Is this the reason you are reluctant to fight in your full might since the beginning, Arjuna?" My voice had turned softer.

"You deserve to raise this question today. It's for my reason you all have been forced to bleed, lose your sons, and even kill the elders you respect. I know that I deserve your curse all the time for this."

"Jyeshtha," Krishna came closer to me. "You are not well. Pray, do not stress yourself thus."

"I have to say this, Krishna. Pray, do not stop me." I looked again at Arjuna. "You are right. You should not fight to make a gambler sit on imperial throne and you don't have to. Keep fighting for yourselves. Not for me."

Krishna looked at me with concern. Arjuna still had the deep frown on his face.

"I won't take the kingdom, Arjuna. Let it be yours . But pray, don't leave it at this stage now. Don't let the war end without a result."

"That's not possible, Dharmaraj." Krishna shook his head. "This war is being fought to make you the emperor and will be continued for the same."

"No, Krishna." I almost whispered. "I don't deserve to rule this country. I don't deserve to be the leader of this army. Arjuna is right. The king who always needs others' protection, who is so weak to save himself from enemies' attack, how can he rule a whole empire?" I felt like bleeding not just from my body but from inside too. As if an old wound at heart had opened after years.

"Better I should retire to forest where I can spend the rest of my life in peace. Let Bhima or Arjuna rule the Pandavas. Either of them will be the best emperor ever."

"Samrat, pray, come out of this illusion now!" Krishna shook my arm. "This is not why you have suffered for thirteen long years and fought for seventeen days. Don't let all this blood and sweat go in vain thus! Don't disappoint those souls who have died for *you*!"

His tone throbbed with pain of disappointment. I felt compelled to meet his eyes. The same pain surfaced there too. I could not bring myself to speak anymore.

"You are the one who knows how to stay calm in every battle, Jyeshtha. Please, gather yourself!" Krishna pleaded again. His eyes still betrayed the hurt.

A pang of guilt passed through my conscience.

It was not for this that Krishna went against his own Yadavas and came to us, willingly! He had always wanted us five to stay united and work together for a greater good. This rift between us would not hurt him any less than the division within Dwaraka.

*Why didn't I care for that?*

Krishna then turned to Arjuna.

"Remember one thing, Arjuna. Your aim is not just getting back your own kingdom but it's as big as restoring Dharma in Bharata. And you need your brothers in this as much as they need you. Dharma needs you five staying together, not fighting within."

His words pierced my conscience harder. I felt ashamed now.

*How could I lose myself to that extent?*

In our own fights we had forgotten the greater aim we were yet to achieve. We forgot the two people who would feel the most hurt to see this. One was in front of us. And the other one was in Upaplavya. The one who had sacrificed her own comforts for the sake of our unity. How could we even forget how Draupadi would feel to hear this?

I pushed the grudge out of my heart. Even Arjuna's eyes had softened now.

"I am sorry, Krishna." I muttered. "Whatever might happen between us, we have no right to disappoint a friend like you." I joined my palms. "I apologise. Both on my and my brother's behalf."

He held my joint palms and smiled, patting them slowly.

"I apologise to you too, Arjuna." I turned to my brother. "I have been out of my mind today. This will never repeat."

"Don't add more to my guilt, Jyeshtha." He held my hands. "It's me who should apologise." He knelt down. Warm tears fell on my feet.

"I don't know what made me speak so harshly to you, Jyeshtha. But I never meant it. Pray, don't take my offence!" He joined his palms.

I raised him. "You are not at fault, little one. The fault is all mine." I smelt the scent of his head. "I should never have doubted your valour that has kept me protected since childhood." I embraced Arjuna who was still in tears. "Forgive me, dear brother!"

Krishna came closer, smiling. "I'm glad that you two corrected yourselves soon. The unity of Pandavas has survived all possible threats. It cannot be so fragile to break so easily."

"It won't." Arjuna's voice was much calmer now. "Let me take your leave now, Jyeshtha. You shall hear the news of Karna's death before sun sets today." He touched my feet and picked up Gandiva.

"Vijayi bhava!" I uttered my blessing.

# CHAPTER THIRTY-ONE

It felt so relaxing to hear the news.

"Tell me once again, messenger!" I asked, partly to feel the happiness fully, partly to confirm that I heard it correct and did not dream within my trances.

"Prince Arjuna has killed Angraja Karna." The messenger repeated. "His Anjalika arrow has just beheaded the Kaurava Senapati."

I took a deep breath. I doubted whether I had ever been this delighted in the past thirteen years. This comfort and content could only be compared with the one during the final ceremony of Rajasuya. The only regret was that I could not witness the most awaited death of Karna in my own eyes.

I rose. "Get my chariot ready, Indrasena. I shall go to the battlefield."

"Samrat, you have not yet..."

"I have recovered." I cut him off. "All my pains have disappeared as soon as I heard this. Take me to the battlefield, Indrasena. I cannot miss to see the corpse I have waited for since thirteen years!"

There was a flicker of shock in Indrasena's eyes. Perhaps because he had never seen me being this happy to hear someone's death. He took a while to observe me, and then went back to obey my order with a nod.

When I reached the battlefield, sun was about to set. The last ray of sun fell on Karna's armour like a gloomy gaze of someone dear to him. Karna's headless body lay on the ground near his chariot whose wheel had stuck to the mud. Uncle Shalya sat quiet, still holding the reins of that motionless vehicle. I looked around for Karna's head.

There it was! Arjuna's arrow had felled it far away.

The tongue that had once called my wife's name was dumb forever now. The eyes that wanted to see her naked had been closed forever! A refreshing feeling washed over me as I saw fresh blood still gushing down his head.

Note of Dhrishtadyumna's conch reached my ear overpowering the mourning noises of Kauravas. The war had ended for the day.

My eyes now turned to a victorious Arjuna. His smile faded as he saw me.

"Jyeshtha!" he hurried to me. "Why have you come here in this condition?"

"I am fine, brother." I assured him. "How could I not come to congratulate you for this feat?" I smiled and embraced him.

Krishna went down the chariot and came closer.

"Arjuna has fulfilled his promise, Samrat." He said. "Karna has not seen today's sunset."

"My penance of thirteen years has borne fruit, Krishna. At least, now I can feel myself deserving to face Draupadi." Arjuna muttered.

His brightened face spoke of his inner peace. I knew how comforting that feeling was. But I could not deserve to face my wife yet. Not before Duryodhana and Shakuni were also dead.

"Our joint penance will bear fruits, brothers. We are just one more step away from victory. And we shall achieve that soon, too." Bhima came forward along with the twins. "Duryodhana won't see more than one sunrise! I promise!" He assured, his eyes shone in a wrath he had nourished within for thirteen years.

"Neither will Shakuni do." Sahadeva added. I saw my brothers nodding, their eyes glowing in content. After thirteen years!

"You should not forget Madraraja Shalya." Krishna reminded. "I have a feeling that Duryodhana might choose him as the next Senapati. And don't think that he would be kind to you just because of your relation."

"I know that. He is the same for us as grandfather and Gurudeva were." I remarked. "He loves us but won't spare our warriors while fighting. We have to be careful about him."

"Better you take the lead tomorrow, Jyeshtha. Let Arjuna protect your chariot." Krishna suggested. "King Shalya is a famed spearman, and very calculative warrior. Only you can handle him the best."

I nodded, realising well that Krishna was asking me to do it so that I could wash away my insult of today's defeat. And it was also true that both Bhima and Arjuna along with our Maharathas were tired enough after seventeen days of war. The king they had guarded these days needed to come out of his shell now.

For proving himself worthy of winning this war!

***

*The eighteenth day:*

Kaurava army looked so scattered today.

Senapati Shalya had formed Sarvatobhadra vyuha. But the soldiers seemed to have already left all hope about winning this war. They often launched unplanned attacks out of the order of their vyuha.

Uncle Shalya was in his full form today. He shuttered my army singlehandedly and kept Dhrishtadyumna and Satyaki on check who tried to stop him. Bhima faced him but he also got wounded. Neither could Shikhandi stand for long.

I drove towards uncle Shalya, having the twins guard my chariot wheels. He shot a serpent-shaped arrow at me. I replied back with the sharpest arrow I had, desiring to hit his inner organs. It worked. The Madra king sank on his chariot, pressing his chest.

I killed the two protectors of his chariot wheels. This made him fume. He quickly steadied himself and showered arrows at me. I cut down his flag and bow. He took another and shot arrows like heavy rainfall. Those arrows pierced my armour. I held my flag post to gather myself.

Seeing me in that condition, the twins came to guard me. But they could not check their own uncle. Bhima came for my help, followed by Satyaki. The Lord of Madra covered them with arrows.

I steadied myself and faced him again. With two arrows I cut his bow into half. My next arrows killed his four horses. I did not stop before claiming the life of his charioteer in my next shot. The king looked perplexed but quickly collected himself and boarded a new chariot. He pierced me hard on my both arms. I replied back with equal blow on his chest. He cut my bow and then, my horses too. Before I could get down, my charioteer Indrasena's body fell down from my chariot.

My heart ached as I looked at his lifeless body. A part of me felt numb. My loyal charioteer, my faithful friend since young years had left me. I could not save the one who had served me like my fifth brother!

I could not even get time to mourn Indrasena. The next moment the protector of my back lost his head. The couple of arrows that claimed his life had come from a different direction.

I looked around. Guru Kripacharya had intervened.

Quickly gathering myself, I jumped to Nakula's chariot. Shalya advanced me with a sword and shield in both hands. His sword could not land on me though. A new bunch of arrows cut his weapons down.

Bhima had come!

"This is why you left the duel with me, Bhima?" Guru Kripacharya snapped.

"It's you who have withdrawn first to help your Senapati, Kulaguru." Bhima calmly replied.

Kripacharya frowned and advanced Bhima again. As both of them started another duel, Shalya picked up a spear and advanced me again. Without much thought, I picked up my favorite javelin that was gifted by Guru Dronacharya himself. Determination had replaced my grief now.

Indrasena would not want me losing my battle. The best tribute I could pay to his lifelong service was Shalya's death and our victory!

The Kaurava Senapati launched his attack. I blocked the blow with my weapon and hit his spear hard. He realised that I could disarm him and stepped back. I went defensive deliberately for a while, locking my spear with his, letting him increase the gap. He tried to circle me from that distance but I quickly stepped back and hurled my spear at him. Its hardened metal tip entered his chest and emerged from his back. His trembling body fell on the ground. Fresh blood gushed down his chest. His limbs stopped moving soon.

"Senapati Shalya is no more!" cried the Kaurava soldiers. Most of them, especially the Madra warriors, started to run away.

Bhima had won over Kripacharya. He was now fighting against Duryodhana. The Kuru Yuvaraja seemed much tired today. As if Duhshasana and Karna's deaths had drawn out all the energy from him.

Bhima hurled a javelin at Duryodhana's chest that made him faint. His charioteer took him away from Bhima. Guru Kripacharya and Kritavarma also followed that direction.

Sahadeva was at his best against Shakuni. His arrows covered the Lord of Gandhara. A wounded Shakuni tried to flee, but my youngest brother did not let him. They began the duel with doubled vigour. I wished to witness the rest of their duel but I could not. Uncle Shalya's younger brother blocked my way.

He seemed desperate and determined to avenge his late brother. Unwilling to spend long with him, I picked up my spear and jolted it through his heart. He gave out a sharp cry before falling dead. The remaining Madras cried out in fear. A familiar note of conch soon overpowered it.

Sahadeva's Manipushpaka.

Shakuni's head had fallen on ground. The dice of deceit had finally stopped rolling.

The Kaurava army saw Shakuni's beheaded corpse and began to flee. There was not much time left for sunset. My brothers had returned from their respective duels.

But where was Duryodhana?

"Coward!" Bhima gnashed his teeth. "Fled with his life!"

Maybe he did. But I could not just spare him like that. Letting him live for another day meant one more day of war, and even more loss in lives and wealth. At this point, we could not simply afford to have the luxury of saving the main enemy for one more day. This war needed to end today itself.

"We cannot allow him to escape alive, Bhima." I said. "Come, let's send away spies to search for him."

# CHAPTER THIRTY-TWO

It had been past midday. Still there was no trace of Duryodhana.

"I never knew that he was such a coward." Bhima groaned.

"And irresponsible too." Nakula added. "He left his entire army just to save himself."

"His army is also not here." Sahadeva commented. "The remaining Kaurava warriors have fled."

"Let them." I said. "Soldiers are not our target. Their leader is."

"But where is he?" Bhima sounded impatient. "All the spies have returned unsuccessful."

"Send more spies to different directions." I suggested. "We cannot give up and complain, standing idle here. We have to find him out and kill him before sun sets for the day."

"Let me talk with the spies." Arjuna nodded and stepped forward. A messenger hurried to us.

"Samrat, the forest-hunters await Yuvaraj Bhima's audience."

"Hunters? Now?" Bhima looked reluctant. "This isn't the time. Tell them to come after sunset."

"I already told them so, Yuvaraj." The messenger said. "But they are insisting on meeting you. They say it's urgent."

Something struck me. These forest-dwellers might help us if Duryodhana had taken shelter there. Maybe they would be able to bring the news sooner.

"Send them." I ordered.

These were the hunters who used to supply raw meat and wine regularly to our camp. I did not have much contact with them as Bhima generally used to do that. It was his task to talk to them regarding the deals and negotiations. They were aware of our timing and never came like this during the battle. Their insistence of meeting us at this afternoon seemed like they had something else to offer us today.

A group of our familiar hunters arrived soon and bowed to us. Their eyes glowed in excitement.

"I have already paid you for today's supply." Bhima reminded. "Why have you come at this time?"

"My Lord, we have seen something while coming from forest." Their leader said joining his palms. His tone was a little louder than whisper.

"Three warriors of the other camp were talking to someone near the Dwaipayana lake." He continued. "I have not heard what they were talking but it seemed suspicious. So we thought of informing you."

I straightened myself.

"Whom did you see?" I asked. "Which three?"

"We don't know their names, Lord. But one of them is an old man, almost looks like a sage. And another one has a bright stone tied on his forehead."

"Ashwatthama!" I muttered. "And Kulaguru Kripacharya."

The third one must be Kritavarma, I guessed. Only these three major warriors were still alive on that side. And it was now clear that they knew where Duryodhana was. There must be some new plan going on between the four.

*Who does not know how desperate a dying lion can be?* We had to stop them before they could come back.

"We cannot thank you enough for this information, friends!" I looked at the hunters. "You don't know what a huge favour you have done to us!"

They bowed again. "We consider this our duty, Lord. You have been so kind to us since the beginning. It's our great fortune if we can come to your help, even if it's a small one."

I smiled as I joined my palms. As they bowed and left, Bhima looked at me with question.

"Jyeshtha, did that mean..."

"Duryodhana is near Dwaipayana Lake, Bhima." I said. "We have to go! Quick!"

***

The lake of Dwaipayana was in the middle of the forest leading to Samantapanchaka. While proceeding through the way, I carefully observed behind the bushes. There was no trace of any movement at all. Neither was any restlessness seen in the birds and animals that could hint a human presence.

Where was Duryodhana hiding then?

I shifted my keen gaze to the lake. A small ripple was forming over the otherwise calm surface. Yet no animal was seen to be drinking water. My eyebrows met.

"I don't think we would find him here." Satyaki was disappointed. "Rather..."

I raised a hand to stop him and indicated towards the unexplainable vibration on the water. "Can you see?"

Satyaki nodded as he followed my finger. "Yes. But what does that..."

"Guru Kripacharya had taught us a vidya of breathing under water, remember?" I looked at my brothers. "Partly adjusting own body parts, partly using a few hollow objects. If practiced well, one can survive under water for a longer time too."

All my brothers' eyes turned to me.

"That means," Arjuna voiced it. "Duryodhana is hiding under the lake?"

"That is the only possibility, Arjuna. Especially when Guru Kripacharya has been found here talking to some invisible person." I explained. "This is why those hunters could not see Duryodhana."

"Whatever it might be, we have to hurry, Jyeshtha." Bhima said, quickly glancing at the evening sun. "Not much time is left for the day."

"Duryodhana is now in such a position that we cannot just go and attack him." I shook my head. "We have to make him come out willingly and fight us."

And I knew that was not going to be easy. I had to hurt his ego enough to bring him back to the battle.

I approached the lake.

"Come out, Yuvaraj Duryodhana! We know you are here."

No response came. My warriors exchanged glances.

"This hide and seek does not suit a warrior, Duryodhana." I raised my voice. "The battle has not ended yet. Come out and fight! You have fought bravely enough in the past seventeen days. Don't earn the title of coward out of fear now."

"I am not escaping the battle, Yudhishthira." A familiar yet broken, tired voice came from the lake, creating more ripples on the surface.

"I have renounced the world." He continued in the same tone. "Now I have no more urge to fight for saving my kingdom from you invaders. Take it and let me enter forest."

Renounced? That very person who could do anything to snatch other's wealth? Was this some new trick planned by the four?

"That is not possible, Duryodhana. Once the war has started, we have to finish it no matter what." My voice was firm. "Both you and I have lost enough of our loved ones in these eighteen days. We cannot let their sacrifices go in vain without a conclusion thus. Let's end this now!"

"It's already ended." His voice was unbelievably calm. "You have won. I have given up my rights to you. Go and enjoy Hastinapura. Leave me alone in peace."

"I have not come here to accept charity from you, Yuvaraj of Kurus. I have come to earn my own rights back." I sensed that my voice had been unusually louder as my brothers looked at me in surprise.

"This war needs to be taken to a conclusion, son of Dhritarashtra. And that can never happen with both of us staying alive." My voice sounded dry.

"Either you have to die today, or I!" I declared.

"Then assume me as dead and leave. No one shall ever put a claim on Hastinapura. You can trust my words."

"I choose not to! You have refused my message of peace one day. I refuse to accept your charity now." I was calm yet determined. "Come out and do fight! Either attain the throne on earth or the heaven of warriors."

"I have interest in neither, Yudhishthira. I have been beyond all these now. You have killed all my brothers, my relatives, and friends. What shall I do winning this empty kingdom?" His voice echoed the void of his life at present.

"I don't want to cherish this widowed Rajyalakshmi anymore. Let her be yours now."

"Stop giving excuses just to save yourself!" I snapped. "A true Kshatriya does not waver from his own words till the end of his life. You were the one who once refused to give us even the soil on tip of a needle. Why are you giving away entire kingdom now? Are you scared to fight against us?"

A large ripple showed up on the water. I knew Duryodhana was breathing in anger. I exhaled. My effort seemed to have worked.

"If you are so much afraid of death, admit it, Yuvaraj!" I continued in same tone. "We shall consider sparing your life. We do not kill someone who is fleeing in fear."

"I am not afraid, son of Pandu. I can still defeat all of you along with Panchalas." Duryodhana roared. His voice echoed from the large trees surrounding the lake. A couple of birds drinking water flew away in fear.

"But you must promise me that you all won't attack me together. I am alone, without chariot and armour. Don't be unfair with me."

"Stay assured." I said. "I am providing you with everything that you need. You will get a chariot and armour, even weapons if you require. I also promise you that only one of us will fight with you. The others won't interfere."

A brief silence followed. Then a splash of water fell on my cloths. The calm water of Dwaipayana turned turbulent as Duryodhana's massive frame began to rise above the surface of lake. Water dripped from his person. The evening sun's ray reflected on golden layer of his iron mace.

"Thanks for the offer, Yudhishthira. But I don't want any charity from you either." He gritted his jaw. "I don't need chariot or armour. And for weapon, my mace is still with me and that's enough." He patted his weapon. "But remember your other promise that you won't attack me together. Come one by one. I'll vanquish all of you."

"I won't break my promise. You can trust me." I evenly uttered.

"I cannot. You have broken all the rules of war in past days." He glanced one by one at us. "It's my request to you, don't launch a group attack on a lonely warrior. That's unfair."

"Now you are remembering fair-unfair when it has come to you?" I retorted. "Where was this sense of morality when you six Maharathas attacked a young Abhimanyu together? He too was alone, Duryodhana. Did you show any mercy on him?"

Duryodhana did not reply. His squinted eyes rested on me, more disbelief surfaced on them. I knew that Abhimanyu's mention had made him even more doubtful regarding my promise.

"But worry not. I'm not going to take that revenge on you now. I know how to stick to my promise. Decide whom you want as your opponent, Yuvaraj. I assure that only he will fight against you. And since you have refused to take chariot, your opponent also will fight on ground to make it fair."

"Samrat!" Krishna nudged me. "What are you doing? This might ruin all our struggles so far!" he whispered, frowning. "It's nearly impossible for any of you except Bhima to defeat Duryodhana with mace. Your habit of gambling hasn't yet cured, Jyeshtha?"

Then, I regained my sense. It was true that Duryodhana with his mace was no match for any of us four or even Satyaki and Dhrishtadyumna. We all had defeated him in past seventeen days. But not in mace-fight. My eyes moved to the twins once. They stood with complete confidence. I dreaded even to think what might happen if Duryodhana decided on either of them in a mace-fight.

Sweat broke on my brow. Did I just make another gamble to prove my fairness to Duryodhana?

"Worry not, Krishna." Bhima came forward, whispering. He subtly nodded at both of us, his eyes held assurance. He then turned to me and side glanced on Duryodhana who was still observing us one by one, maybe still confused about whom to choose.

"Leave this sinner to me, Samrat!" Bhima said aloud. "I have killed all his brothers in this very hand." He flexed his arms. "His death too is destined in my hand. Let me fulfill my vow today!"

"You wretch!" Duryodhana cried out and rushed to Bhima. "My brothers' killer, cannibal Rakshasa! I won't spare you today!"

I exhaled, thanking Bhima's presence of mind. Even more thanks to Duryodhana's ego that had not seen the huge opportunity I had mistakenly opened to him. Perhaps that was the effect of absence of Karna and Shakuni.

The two warriors faced each other, whirling their maces in the air. I straightened myself.

"Wait! Do not fight here."

My head turned to the left from where the known voice came.

Balarama! Now, at this place? His visit of pilgrimage was over?

Both Duryodhana and Bhima put their maces aside and bowed to Balarama.

"Nothing could have been better than your arrival before our battle, Gurudeva." Duryodhana beamed. "Now I don't even have the slightest doubt of winning."

Something felt odd. If I remembered it correctly, Balarama did decide to return from Samanta Panchaka only after the war was over. He said that he did not want to witness this bloodshed between the two groups of his relatives. Then what made him come today just before the final battle?

Could Duryodhana have sent a message asking for his presence?

I did not get time to think more. Balarama was narrating the glory of Samanta Panchaka and insisting of letting the battle happen there instead.

"This uneven ground of Dwaipayana is not suitable for mace fighting." He said. "The plains around Samanta Panchaka will be the best for it. Also it's better to have the concluding battle of Kurukshetra on that sacred field blessed by Lord Parashurama himself."

"I have no objection." Duryodhana said.

"Neither do we." I gave my assent.

# CHAPTER THIRTY-THREE

The battle had begun.

We stood at a distance, maintaining the promise I had given to Duryodhana. Balarama sat on a rock, keeping his keen gaze on both of his students.

Frequent clash of both the maces caused sparks. The fight seemed never ending. It was true that Bhima was much more powerful and his mace too was heavier. But Duryodhana's skill and special twists could turn it towards him at any moment. I doubted whether Bhima's strength would be able to handle Duryodhana's well-trained strategies.

I held my breath as Duryodhana hit Bhima on his head. But my brother fought back with more wrath. He struck Duryodhana back, so hard that the eldest Kaurava fell unconscious. I let out the breath and exchanged glances with the others. All looked confident except Krishna. He still had curves of worry on his usually tranquil brow.

Duryodhana recovered soon enough and launched a powerful blow on Bhima's head. My brother still persisted before his opponent hit him harder on the chest. I saw fresh blood gushing down Bhima's armour. With the next blow, Bhima's armour got broken completely. He staggered a little before steadying himself again. At that moment, he looked way too exhausted.

As if the single duel was draining out all his energies!

"This is why I told you not to take this risk." I heard Krishna sighing. "You don't know how religiously Duryodhana has practiced on mace in thirteen years. He used to come to Dwaraka often to learn newer advanced techniques from Dau." He shook his head. "I don't think even Bhrata Bhima can defeat him in a fair way. We need some trick here."

I shook my head, realising what he meant. "No, Krishna. I have promised Duryodhana a fair battle. This will be a huge deceit if I break it now."

"You won't have to break it." Krishna smiled. "Your brother will. Or rather, he will just fulfill his own past vow."

I looked at his face with surprise. His eyes sparkled. He must be having an idea.

And then, I remembered.

"Are you too thinking what I am?" I whispered. My eyes stuck to Duryodhana's left thigh. My breath raced.

*How could I even forget that he once asked Draupadi to sit over there?*

"You got me, Jyeshtha." Krishna nodded.

"But it's against the norms of mace-fight to hit below naval."

"What did I just tell you? You have promised Duryodhana a one-on-one fight. Nobody is going to break that. But Bhrata Bhima is still free to do anything while fighting the duel, right?"

I nodded. Krishna was right. Duryodhana's demand had been fulfilled. Now it was time to let my brother fulfill his vow. But did Bhima even remember that he vowed to break Duryodhana's thighs? The way he was trying his best and yet could not overcome his opponent did not tell me so.

"Bhima needs a reminder, Krishna." I said. "Do remind him of his promise!"

Duryodhana had hit Bhima's head again. But Bhima showed no sign of weakness. His next strike launched on Duryodhana's chest, covering him with blood. Duryodhana visibly fumed. He raised his mace that struck Bhima as hard as it could.

Bhima fell on the ground. Duryodhana's loud laughter echoed from the trees beside Samanta Panchaka.

"Arise, Bhrata! You can do it!" Krishna drew Bhima's attention and patted his own thighs repeatedly. Bhima's eyebrows met for a while. And then, they evened. He nodded as he rose with double enthusiasm.

Duryodhana steadied his mace while Bhima suddenly jumped out in air. I straightened myself. Duryodhana's strike got wasted due to Bhima's sudden leap. I could sense that Bhima had done this deliberately, to make our plan work out.

And it did. Duryodhana too jumped out to make Bhima's next attack fail. Within a blink of eye, Bhima's heavy mace launched its best ever blow on Duryodhana's left thigh first, followed by the right one as the latter cried out in pain. The next moment Duryodhana landed on earth, blood gushing down both his thighs. His deafening yell reverberated from everywhere.

He did not seem to have the strength to arise anymore.

The Panchalas hailed Bhima aloud. I let out the breath I held for long. But the feeling of satisfaction was short-lived, owing to Balarama's sharp cry.

"Haven't I taught you that hitting below the naval is prohibited in mace-fight?" he fumed. "How could you do this?"

Bhima remained silent, lowering his gaze. I knew he would not be able to argue with Balarama. The only person who could stop Balarama was Krishna.

"Unjust warrior! You have insulted me, your Guru, along with your own valour!" Balarama continued in the same tone. "What Dharma empire are you five going to establish on this piled up unfairness?"

"Dau, pray, listen to me!" Krishna softly nudged him. But Balarama raised his palm.

"I have nothing more to listen from you or these five. I know you will still find ways to defend this. But for me there is no apology for my own student who did not honour my teaching. Bhima has made me ashamed. I can't let him go unpunished!" He raised his plough on Bhima. Krishna hurried and held his hand.

"Didn't Duryodhana make you ashamed, Dau? What punishment did you give him then?" Krishna's extremely calm voice made Balarama look at him.

"If Duryodhana's behaviour with Draupadi was fair, then what Bhima did is also fair. You might have forgotten, but it was your beloved student who dared to show his naked left thigh to a married woman, his own sister-in-law." Krishna continued looking through Balarama's eyes. The elder Vaasudeva just looked away, lowering his plough.

"Had Bhrata Bhima not vowed to break these thighs back then, Draupadi might have been assaulted even more. Was he wrong to protect his wife, Dau? Is he wrong to fulfill his oath as a Kshatriya?"

"I told you, Krishna, that you would have your own logic. But even then I cannot agree with this. Vow could be fulfilled after Duryodhana's death as well. The truth is that Bhima took unfair way just to win this war. He will have lifelong infamy for this!"

A weird silence followed. Even the Panchalas' hailing had stopped.

"I hate staying here even for a while!" Balarama rested his plough on his broad shoulder and turned to leave. His heavy footsteps gradually faded away towards west. As soon as the last trace of his long plough disappeared from our vision, Bhima pounced on a blood-drenched Duryodhana who was shivering in pain.

As if he was waiting for this opportunity!

"Wretch! You showed that thigh to my wife, remember?" Bhima roared. "You laughed at us while we left for exile. Now see us enjoying this sight of yours!" His left foot landed on Duryodhana's head and kicked him hard, making him vomit blood.

"Bhima! Stop this!" I rushed to him and pulled him away with some effort. He gasped, glaring at Duryodhana.

"No sane person does this to a dying man! Stop!" I snapped.

"Why should I?" he flared up, meeting my gaze. "This is the one who fed me poison. This is the one who wanted to burn us alive. This beast had assaulted our wife and robbed us of our kingdom. What honour does he..."

"I know everything, Bhima." I cut him off. "But he has just received his punishment. Your vow and vengeance both are over now. Stop insulting a dying warrior thus. This doesn't suit you."

Bhima pursed his lips and looked away. I sank on a rock, imagining what could have happened had Bhima kicked

Duryodhana's head in front of Balarama. Maybe I would have to lose my brother as well today.

Duryodhana was still alive, yelling in intolerable pain. I rested my eyes on him. Something churned inside me. There was no feeling of victory yet. Rather I sensed emptiness. A strange void lay around me.

Was I angry with Bhima? Not really. I knew well how much my brother had suffered since his fifteenth year due to Duryodhana. I could not hold grudge on him for expressing too much of anger. It was not his act but my own self that questioned me.

*Whom was I going to rule in this empty Bharatavarsha?*

What was the fruitfulness of so much blood? Losing almost all the elders who could have guided us? So many young lives who could have become great warriors and rulers one day? What was our right to let all of them get killed?

Duryodhana was right. Who desires to enjoy a vacant kingdom bathed in blood and tears? What feeling of victory would be there in Hastinapura palace now, with hundreds of widows cursing us?

I heaved a sigh. It seemed like Duryodhana only had won. Heaven of warriors waited to welcome him. And in my share there was only this emptiness.

"Jyeshtha!" Krishna's warm arm held my shoulder.

"This Bharatavarsha has become a crematory just in eighteen days, Krishna." I muttered. "What empire are we going to build on this?"

"We were prepared to pay this price of blood, weren't we? Lord Dharma is also the God of death, Jyeshtha. It's never easy to appease him."

The God of justice had taken too much of offerings to become appeased!

"Jyeshtha, our mission has been fulfilled." Krishna tried to cheer me up. "Dharma has won. This is not the time to sit dejected, brother. We have to work on the reconstruction of whatever was damaged in past thirteen years."

I nodded as I rose. Responsibility has no luxury to sit quiet and feel pained.

My gaze fell upon Bhima first, followed by the others who stood cheerless, probably for my reaction. I regretted for expressing my feeling. These brothers and friends of mine had put their lives at risk and lost their dear ones for my sake. I had no right to ruin their moment of celebration now.

I approached Bhima and embraced him with a smile.

"Congratulations for your feat, brother! You have freed us from our enemies."

Bhima's face lit up. Arjuna and the twins came forward and touched my feet. I lifted them and drew them in my arms.

"Congratulations, Senapati! You have won this war!" I beamed at Dhrishtadyumna and glanced at the other Panchalas and Satyaki. "Thank you all, my friends! Without your help we could never have achieved this victory. You all deserve my heartfelt gratitude and reverence."

"We have done everything to make you the emperor." Dhrishtadyumna beamed. "Our true moment of victory will be to see you on the imperial throne, dear brother." He picked up his conch. Notes from all Panchalas' conchs played in the air of Samanta Panchaka. Krishna joined in, playing the note of victory in his Panchajanya.

The horizon in front appeared multi-coloured as my brothers and Panchalas waved their upper garments in the air. Mixed notes from familiar conchs declared the result of this eighteen-day long war. That sound of celebration coupled with the loud cry of our enemy seemed to send away the news to all our late warriors in heaven through the setting sun.

*Their sacrifices had paid off!*

"This country is again yours, Samrat Yudhishthira!" Krishna uttered with smile.

# CHAPTER THIRTY-FOUR

The deserted Kaurava camp looked so haunting.

I closed my eyes to imagine how cheerful this very place might have been even a few days ago. Twangs of bows and frequent war cries used to reverberate from every corner of this camp. The dancers and singers used to tune the camp with pleasant melodies to entertain the tired warriors during their evening breaks.

Today it was all over.

A strong breeze passed by, making a whistling noise. As if the haunting silence was crying over the empty tents!

In my mind I could hear countless widows lamenting at every corner, pointing their fingers at me. I heard the grieving mothers scream.

*You are responsible for all our losses, Yudhishthira!*

A shiver ran through my spine. I jerked my eyes open. A part of me wondered how I would bear with the empty palace of Hastinapura if this very camp was making me feel thus.

I did not want to come here. My heart ached for Grandfather Bhishma who was still alive with all his pain. That hundred-and-two-year-old sire of Kurus still refused to give up in his battle with God of death, maybe just to hear the end result of this war.

He deserved to know what happened to the fate of his clan!

I wanted to meet him first, to let him know that his blessings had come true. But that could not be possible. Owing to the tradition, victors of war were supposed to spend the night of victory in the enemy camp. Keeping the Panchalas and our sons to protect our camp, we had come here along with Krishna and Satyaki.

To celebrate our victory in this dreaded emptiness!

A shadow shorter than mine showed up on the ground. A familiar delicate hand held my arm.

"What bothers you, Samrat?" Draupadi softly asked.

"This emptiness is unbearable, Samragni." I mused, looking at the empty tent of Duryodhana where we stood. "Don't you too feel the same?"

"Emptiness has no place where Dharma rules." She evenly replied. "This camp has been a big, dark void in absence of morality. But not anymore. Your victorious presence has removed that today, Dharmaraj."

"Void lies in my very heart, Krishnaa." I muttered. "And nothing can ever remove that. I have to live the rest of my life with the guilt of causing such a bloodshed in my country." I heaved a sigh.

Draupadi's gaze rested on my face. "The blood that has flowed in these eighteen days has not gone in vain, Samrat." She calmly reminded. "Bharatavarsha has been free from Duryodhana's grip. Dharma has won."

"At the cost of lifelong curses of all those who have lost their loved ones." I remarked. "This was not what we dreamt for, Samragni."

She frowned. "Why do these thoughts bother you now, Yudhishthira? This is the time to accept our duties again. Not to regret over the past."

"I know. I won't ignore my duties." I said. "Prativindhya is able enough in his wisdom and sense of responsibility. His brothers are great warriors and dedicated to his guidance. They will successfully take over our remaining responsibilities." I paused to observe her reaction. "What if we leave the empire in their hands and return to forest?"

Draupadi observed me for a while, as if reading my thoughts.

"The boys are still much younger for ruling an empire themselves, Samrat. We need to be there to guide them." Draupadi said. "Not to forget that they did not have us by their side during growing up."

I did not comment. I also had mulled over these points.

"We just have to start, Samrat. At least till our children become eligible to replace us." She spoke. "And adding to it, I don't want to put the burden of our guilt on their young shoulders just because we are tired to carry it. We should not be so selfish, Aaryaputra."

She was right. We had been enough selfish to our kids. We had deprived them from our love and care for thirteen years. At the end of it we just dragged those inexperienced young boys to such a massive war. And now, to pass on the responsibility of our empire to them just to escape our own guilt - it was unthinkable. I could not fail as a father thus.

"Stop searching for ways of escape, Samrat." She said again. "Re-establishing the empire of Dharma was your mission. You only have to fulfill it."

I nodded, letting out a sigh. "True, Krishnaa. I should have realised this earlier that I still have a lot of duties pending. Not just to this empire but to my own kids."

I saw her exhale in relief. My conscience reminded that I had duty to her too. To bring her happiness back after all the loses we had faced.

"The boys have done a lot for their parents, Draupadi." I added. "Now we must do something for them. Maybe starting with their marriages, for an auspicious beginning?" I smiled a little.

"I thought the same." Draupadi beamed now. "We need to find out suiting girls from good families."

"Even if that is not a royal family." I added. "Many of our soldiers who died for our sake have left their orphaned young daughters. Why don't we get someone from them as our daughter-in-law?"

"That's a nice idea, Swami." She agreed. "But this is not the time for it."

I nodded, realising what she had meant. "I understand. Now our foremost duty is to bring back peace and prosperity in this broken land. It's true that we cannot bring back the dead ones. But at least we have to give our best for filling the financial losses. Our personal celebrations can happen only after our empire reaches stability."

“The condition of treasury, I fear, is not ready to serve our purpose, Samrat.” She thought aloud. “First we need to gather enough wealth.”

“I know. We need to build up the empire once again from scratch. But with you by our side, I know we can make it again.” I smiled, brushing her hair. She did not object. It was after years we were so close, not just physically but emotionally too.

“You are our Shakti, Samragni. You are the inspiration behind all our actions and successes. This victory is yours. And the reestablished empire of Dharma will also be the result of your tapasya.”

She shook her head. “The tapasya was not mine alone but yours too. We six have achieved it together. And we only have to maintain it. But before everything,” She paused and smiled. “We need to be well ourselves for keeping others well.” She held my hand and led me towards the bed.

“Have a good sleep now.” She softly said. “You have not slept well in the past seventeen nights.”

“Neither have you.” I said, making her sit beside me. Draupadi’s nod showed her acceptance. Exhaling, I put the lamps off. As soon as the darkness engulfed the chamber, I sensed her arm resting on me. Just like she used to do thirteen years ago.

I took a deep breath. It felt so relaxing that all the barriers and distances between us had begun to disappear.

*Maybe I had finally deserved to earn her trust again!*

***

“What else do you want now?” aunt Gandhari’s face tightened in hatred. I thanked my stars that she had not opened her blindfold to see me.

*There is nothing more disastrous than the curse of a grieving mother!*

“My all sons are dead. The last one, my favourite child, is lying on his death-bed.” She continued in same tone. “Hasn’t your wish been fulfilled yet, Samrat Yudhishthira?”

"I came to seek your apology, Mata!" I joined my palms, lowering my gaze at her feet. She did not speak but kept heaving heavy sighs.

I knelt down at her feet. "I am the killer of your sons. I am your sinner. I shall accept whatever punishment you decide for me. Curse me if that soothes your heart. But pray, forgive me!"

"Forgiveness!" she retorted. "Apology cannot be sought from the height of imperial throne, Chakravarti Samrat Yudhishthira. It requires one to stand at the same level of anguish the other person is suffering. And you cannot do that. Because you are now a victor, an emperor. Not a childless parent."

The way she uttered the last sentence made my heart shiver in some unknown fear.

"Mahadeva forbid, Samrat, the day when you will lose your son, you will realise my pain!"

I stepped back as if thunder had struck me. And then, I saw widowed wives of Duryodhana and his brothers standing around.

"You have killed our sons!" they cried. "You too will get the same returning to you!"

I saw more women coming behind them. Women from all classes and all kingdoms that participated in both sides. I was shocked to see Subhadra standing with them along with queen Sudeshna. None of them was speaking. But their unuttered thought kept echoing in my mind, reminding me that their children had died for my reason.

*"You will have to face our curses, emperor!"*

"No!" I screamed. The next moment I discovered myself sitting on bed, bathed in sweat.

"Samrat! Are you alright?" I heard Draupadi's concerned voice.

"Where are they, Krishnaa?" I looked around, searching for the women. They were nowhere now.

"Who?" her brow arched.

"Those women? Mata Gandhari, sister Bhanumati, all of them were standing there." I pointed at the blank wall of tent. "Where did they go?"

"Whom are you talking about? No one is here except us." Draupadi shook my arm. "You must have been dreaming."

*Dreaming?* Was it a dream? Or an indication of...

I could not think anymore. I rushed outside where my chariot was standing. Our charioteers must have been sleeping now, and so was my brothers and Krishna.

It was not possible for me to wait. I pulled out a horse I found closer and rode on it. The speed of the horse felt much slower. More the horse advanced, more my heart raced as if war drums were being beaten within me.

The first ray of dawn fell on my eyes as I pulled the reins. The sight in front of me held me in a pause.

Where was our camp? I must have lost my direction in darkness.

*My camp was supposed to have been celebrating the victory with showers of flowers. Not such ashes!*

*Conchs and trumpets were to be played around in my camp. Not these yells of vultures!*

I went down my horse, almost in trance. My feet touched a human body. Seemed like the man had been guarding this area till his last breath. I felt like I knew the colour of his blood-smeared robes and the half-burnt crown that fell beside. But could not identify the face.

Who could it be? I looked again at the mutilated body and face.

*My Senapati was to be smeared with sandalwood paste now. Not with blood! This had to be someone else!*

But then...

Why did the body marks feel so familiar? My heart pounded as I caressed the corpse. A broken sword lay beside him. Its gem-studded sheath had loosened from his waistband. My hands froze as my eyes stuck on that.

*This was the sword I had gifted to my Senapati as a mark of honour!*

*My valiant commander, my caring brother-in-law could not even live a day more to celebrate his victory.*

But how? The war was over. Who had attacked at the darkness of night thus? Why didn't Dhrishtadyumna send warning notes to me?

I looked around restlessly to find an answer, only to discover more burnt bodies lying everywhere. The soil was coloured with black and red. Chopped off limbs were scattered everywhere. Sparks of dying fire were still burning at some corners. A strong odour of burnt flesh had overpowered the ambiance.

*Was I still on the battle ground? Or still dreaming?*

My all senses refused to believe in what I saw. I shut the inner voice which repeated to me that what I dreaded to believe was true.

It could not be so! What sin have I committed to get this punishment?

A group of vultures cried out. Their sharp noise pierced through my senses. The chorus of all those childless mothers of my dream echoed in my ears.

"*You have killed our sons! You too will get it back!*"

My heart skipped a beat.

*Was my son alright?*

I sprung to my feet and rushed to the right side, ignoring the corpses lying everywhere in my path. His tent was supposed to be here. All I could see was ashes, and weapons scattered on the ground. My knees felt weak. I sank where I was.

"Janaka! You came?" a feeble voice called me from the pile of ashes. There he was. A long sword pierced through his stomach. My twenty-four-year old son lay on a bed of his own blood.

Just like Duryodhana!

*This is what you wanted, Mata Gandhari!*

"Prati!" I hurried and picked up his bleeding head on my lap.

"How all these happened, child?" Even my whisper sounded like a yell.

Prativindhya did not reply. He raised his head a little, his bloodshot eyes searched behind me. I knew he was searching for Draupadi.

"You will see your mother, Prati. First I need to call the physicians for..."

"No." He cut me off. "This wound is not to be cured. Let me go, Janaka. Convey my last Pranama to mother."

He tried to join his bleeding palms, but his energy gave up. The half-joined hands fell apart besides his body as his head rolled at a side.

My punishment had been completed.

My intelligent son knew that his father would be forever blamed for this war. He had washed off my sins with his own blood. *With my blood!*

***

"Now arise, Yudhishthira." I felt a warm hand on my shoulder. The consoling voice seemed to be coming from a distance. As if from some other world where I did not belong anymore.

I did not know how long I sat thus, carrying my dead son on my lap. The same lap that had cradled his newborn tiny form once, now held his lifeless body.

"Samrat!" That voice nudged me again, probably fearing that I was not in my sense. This time, I identified the voice as Satyaki's. I slowly turned my head to him. He still held me, with concern in his eyes.

"See, Satyaki, my own blood has paid for all my sins with his blood." My voice was completely calm.

"They say a child has to pay his parents' debt. My son has shown that with his life."

Satyaki just patted my back. I heard him sighing. Something churned within me remembering that even his sons had died in the war.

"Jyeshtha, pray, calm yourself now." Krishna softly said, squeezing my shoulder. "Think about Draupadi once. Who would console her if you five give in to mourning thus?"

I slowly raised my gaze from Prativindhya's face. The sight in front was even more unbearable. My eyes fell on Draupadi first who kept calling and talking to Sutasoma's headless body, hoping for a response. She carefully wiped blood from Shatanika's face and body that had been mutilated to an extent of beyond reorganization.

Besides her sat a grieving Arjuna, trying in vain to wake up Shrutakarma. Sahadeva's all calm was gone. He kept patting Shrutasena as if to make him fall asleep. Nakula stood at a corner, completely broken. The powerful Bhima sat numb, caressing Sutasoma's chopped head. None of them even seemed to have any energy left in him for consoling Draupadi.

"Who is it, Krishna?" I muttered. "Who has dared to turn my camp into a crematory overnight?"

"Ashwatthama. He has completed the incomplete task of his father." Krishna softly remarked. "With active help of Kripacharya and Kritavarma."

*Guruputra Ashwatthama! This is why Dhrishtadyumna has been killed so brutally?*

I looked at Dhrishtadyumna's body again. He did not have any weapon's blow on his body. It seemed like he had been killed only with hard kicks and punches. Besides him lay Shikhandi, his inner organs had come out of the body. The vengeance Ashwatthama carried within had left its mark everywhere on the corpses of Panchala princes that lay scattered around me.

And our sons? Did they also have to die just because of carrying Panchala blood through their mother?

"No more Panchala is alive now. Only Dhrishtadyumna's charioteer could escape to give us the news." I heard Krishna.

"Cowards!" Satyaki gnashed his teeth. "Only assassins do such ruthless mass killing in the hours of sleep! Not warriors!"

He kept cursing the three invaders. I could not hear anything. The death of Guru Dronacharya flashed in my mind's eye.

It was I who had caused Gurudeva's death. Ashwatthama had avenged his father well. He did not kill me. He chose to kill my child whose death would kill me alive.

"They have not won with valour. They won with deceit. An inhuman deceit to wake sleeping people up only to kill them!" Satyaki screamed. His eyes glowed in wrath. The next moment his open sword flashed in the morning light.

"I won't spare that Kritavarma!"

Krishna held his hand.

"Patience, my friend. Not to make another mistake in rush."

Bhima left Sutasoma's head and sprung to his feet. His crimson eyes sought revenge.

"You can still keep patience, Krishna. But I cannot." Bhima groaned. "We cannot! Either Ashwatthama will die today, or..." he did not finish it and left with hurry. Within a while, I heard neigh of the horses of his chariot.

"Stop him, Jyeshtha! Stop him right now!" Krishna's eyes betrayed worry which was so rare in him. There was something in his tone that shook me up. I put down Prativindhya's head and rose. But the sound of chariot-wheel had faded away by then.

"Bhrata Bhima's life is at risk." Krishna warned. "We have to follow him! Come!"

## CHAPTER THIRTY-FIVE

We did not have to go far. Ashwatthama was found in the vicinity of our camp, sitting with Maharishi Vyasa.

"I have just received the news, sons." Maharishi's old eyes betrayed pain. "I was coming to congratulate you for the victory. Could not even think that I would have to see you in this condition!"

"This is the killer of our sons!" Bhima cried out, pointing at Ashwatthama. "Why are you not punishing him, Maharishi?"

The seer grimaced as he took a glance at Ashwatthama.

"He has taken my refuge, Bhima. I'm bound to protect him now."

"Refuge? Why, Guruputra? Do you fear to die?" I fumed. Ashwatthama seemed much disturbed as he observed us with our weapons and chariots.

"Arise, fight with us!" I said again.

"I..I have taken sannyasa." He fumbled, avoiding eye contact with us. "Maharishi has given me shelter at his feet. Leave me alone."

"Where was this renunciation at last night, Ashwatthama?" I snapped. "Now you're searching for shelter in fear of your own death? Do your valour and courage come only for killing people in darkness of night and then disappears with daybreak?"

Ashwatthama looked up to meet my gaze now. His face flushed.

"Come and fight if you don't want to be called a coward!" Bhima cried.

Ashwatthama picked up his bow that lay beside him and sprung to his feet. He kept chanting a hymn on the arrow he placed on his bowstring.

"Maharishi!" Krishna came forward. "Ashwatthama possesses the most poisonous Brahmashira weapon. Stop him from using that on Pandavas!"

Maharishi did not get time to stop him. Ashwatthama had released the arrow.

"Arjuna!" I turned to my brother.

Arjuna picked up an arrow and placed it on his Gandiva. "May my weapon nullify this!" He prayed before chanting the code of Brahmashira. I knew that he was chanting a different code to activate an antidote.

"Don't, Arjuna!" Maharishi cried. "Two Brahmashiras can intoxicate the air if their smokes collide."

Then, I remembered. Though the poisonous smoke produced from Brahmashira could be nullified only by an antidote smoke from another Brahmashira, the side effect of that encounter was bound to leave harmful residues in the nature. The effect could be as disastrous as drying up all water element from the air, converting the place to a desert.

I did not want to destroy all creatures of this land. But what else was the way now?

Arjuna put down Gandiva and joined his palms.

"I don't want to disobey you, Maharishi. But please make sure that I or my brothers are not harmed too." He requested. Ashwatthama's weapon had spent sufficient time in air that was required for its activation. Smoke was about to emerge from its tip. I held my breath.

Once the smoke was produced, there would be no counter of it!

"Revert your weapon, Ashwatthama!" Maharishi ordered.

"I haven't released it for reverting, Maharishi." Ashwatthama denied. "Pandavas' end is confirmed."

"Vengeful Brahmin, I won't let you kill Krishna or Pandavas." Maharishi Vyasa's eyes turned crimson. "Call it back right now!"

"I cannot. Father has not taught me the reverse code." Ashwatthama admitted.

"Then why did you release it, fool?" Maharishi chided. "You have to stop it now."

"I know the code of changing its direction."

"Then use it." Maharishi ordered. "Target at anywhere except the Pandavas and Krishna."

Ashwatthama's lips moved in a whisper. The arrow turned to the left, towards our devastated camp. That very moment it struck me what Ashwatthama had planned to do.

"Krishna! Women are there in the camp, unprotected!" I cried.

Krishna's face grew pale. The next moment he rushed towards the camp, followed by Satyaki.

"You sinful Brahmin, how lower will you stoop?" Maharishi snapped. "I wanted to forgive you since you sought my refuge. But not anymore."

"What wrong have I done?" Ashwatthama argued. "You only asked me to alter the direction."

"Foolish Bhaaradwaja, you should have thrown that poison to a deserted place. How could you even think of shooting it at the women of Pandava camp?"

Ashwatthama's lips curved into a cruel smirk.

"I have released my weapon to harm Pandavas, Maharishi. And I have fulfilled my intention. Let these five brothers stay unharmed as you wish. But their family will suffer the effect of poison for sure."

"Live in that dream, son of Drona. Krishna has gone to save them. Pandava women would be fine. But *you* won't be!" Maharishi raised his finger, his serene frame shook in uncharacteristic anger.

"You have to suffer the consequence of this sin of hurting women, especially a pregnant woman and her baby." He approached Aswatthama and removed the gem he was wearing on his forehead.

"You have lost the rights of good fortune and fame. This provider of fortune is bound to desert you now. You have committed enough sin to earn mass hatred, son of Drona. You'll have no escape from it! The rest of your life will be worse than burning in hell. Go wherever you like with this burden of infamy."

I felt aghast. Maharishi was sparing his life? Was this much punishment enough for what he had done?

"Maharishi," I stepped forward. "It's risky for us to leave him alive after what he has done. Pray, don't set him free."

"Don't worry, Yudhishthira. He has no power left in him now. All his weapons have been destroyed and exhausted. He cannot harm you anymore." He assured us and turned to Ashwatthama. "Now leave! Keep roaming in forests till death comes to claim you."

He joined his palms and slowly left.

"Come, Yudhishthira. This gem is yours now." Maharishi looked at me.

"Apologies, Maharishi. But I don't want to use something that belonged to my son's killer." I denied. "Pray, keep this with you."

"This gem is not to be kept with a sage but a householder. It has the ability of providing fortune to the place where it stays. For the wellbeing of Bharatavarsha, it should stay with you only, Samrat."

He came closer to me and tied it on my crown.

"Hail Chakravarti Samrat Yudhishthira!"

***

My heart raced each moment while I was back to the camp.

Krishna and Satyaki were enough to protect the women, I knew. But Brahmashira was not an ordinary weapon. It could intoxicate even the air and water along with the person on whom it would land. I feared whether Krishna and Satyaki were alright in their effort to save the ladies.

I rushed into the burnt camp, my eyes desperately searching for Draupadi. My breath raced more as I did not find her or Subhadra. Neither did I find Krishna anywhere.

*Has everything ended?*

Uttara! Our Abhimanyu's unborn child! Where was she?

"Jyeshtha!" I heard Arjuna calling out to me. Following his voice, I reached a lone corner behind the camp. It was a deserted cottage, with every single passage of air tightly closed. Satyaki stood guarding the place. I hurried in. Krishna was instructing Subhadra who was busy nursing an unconscious Uttara. Draupadi was helping her.

*What has happened to Uttara?*

"Krishna?" I dreaded even to ask him.

He looked at me, smiling a little. "Stay assured. The danger is over."

Over? My gaze dropped to Uttara once and then returned to Krishna.

He understood my unvoiced question. "We could save the ladies at the last moment by hiding them here. The smoke fell on Uttara since she could not move fast."

"Did Uttara inhale it?" I held my breath.

"Not much." Draupadi looked at me. "Krishna has saved her at the right time. She will be fine soon."

"And the baby?"

"Alive. Don't worry." Krishna assured. "I have got it confirmed from the royal physician."

I let out the breath that I had held, and sank on the ground. At that moment it felt like enough blessing that at least Abhimanyu's child was alright. I saw Uttara opening her eyes slowly, making everyone exhale.

"Mata?" She looked at Draupadi and Subhadra, clueless about the changed place.

Subhadra took her head on her bosom and wept silently. Krishna patted his sister's head before he rose.

"Come, brothers. We have to arrange for funerals of all these people."

# CHAPTER THIRTY-SIX

Is there any greater curse than lighting the pyre of your own son?

I had witnessed deaths since I was sixteen. I had lit my father's pyre in my own hand. All the close friends and relatives' pyres had been burnt in front of these very eyes. But this one was unbearable.

*After these flames die down, there will be no more trace of the body that had been born from me! My son will turn into a small pile of ashes!*

"Hold yourself, Jyeshtha!" Krishna squeezed my back.

"I have lost this war, Krishna." I muttered. "See, there lies my victory, burning within flames!"

He did not comment. He knew when the other person needed a silent listener.

"To make Dharma win, I myself became a loser. In the process of winning an empire, I have killed the future." I spoke again. "We have let our entire next generation get killed for our sake. We have no escape from this lifelong regret."

"They have fulfilled their duties to their parents, Samrat. They have attained the heaven of warriors." He calmly reminded. "You are wise. Pray, do not grieve those valiant young souls."

"But I could not do my duties to those boys, Krishna. I couldn't give my son a childhood he deserved. My nephews stayed deprived of their fathers for my reason." I pursed my lips. "I am a failed father, a failed uncle who has only taken from his sons but could never do anything in return."

"If that's your regret, you can still pay for that." Krishna's calm voice made me look at him.

"You are the father of this empire. The entire Bharatavarsha's people are your children. Find your late son and nephews in them

, Lord of Bharata. Let your service to the subjects fulfill your incomplete duties to those boys." Krishna said in encouraging tone. "Let your own pain merge with theirs. Find your solace in reducing their sorrow. That will be your true penance now."

I listened quietly, still staring at the dying flames.

*Maybe Prativindhya too wanted this only.*

He had paid for my sin. He won't like me shying away from my penance. The least I could do to honour his sacrifice was to dedicate myself in this way of atonement that Krishna advised.

"Don't hold anymore regret within, Jyeshtha." I heard Krishna again. "You have to heal yourself first to rebuild your empire of Dharma."

I took a deep breath as I nodded. The flames had died down now, leaving behind ashes. I moved closer and caressed the remaining of my child, trying to imagine that his soul had merged with my subjects of Bharata.

*I shall not fail you anymore!* I promised to the ashes.

***

The tent was almost dark, with only one lamp glowing at a corner that refused to give up even in the strong dusty air of Kurukshetra. No one except the physicians and servants was allowed to enter here.

I walked in slowly, leading my brothers and Krishna. The guards saluted me and left the entrance. I reached the bed where the old feeble body lay with all his severe injuries.

"Pitamaha!"

He managed to open his weary eyes. They rested on my face for a while, trying to recognize me in that weak light.

"Yudhishthira!" his lips curved into smile. "You came!"

I knelt down and clasped his feet. "I came to seek your blessing, Pitamaha. For serving your beloved Hastinapura."

He squinted his eyes and stared at me first, then at my brothers who stood around his bed with joined palms. I understood that his brain was not working fully due to excessive bleeding.

"The war has been over, Pitamaha." I said. "Your blessing has come true."

"You...you have won?" his face brightened up. My brothers knelt down around the bed now.

"Give us your blessings, Pitamaha." Arjuna bowed. "And forgive our sins!"

Grandfather's shivering hands raised in the air and touched Arjuna's head first, followed by Bhima's.

"I prayed to Mahakaala not to take me away unless Hastinapura gets back the rule of justice." His voice was almost like a whisper. "He has listened to me." His eyes now fell on me. "Come near me, son."

I rose from his feet and went closer. He called for a servant who entered with a golden plate, carrying a gem-studded golden crown. It looked old but still had a regal aura around it.

"This is your father's." Grandfather said, picking it up with much care as if he was holding my father. "After his retire to forest, I kept this with me, hoping that he would come back one day for sure."

He heaved a sigh. My eyes went moist. Partly in father's memory, partly in empathy with grandfather.

He too had witnessed his son-like younger brothers' and favourite nephew's death. And now, his grandsons' death too. I connected to his lifelong pain within a while.

The pain that I too was going to inherit!

"Pandu had not come back. Still I have never given this to Dhritarashtra. I saved it for Pandu's heir. For you."

Grandfather raised his head a little. His hands shivered. I lowered my head to make it easier for him. After a little struggle, he managed to place it on my head.

"Hail KuruRaja Yudhishthira!" He beamed despite the continuous bleeding. "Hail Samrat Yudhishthira!"

I bowed to him. He closed his eyes, his face holding the smile of content.

"Now I can die in peace."

"Pitamaha!" Arjuna held his feet, weeping.

"My time is over, child. Let me go." He slowly uttered, raising his palms again. "May your rule be the best one in the history of Bharata!"

His weak frame shivered as his white head fell back on the bed. I held his feet to offer my last reverence. His head tilted at one side, still carrying the smile on his face. A chapter in the history of Kurus had ended.

Arjuna hid his face in grandfather's feet and cried. I patted his head.

"He has gone with content and peace, Arjuna. Let's complete our last duty to his journey to heaven."

***

I was still in doubt that how would I face uncle Dhritarashtra and aunt Gandhari. But grandfather's last rites had managed to bring that opportunity. At least we stood together, though I knew they had not liked our presence in front of grandfather's pyre.

We went to Ganga for floating grandfather's remaining. Uncle Dhritarashtra wept like a child who had lost his father. He could not stand straight on his feet while rising from the water. His weak frame kept trembling. I hurried and held him with both hands.

"Hold me, Uncle." I softly said.

He shook his head, waving his hand. "Leave me, Yudhishthira. I have to hold myself now. The ones who could have given support to me, are all gone, thanks to you five." His jaws gritted.

Hiding a sigh, I stepped back. I told myself that it was normal. He still needed time to accept us.

Uncle Vidura patted my shoulder and rushed to hold his elder brother. My mother stood behind, holding aunt Gandhari in her arms.

"Everything is over, Vidura." Uncle Dhritarashtra sobbed. "Everyone has left this old blind father."

Uncle Vidura kept consoling him. I felt bad for Yuyutsu. He was so concerned for uncle and aunt that he alone went to visit them right after Duryodhana's fall. And uncle didn't even care to remember that his one son was still alive!

Had he disowned Yuyutsu just because he had fought for me?

"Gather yourself, Jyeshtha!" Uncle Vidura squeezed his brother's shoulders. "Your sons have attained heaven of warriors that every Kshatriya desires. Do not grieve them."

Uncle Dhritarashtra impatiently shook his head. "They cannot attain heaven unless their last rites are properly done. Even their sons have died, Vidura. Now only I'm left to perform tarpana for them."

Something churned within me. Even I had to perform jalapradana to my son. The son who had not even have a marital bliss to beget an heir.

"Vidura, arrange for the water oblation." Uncle Dhritarashtra ordered. "I have to secure heaven for my sons and grandsons."

Uncle Vidura nodded and looked at few maids waiting there, indicating them to bring the wives of all late princes. The ladies wrapped in white robes arrived at the riverbank, led by Bhanumati. They were without jewelry, their hair opened. My heart raced, remembering my own nightmares. At one side stood my beloved sister Dusshala, clad in the same white.

This was the sister for whose sake I had once forgiven Jayadratha! So that she was spared from wearing this white! Lump formed in my throat. I could not lift my eyes to meet any of their gazes. I dearly wished that I could leave that place.

"Look, emperor Yudhishthira! Look at your achievement!" I heard aunt Gandhari retorting.

"This is what you wanted, didn't you?" She snapped. "Just like your wife's hair was opened and dragged, you wanted my daughters-in-law also to have this condition one day."

I shut my eyes. I knew this would come to me whenever I would meet her first.

"Now you are satisfied, right? All your wishes have come true. Go, enjoy your throne now!" She screamed again. My brothers and Krishna stood behind me but she did not even turn to them once. I could sense that all her anger was on me and not on Bhima. And that was justified.

I joined my palms without looking up. "Pardon me, Mata!"

"I could have, Yudhishthira, have you been a little kind to me and your blind uncle." She sighed. "Trust me or not, I did pray for your victory. I wanted Duryodhana and Duhshasana to get punished for their sin to Draupadi. I too am a woman, Yudhishthira. I didn't forgive them for what they did."

I knew that. I had heard that she had not even blessed Duryodhana for winning the war. Perhaps the righteous soul in her wanted us only to win. But the mother in her certainly did not wish to lose her sons.

"But why did you kill all my sons? What did the others do to you? Do you remember Vikarna? He was the only one who protested against Draupadi's humiliation when even you, her husbands, were silent." She broke into tears now. "Couldn't Bhima just spare at least him?"

Yes, we *were* grateful to Vikarna. But he too did participate in the side of the same brothers who committed that crime. All of them did.

The reply came to my throat. But I chose not to voice it.

"I agree that Duhshasana was wrong, very wrong. But was it fair to drink a human's blood? What does your Dharma say, Dharmaraj Yudhishthira?" She burst out again.

And where was your Dharma when my wife was dragged to the court from your very mansion? How could you keep quiet and let it happen? Why didn't you stop your son that day?

A part of me screamed while the rest struggled to send it back. *Speaking that would be too harsh to a grieving mother!*

"I have not drunk his blood, Mata." Bhima came forward. "At the end of everything, he was my brother. And brother's blood is like own blood. No one can drink that."

I looked at him, knowing that he was speaking truth. I myself had seen him spitting out Duhshasana's blood soon after taking it in his mouth.

"Duhshasana's blood has not gone down my throat, Mata." Bhima continued. "I just had to touch it with my lips because of my vow. And you know well why I had to take that vow on that cursed day."

Aunt did not reply now. I heard her heavy sigh.

"We tried our best to avoid this war, Mata. At least," Bhima sideglanced at me. "Jyeshtha certainly did. It's your firstborn who chose not to listen. If you could not stop him then, you should not blame us either."

I thanked Bhima within my mind. This was something I could never have uttered to my mourning aunt, despite of knowing that all of it was true.

"Mata, we have made you childless. We also have received the Karmaphala by being childless ourselves." I softly said. "This war has left no one happy, Mata. No one has been the victor. We all have been lost."

"Maharani," Uncle Vidura called. "Priest Dhaumya is calling everyone for performing the water oblations."

Aunt Gandhari nodded with a heavy sigh, and turned her head to me.

"Come, Yudhishthira." She said in a calm voice now. "Let all the surviving Kurus unite to give oblations to the departed ones today."

***

The sight of Ganga was so disturbing with all the mourning women and men offering water to their dead relatives. The river shivered in ripples as hundreds of widows went down to pray for their husbands' soul. Their tears mixed with the water in their cupped palms. Their laments echoed from the riverbank.

Uncle Dhritarashtra wept uncontrollably while offering oblations to his sons. Sanjaya and uncle Vidura held him. With my brothers I performed the water rites for our sons and cousins. Draupadi offered water to her father and brothers. Knowing that Uttara was not in the condition to take so much stress, I myself performed the last rites for king Virata and his sons, with Aacharya Dhaumya's approval.

Hundreds of offerings kept floating on the water. Hundreds of eyes kept shedding tears and bid their farewell to their loved ones.

With the turbulence generated within her current, even Devi Ganga too seemed to be mourning.

Pushing away the last arghya to the river current, I rose. Sun was about to set.

"Wait, Yudhishthira. You need to give one more offering." À familiar female voice said. I looked up with surprise. It was my mother.

Did I forget anyone? I turned to the river once. Uncle Vidura was leading uncle Dhritarashtra to the riverbank. There was no doubt that water oblations had been duly paid to all our cousins and their sons. Whom did mother talk about then?

"Have I left out anyone, Maa?" I asked her. Mother looked away, avoiding my gaze. She was hesitating.

"You should pay an offering for Angaraja Karna too, son." She managed to speak. "He has no son alive to perform his water rites."

My jaws clenched even in this grieving ambiance.

"That is not possible, Maa." I said, looking away.

"Why not?" She insisted, coming closer. "You have performed the rites even for Duryodhana and his brothers. You have admitted that all rivalry ends with death. Why cannot you forgive Karna then?"

"It's not about forgiving, Maa. Jala pradana sanskara can be performed only by family members." I was grave. "I have no relation with..."

"*You do have relation with him*, Yudhishthira. And that's even closer than Duryodhana's relation with you." Mother's voice sounded sharp despite her grieving tone.

"Karna was your uterine elder brother. My firstborn."

# CHAPTER THIRTY-SEVEN

Uterine brother!

It took me a while to let mother's words sink in. All my senses strongly refused to believe the new information that had gone into them.

*I must have heard it wrong!*

Duryodhana's best friend Karna, the man who had abused Draupadi, Arjuna's arch rival Karna, - he was my brother? *It cannot be!*

"What are you saying, Maa?" I protested. "Karna was son of suta Adhiratha, uncle Dhritarashtra's former charioteer."

"No." Mother firmly shook her head. "Adhiratha and his wife Radha found him floating in river and raised him as their own son. He was not born to them."

I tried to recall. Yes, there was a rumour about that as I had heard since our Gurukula days. People, especially Duryodhana and his brothers, used to say that such a valorous warrior could never have been born to a suta family. But that was all I had heard. There was no proof of Karna not being Adhiratha's son except that rumour.

"How can you be so sure?"

"Because it was I who sent him afloat the river." Mother whispered, avoiding my gaze. "He was born to me before my wedding with your father. I could not keep him with me." Her face held a deep pain that I had rarely seen.

"But I kept gathering his news. My spies had brought me the information that suta Adhiratha had adopted him." She continued, collecting herself. "I knew that my son was growing up here, in this Hastinapura. I had recognized him as soon as I saw him."

Something struck me. A part of me suddenly discovered that I was in front of an unkind truth of my life. A truth that was so unsettling, so discomforting, yet inevitable.

This was the same Karna for whose death I had been so eager! Whom I had hated with all my life, cursed for thirteen years! The one whose death I had celebrated the most! He was my own blood? My elder brother?

"Then why did you hide this from the world, Maa?" I was stern. "Why have you never let us know? Do you realise what a huge injustice you have done to your own firstborn? To us?"

My entire body shook in unnamed emotions. Maybe it was anger, maybe guilt, maybe something else.

"I have forever craved to have a father-figure above my head. I have wished to have someone who could have saved me from my burdens since childhood. Why didn't you tell me that I do have one elder brother?" My voice was gradually turning harsh. "Why did you deprive me from my brother's love?"

"I had no other way, Yudhishthira. Revealing this could have been troubling for you five in Hastinapura. I had to suppress it for your good." Mother muttered. "I had promised to myself that the truth would remain with me till my death. Had Karna have anybody else alive to perform his water oblations, you would never have known this."

"You have not done this right, Rajamata Kunti." I groaned. "You have been unfair to all your sons. You have let the lifelong hatred and rivalry prevail between us and him. Despite of knowing everything, you never tried to stop this conflict among your own sons."

"Who told you that I did not?" She looked hurt. "I went to Karna before war. I asked him to join you. But he did not listen to me."

"That means, he knew his true identity?"

Mother nodded. "He did. He had promised me not to kill four of you. And he kept his promise."

Slowly, things began to connect in my memory. Karna's unusual sparing of my life, despite of getting complete opportunity to kill me. Now I knew the true reason behind that.

He had spared me to fulfill his promise to my mother. *Our* mother!

"You revealed it to him but not to us?" My voice betrayed hurt as I stared at mother.

"I would have revealed to you too, had Karna agreed to reconcile." Mother's voice turned grave.

"I went to make him unite with you, his own brothers. I tried to bring him back to where he truly belonged. I tried to save his life." She heaved a sigh. "But it had been too late by then. His soul had already been sold to Duryodhana. He could not come back to you even if he wanted."

Perhaps, it was even beyond that. Maybe he could not abandon his foster parents who had raised him with all love and happiness. Either way, he had done it right. It was never a small thing to refuse own mother and brothers just for the sake of fulfilling responsibilities. Not everyone could do this. For the first time, I felt a flicker of respect for the Lord of Anga.

"I did not let you know. Because I did not want to throw you in a moral dilemma before war." Mother patted my shoulder. "Fighting this war was your Dharma, my child. And I ensured that no single doubt holds you back on the battlefield. I wanted you to fight for your rights as much as I wanted to save Karna's life." Her voice turned softer. "I did my duty to both my sons, Vatsa. You listened to me. Karna did not. Even a mother cannot help a stubborn child if he refuses to see his own good."

"You have done your part. I could not. I shall never get another opportunity to undo my sin of killing my elder brother. Another sin that has added to my share even without my knowledge." " I slowly uttered, meeting her gaze.

"You gave me a life full of regret and remorse, Rajamata." I looked away, biting my lips. My heart felt like being stabbed with sharp sword.

Mother's words, her voice, everything sounded selfish to me now. This was the mother who preserved her secret within despite of seeing her sons fighting against each other. And now she had revealed it only to make her firstborn receive his last rites.

I knew I would never voice my feelings. But in my heart, I could not forgive her.

"Yudhishthira, you are misunder..."

"I did understand you right, Rajamata!" I raised my palm. "I do not feel like talking about this anymore." I slowly walked away from where she stood. Karna's beheaded body shown up in my mind's eye.

*How could I never feel any pull of blood to him?* My vision went blurred. I stumbled over a rock while Krishna held my hand.

"Calm down, Jyeshtha. It's not your fault that you did not know the truth." He softly said. "Neither was it wrong for you to hate someone who humiliated your wife. Pray, don't feel guilty for this."

"I never thought that I would end up being in debt to Karna too, Krishna!" my voice had chocked. I felt Krishna's warm caress on my back.

"He spared my life and my brothers' lives to fulfil his promise. And I could never know! I kept on loathing my own brother and prayed for his death. I have got him killed for winning the war. What is the remedy of this sin?"

"You did no wrong, Yudhishthira." I heard mother. "You have punished a sinner. As the emperor of Bharata, that was your duty."

"Who is the emperor, Mother? Wasn't Karna the real heir of Hastinapura's throne? The eldest of Kuru scions? Did I kill the rightful owner of the empire and am going to take it myself?"

"No." Mother's voice was firm. "Karna was not a Kuru scion. Your father, king Pandu, had no knowledge about his existence. He never gave Karna his identity with due rituals. Adhiratha did that. As per the norms of Shastras, Karna belonged to Adhiratha's clan. Not the Kurus'."

I listened with no comment. Mother was not wrong. A child can belong only to that clan which gives him their gotra in proper Vedic way. If my father had not done that to Karna, he could not be a Kuru. A part of me felt relaxed.

At least, I was not going to snatch anyone else's birthright!

"The Kuru throne is yours, Yudhishthira, you being the eldest of Pandu's acknowledged heirs." Mother said again. "And, believe this or not, but Karna also wanted you only to rule Bharata."

I looked up to her. This was shocking.

"You heard me right." Mother continued. "With all his rivalry with you five, he had this belief that you alone deserve to rule Indraprastha as well as this empire. Not he himself, nor his friend Duryodhana."

Lump formed in my throat. He had this much trust on me? Why had I never known this side of the man I hated the most? Why did fate never allow me to experience such an elder brother's affection?

"And he was right." Krishna said. "He or his friend was not the ruler we need for the empire of Dharma. You are."

"As a ruler he might not have been significant to anyone. But we never know, maybe as a brother he could have been. If he could know his truth earlier." I muttered.

"Wrong. Nothing would have changed even if he knew earlier. You really think that he could be a great elder brother to you, Jyeshtha?" Krishna frowned. "He had fought against you, hurt you, insulted you even after knowing that you are his younger brothers. He had never abandoned his vow of killing Arjuna. He had caused death of his own nephews knowingly. Could you do that if you were in his place, Jyeshtha?"

My four brothers came near me.

"You always are the better one, Jyeshtha. Be it as a ruler or as a brother." Arjuna patted my shoulder.

"Even if we learnt this earlier, Karna would never have been able to replace you in our hearts." Bhima added. "He could never have been the brother you were to us since father's death. The love and respect we have for you could never be his. Maybe he too knew this and hence refused mother's request to join us."

I let Bhima draw me closer to him. The four brothers secured me in their embrace.

"Maybe he had realised that it was better to fight us rather than to live with us bearing lifelong hatred." Arjuna commented. "He has done what he felt right, Jyeshtha. You should not feel guilty for that."

I looked at them. Their eyes shone in love. The love that had remained unaltered even after discovering another elder brother. The love that was not affected with regret of killing Karna. My throat chocked in gratitude.

"What has happened was for good, Jyeshtha." Krishna said again. "Pray, arise now, and do what your elder brother wanted. Accepting the throne of Bharatavarsha will be the best homage to his soul."

I slowly nodded, remembering that I had to perform the water oblations. The last sanskara that only I could do now in the absence of his sons. The only atonement I could do for killing him!

I went back to Ganga for performing my first and last duty to my elder brother. In the water cupped in my palms, I saw Karna's face. The very face I once even hated to visualise. The very head I craved to see separated from his body!

"Forgive me, Bhrata!" I whispered to the face.

## CHAPTER THIRTY-EIGHT

Was this the same Hastinapura that I knew?

The court hall felt so empty, with no familiar figures sitting with white robes. All the empty thrones meant for Kuru princes kept mocking me. The sight of the place where Karna used to sit stabbed my soul. Unstoppable yells of widows and orphaned children echoed from every wall of the palace. As if the entire mansion was cursing me!

*This was unbearable!*

"Finally we are here." I heard Bhima. "Where we were meant to be. To rule the entire Kuru kingdom which is our father's."

"I have something to tell you all." I softly uttered, drawing their attention.

"I won't take this kingdom. Let Arjuna rule Hastinapura as well as the empire." My voice was calm. "After his coronation, I shall retire to Himalayas for penance."

Arjuna's eyes widened in shock. The twins looked aghast, while Bhima was clearly displeased.

"Have you gone insane, Jyeshtha?" he snapped, frowning.

"I am completely in my sense, Bhima." I repeated in the same tone. "It's not possible for me to accept this throne anymore. I want to repent for my sins for the rest of my life."

"How wonderful!" Bhima retorted. "If this was your intention, why did you make us fight for eighteen days? Why did we suffer so much?"

"You fought for justice. Not for me." I replied. "Our aim has been achieved. It does not matter now who sits on the throne."

"It does matter. The achieved aim has no meaning unless we can follow the same pattern of administration that we used to do. You have no right to break it now." Draupadi stared hard at me.

"Pray, don't be so immature at this stage, Samrat. You know these four even more than me. How could you even think that they would sit on throne in your absence?" She said. "If you leave for penance, they too will follow you. What would happen to this empire then?"

"Jyeshtha," Arjuna came closer and held my hand. "I feel that something bothers you. You can empty your heart to us. We shall take the share of your pain. But pray, don't leave us thus!"

His loving words did not console me.

"Samrat, I can understand what pains you." Draupadi's tone turned soft. "But renunciation is not a solution. Have you thought of all these orphaned widows and children of Hastinapura? Of the whole Bharatavarsha? It's our duty to protect them now. How can you leave them unprotected thus?"

"Do I deserve to protect them at all, Samragni?" I heaved a sigh.

"It's me who has rendered their misfortune. I have caused destruction of my own clan. I got my elders, even my own brother, killed for my own interest." I shook my head. "This huge sin needs to be washed off."

"Which sin, Vatsa?"

We turned to the entrance of sabha. Maharishi Vyasa had come.

"You have not killed your kinsmen. You have punished the sinners and their silent supporters." He reminded. "You have done your duty as the Lord of this country. Rather it would have been a sin had you refused to kill them just because they were your family."

I looked down. "My son, my nephews, Satyaki's sons, king Virata's sons, - they have not sinned, Maharishi. My in-laws of Panchala have not sinned. How will I forgive myself for causing their deaths? Especially the young ones who could be this country's future? Our future?" my empty heart cried out to him. "Which Bharatavarsha am I supposed to rule, Maharishi, that has no future left to care for her?"

"If there is no future, build a new one, Samrat Yudhishthira!" Maharishi's grave voice sounded like an unavoidable order. "You are the emperor. It's your responsibility."

"I have no more power left within to carry out with this." I joined my palms, lowering my gaze. "Pray, allow me to handover my duties to my brothers."

"You want to escape your responsibilities, Dharmaraj?" His displeased tone whipped my conscience.

"Karma allows no one to flee, Yudhishthira. You have to pay for the debt you have on every single person who fought this war. The duties of imperial throne are now your true penance, Samrat. Not the isolation of forest."

I lowered my head. A sense of doing wrong hit me. Was I being selfish only to care for my own penance and not for my subjects'?

Just like my father did once?

"Yudhishthira, your sons, your friends' sons, - all have died to make you ascend the throne. They had dreamt of a peaceful, righteous Bharatavarsha under your rule. All your soldiers, your Panchala relatives, even the Kuru elders of the other side, had died with this wish in their hearts." Maharishi patted my back. "Will you let all their blood and sweat go in vain, child?"

I could not reply. This was something that Krishna too had told me. I remembered my promise to my dead son. I had promised to fulfill my incomplete duties towards him.

"A lot of blood has flowed, Vatsa. Rivers of tears have flowed. Now it's your turn to stand up for all these. Don't let all their sacrifices go in vain." The Maharishi softly said. "Accept the throne."

I felt like hearing not Maharishi's voice but Prativindhya's. I felt as if he and his brothers were pleading to me. I could feel Dhrishtadyumna's request in my mind's ear. All Panchalas', Chedis', Matsyas' voices kept reverberating from the walls of this empty palace.

*Accept the throne!*

Maharishi held my shoulder.

"I can understand you have guilt stuck deep in your heart. If you want to get rid of it, support rebuilding of those kingdoms that have lost their heirs and wealth in war. That will make you feel better. But do not disregard your duty."

I bowed to him. "Pardon me if I have offended you, Maharishi. I shall not disobey your order."

Maharishi smiled now. My brothers exhaled in relief.

"Bless you, Vatsa!" Maharishi beamed. "I shall talk to Dhaumya for finding the most auspicious moment. I myself shall coronate you, emperor of Bharata!"

***

I was not surprised to see Guru Kripacharya coming back to Hastinapura.

"You have arrived at the right time, Kulaguru." I bowed to him. "I did not want to get coronated in your absence."

"Yudhishthira, forgive me, son!" he avoided my gaze, joining his palms.

"I know what I have done is unpardonable. Still, forgive me if you can. I assure you, I shall leave soon after getting your pardon." His eyes betrayed guilt. I sighed. The old teacher of ours had finally realised that he had helped killing his dear students' sons.

"Your realization itself is enough, Gurudeva." I held his palm. "Pray, don't leave us anymore."

"No, Yudhishthira." He shook his head. "I cannot face you with the memory of my sin. I tried to flee with my life, fearing that you five would kill me. But I could not. This burden of guilt is even worse than death, Vatsa. I had to come back to get rid of this."

I listened quietly. I had heard that Guru Kripacharya had escaped in fear.

"Do punish me if you wish. Kill me if you must." Gurudeva continued. "But free me from this guilt. I cannot take it anymore."

"True remorse, true repentance is not in escaping, Gurudeva." I calmly said. "It's there in bearing the responsibility. We can never flee from guilt. The most we can do is confronting the guilt with a positive Karma that nullifies our sin."

A part of me knew that I was not telling it to him but to myself.

"Gurudeva, if you truly want to get rid of your remorse, please consider taking back your responsibility."

"Which responsibility do I have here now?" Kulaguru muttered, looking away.

"We have lost almost all our elders. We need you to guide us. Our unborn grandchild needs your teachings and blessings for becoming an able heir of Kurus. Let him become your disciple and grow with your guidance."

His gaze returned on me, following a long stare. His old eyes betrayed disbelief.

"It's my request to you, accept your responsibility, Gurudeva. Let your teachings to Abhimanyu's child be your true penance towards our sons."

"You proved once again why you are called Ajatashatru, the one without enemies." He sighed as he nodded. "I accept your wish, Samrat. I shall keep serving Kuru heirs till the end of my life."

"Come, Jyeshtha." Krishna called me. "The muhurta has arrived."

I nodded and approached the throne with Draupadi by my side.

This was the fourth coronation of my life. But so different from all the previous ones. Those ones were never as empty as this one; neither did they feel so cheerless. I missed blessings of all the Kuru elders, and greetings of my friends. The ones who made me feel complete in my Rajasuya.

Those who have sacrificed their lives to make me sit on this throne could not witness this!

Aacharya Dhaumya's chanting of Veda mantras brought me back to the present. Krishna was pouring water on my head from his Panchajanya conch. Notes from my brothers' conchs reverberated from the walls of assembly hall.

The imperial crown was brought on a golden plate. With due rituals Maharishi Vyasa put it on my head. The court nobles hailed me. Shower of flowers accompanied the hymns and notes of conchs.

I indicated my wish for a silence. As the noise faded away, I rose from my throne.

"Honourable court nobles and people of Hastinapura!" I addressed them with joint palms. "I promise to all of you that I shall do my best to fulfill your expectations from me. I shall strive to carry forward the legacy of Emperor Bharata, my illustrious ancestor, who had once cared for Hastinapura as well as this Bharatavarsha in the most successful way ever. I promise to unite this broken country again under a peaceful rule."

Everybody listened attentively.

"I also announce that from now on I'm accepting the charge of administration for all those orphaned kingdoms that have lost their rulers. For those principalities who have very young heir or no heir at all to succeed them. Till their heirs become eligible to rule, the responsibility of all those kingdoms will be mine."

"Hail Samrat Yudhishthira!" A chorus broke on the silent sabha. My eyes fell on uncle Dhritarashtra who stood at a distance, visibly broken.

"And last but not the least, I promise that my revered uncle, Maharaj Dhritarashtra, will continue to have the same honour as he used to have for so many decades of his rule. My coronation should not lead to his disrespect and negligence in Hastinapura. It's my request to all of you to treat him with the same respect as you have done before."

"Hail Dharmaraj Yudhishthira! Hail Ajatashatru Yudhishthira!" everyone cried, and went back to their celebration.

And then, I could sense the presence of all whom I missed. The festivity around me had gone faded from my eyes. I felt as if Prativindhya was standing in front of me, smiling wide. Besides him stood his brothers and Abhimanyu, hailing my name. I saw Dhrishtadyumna and Shikhandi playing their conchs, declaring their victory. King Virata and his sons congratulated me. My eyes filled before I knew.

*May I be able to value your sacrifice!* I closed my eyes in silent prayer.

# CHAPTER THIRTY-NINE

Uttara's health suddenly deteriorated.

She was not well since she was exposed to the poisonous fumes of brahmashira. Though the physicians had assured us that the fetus was alive, they had feared that it might be at some risk. As the time of her childbirth neared, things worsened even more. There was no response from the fully developed fetus which was supposed to kick and show movements before birth. All the royal physicians worried that something unwanted might have happened.

Subhadra sat in fervent prayer, stopping even the intake of water. She refused to eat anything until her grandchild was born healthy. Unsuccessful to break her fast, Draupadi finally came to me.

"I cannot see this anymore, Aaryaputra." She sighed. "If something unwanted happens, I fear that we won't be able to save Subhadra as well!"

"Send message to Krishna, Draupadi." I proposed. "His presence is necessary right now."

She agreed. But the distance of Dwaraka was considerably long. When Krishna finally arrived near the end of next fortnight, Uttara was already in the labour room. Draupadi sat beside an almost unconscious Uttara, spending sleepless nights. Subhadra sat unmoved in puja room. With my brothers, I waited outside the chamber. Each moment felt like a year. Arjuna's pain and panic was visible in his eyes which was hurting me even more.

I could not even sit at a place, restlessness growing in me each moment. I could only pray to all Gods that all went well.

Krishna was equally worried when he met me. I asked him to go to Subhadra first.

Uttara's cry stopped, and we heard a group of conchs being played. Midwives were celebrating the childbirth. But there was no cry of newborn baby along with that.

*Is everything fine?*

I strained my ears. The conchs had suddenly stopped. I still heard no baby cry. Neither did any midwife come to me for delivering the news.

*This was unusual!*

"See what has happened." I sent out a maid to check. She returned after a while, her head lowered.

"Devi Uttara has given birth to a boy." She managed to utter.

"Then why did the celebration stop?" I asked, my heart racing in fear.

The maid did not reply.

"Pray, speak out! Is the baby fine?" I urged.

"The baby is a stillborn, Samrat." She said, still looking down.

For a moment, I went numb. It took me a while to feel the meaning of those words I had just heard.

To realise that I had just lost my grandnephew. My sole heir.

Did all our fears just come true? A part of me still refused to believe that it did.

I dreaded meeting Arjuna's eyes. What would I tell him now? That I had failed to save Abhimanyu's son as well? Would he ever forgive me?

My trance shuttered as I heard Subhadra crying out.

"My Abhimanyu's last sign is also gone. What for should I stay alive?"

My chest pained. This girl had never ever spoken in such a loud voice. I could feel how much empty, how much broken she was feeling from inside.

"You told me that the baby would be alright. Give me my grandson back, Bhrata!" I heard her again. "Save my clan!"

Krishna must have spoken something softly to her which was not audible from here. Few moments passed in silence. I exchanged glance with Bhima, wondering what was going on inside.

"Krishna Vaasudeva has gone inside the labour room." A maid informed. "He has asked you all to stop worrying. He is looking into it."

It was extremely unusual for a man to enter labour room thus. Krishna might have gone to make a last effort to save his beloved nephew's son. But that could not calm me. I knew Krishna could turn almost impossible into possible as he had done many times. But reviving a dead child was not possible, even with all his intelligence and knowledge.

I did not know how long I was at that state until I heard a newborn's loud cry. A louder note of conch followed.

Was I dreaming?

"Congratulations, Samrat!" The chief midwife came out now, bowing to me. "The baby is alive and healthy."

I still could not believe my ears. Did I hear it right? Or had I passed out and it was all my imagination? If it was the latter, I feared to wake up from my trance.

"Relax, Jyeshtha. Everything is fine now." I heard Krishna's comforting voice. He stood with his usual calm smile on his face.

"How have you done this, Krishna?" I stared at him with disbelief. "Are you truly a God as many beilive?"

He chuckled. "I am a human , brother. Your grandson was not born dead."

"Then why did they..." Arjuna could not finish. His face was still pale.

"They mistook it. The baby was born motionless. Brahmashira's poison must have affected his nerves. All he needed was a few careful movements and that's all I did." He smiled. "Now the boy is perfectly fine and healthy. You are hearing his cry, right?"

That was true. The baby's cry was getting louder. As if he was compensating for the moments he had not cried.

"A strong boy indeed." Krishna said with a proud smile. His assurance and relief made smile break on my face too.

"You proved again that your knowledge and presence of mind is miraculous." Arjuna came closer and took Krishna in his embrace. "Thank you, my friend! Thank you for everything!"

"Is Uttara alright, Krishna?" Bhima enquired.

"She has not yet regained her sense. But Subhadra is taking care." Krishna assured.

"Ask Subhadra to eat something first, Krishna." Rukmini came forward. I had not even noticed her for so long.

"Jyeshtha, let Subhadra and Draupadi take some rest now." Rukmini looked at me. "They have been under huge stress since months. I'm staying with Uttara."

I smiled with a nod of acknowledgement. As Rukmini went inside, Krishna turned to me.

"This boy is born when the Kuru clan is at the risk of getting ended. He has saved his clan from dying down. Let him be known as 'Parikshit', the one who has protected his clan from extinction."

***

After a week, Aacharya Dhaumya observed Parikshit's naming ceremony with due rituals. Maharishi Vyasa himself was present along with his four disciples, to give blessings to the child.

Hastinapura celebrated as a happy family after long. The newborn baby had brought a feeling of relief and pleasure around the entire Kurujangala. Everyone seemed to have received a new life after so much pain and tears. Even the widows of Duryodhana and his brothers kept aside their silent indifference and showered their love on Parikshit. The little one played in all his grandaunts' arms.

*Bless Parikshit for uniting us again! Finally, the conflict between Kuru family seemed to have been over!*

After the rituals were over, I entered the royal court along with my brothers.

"Honourable court nobles, ministers and citizens of Hastinapura!" I addressed them all. "I thank you all for attending the first ceremony of my grandnephew. Keeping Maharishi Vyasa as witness, I declare Rajakumar Parikshit as the heir of my imperial throne."

Silence followed.

"On the occasion of his arrival, I also announce that from now on, an allowance will be provided to all those families who have lost their men in the war of Kurukshetra." I exchanged a glance with Draupadi who nodded with emphasis. We had already had a talk regarding this.

Something we could not get time to do after Rajasuya despite our wish! Now it was time for that!

"I promise that no discrimination will be done on the basis of their participation. This allowance will be given to all martyrs of the war, irrespective of the side he had chosen to fight for." I finished.

"Sadhu! Sadhu!" the court nobles hailed me.

"Samrat, I also want to make an announcement." Uncle Dhritarashtra said.

I nodded and stepped back to my throne, letting him take the central position in the elevated dais. He slowly steadied himself with the help of Sanjaya. I wondered what he wanted to say.

"My dear citizens of Hastinapura, and all the court nobles present over here, with all your permission, I want to leave for vanaprashtha with my wife and brother Vidura."

Shocked, I looked at him. I had never even imagined that he might take this decision. I turned to my left. Aunt Gandhari was standing there beside Draupadi. Mother was holding her. On the other side, uncle Vidura also stood quietly.

That meant they were already prepared to depart?

"I apologise to you for every wrong that I and my son Duryodhana might have done to you. I am keeping you all in care of such an emperor, who is the best to handle an empire of Dharma. Stay assured that you all are secured under Samrat Yudhishthira's rule. The person who has the nobility to care for the defeated former king, the person who can respectfully protect the women of his dead enemies, - is the perfect one to sit on Bharata's throne."

I looked at him, wondering when he had changed his perspective so much about me. Perhaps this was the first time I heard him praising me from heart.

"Keep living a new life under his rule, and let me take your leave. And..." his voice shivered now. "If possible, please forgive my Duryodhana!" He joined his hands, his body kept trembling. Fearing that he might lose his balance, I hurried and held him.

"Uncle, are you alright?"

He could not speak, just stared at my face with blank eyes. I did not feel right. His pulse kept falling. It seemed like he would pass out any moment.

With help of Sanjaya I got him seated at a comfortable position. Draupadi fanned him. I sprinkled cold water over his face and body. It took quite a while for him to regain normalcy.

"Uncle?" I called anxiously.

He slowly turned his head to me. His eyes were moist.

"I am fine, son. Your love and care did not let my heart stop beating." He smiled a weary smile.

"Your love has won me, Yudhishthira. Whole life I have loved only Duryodhana and kept ignoring you. But trust me, he had never given me this much respect and care as you are doing!"

"Pray, do not talk, Uncle. You are not well." I softly said.

He shook his head. "I have to say this before leaving, Vatsa. Today I realise what a grave mistake I have done in my entire life."

Despite my resistance, he raised himself more, and held me in his embrace. For a while I lost myself in emotions. It felt like after decades I had received my late father's love once again.

"I admit that I have done injustice to you, Yudhishthira!" he softly uttered. "You are as much my son as Duryodhana was. I have never accepted this truth. The fatal war was just the consequence of that fault of mine."

*It has been too late, King Dhritarashtra!* I hid a sigh but could not voice it and break the guilt-stricken old man even more.

He stood up slowly, keeping his support on Sanjaya's shoulder.

"Honourable ones, I admit my fault in front of you all." He joined his palms. "Please pardon me and let me go."

"We have not kept anything in mind, Maharaj." One of them said. "Pray, change your decision!"

Uncle shook his head. "I don't want to get attached to this material world anymore, noble ones. Now we have to go."

"Pray, wait till your health gets better." I pleaded.

"I am able to walk now. Worry not. Also, Vidura and Sanjaya will be with me." He assured. "Don't stop me anymore, Yudhishthira. One should not be stopped after he has taken the sankalpa of vanaprastha."

I sighed with a nod, and let him proceed.

The court nobles stood up respectfully, giving them way. Uncle Dhritarashtra kept his support on uncle Vidura and slowly proceeded towards the gate. Sanjaya followed them from a distance. Mother moved forward and held aunt Gandhari's arm.

"Allow me also to follow you, elder sister."

"Maa!" I exclaimed in shock. But she looked determined.

"I too am at the age of vanaprashtha, Yudhishthira." Mother calmly said. "I have no more need here."

"If this is what you were to do, then why did you encourage us to fight this war, Maa?" I was hurt. "Why did you want us to win our kingdom back? For leaving us thus when we need you the most?"

"I did want you to fight for yourselves, son. Not for myself. I inspired you to win your kingdom because that was my duty. To you and your father." She said in the same tone. "Now my duty is over. My sons are settled in their father's kingdom. My husband's unfulfilled dream has come true. Justice has been established in Bharata. Now my work is over." She evenly said. "Don't stop me!"

I did not try anymore. I knew well how firm mother could be in whatever she decided. But a part of me still bore the hurt and guilt.

Was she unwilling to rule as queen-mother because of my words of that day? Was it because I did not empathise with her loss of her firstborn? I could not bring myself to voice it.

She was such a queen whose wish could never be questioned but obeyed with silence.

Mother walked ahead, without speaking anymore. I stared at the path she went along. Until little Parikshit's baby voice brought me back. I saw him playing in Uttara's arms who stood beside Draupadi.

*The past had left, leaving the responsibility of future in our hands.*

CHAPTER FORTY

# EPILOGUE

*Thirty-six years later*

"This cannot happen!" I shook Arjuna's arms. "Tell me this is a lie!"

Arjuna shook his lowered head, still unable to gather himself. "I would have been the happiest if this was a lie, Jyeshtha!" his sigh sounded like sobs. "I have performed his last rites in these very hands!"

My grip on him went loose. I sank on the nearest seat, trying to sink the news in my head.

Krishna was no more! My cousin, my friend, my greatest well-wisher had left this earth! With him, died the entire Yadava dynasty. The unkind ocean had taken Dwaraka back to its womb.

I remembered that once Krishna had told me that he would rather die than taking a single breath in an earth which won't have his dear Arjuna. He had kept his promise!

"Have all of them died, Arjuna?" I whispered as if I was not asking him but myself.

"Every single man of Dwaraka. Only Krishna's grandson Vajra has survived." Arjuna said. "I have kept him in Indraprastha for safety."

"And the ladies?" I managed to ask. "Krishna's wives? Our aunts? The wives of Pradyumna and his brothers? What happened to them?"

It broke Arjuna even more. "I could not save them, Jyeshtha! Most of them burnt themselves on their husbands' pyres itself. A group of Abhira robbers abducted the remaining ones in front of my very eyes."

He paused, perhaps struggling to speak more. I could feel that his unbearable mental pain had affected even his limbs, leading to this shocking failure that happened for the first time in his life. He had lost his focus, his strength. He had lost his second soul.

"Krishna had sent me a last message asking me to save the women. I have failed to fulfill his wish." He uttered before collapsing on the floor.

I had no word to console him. A weird emptiness took over me. In these past thirty-six years I had seen many deaths. I had lost my mother in a forest fire. I had lost my uncle Vidura who was like a second father to me. Uncle Dhritarashtra and aunt Gandhari had also left the earth along with them. But none of these could break me this much.

*Today I had realised once again what Krishna was to me. To us!*

I made up my mind. Krishna's absence seemed like a sign to me. A message from Mahakala himself that our time had come, too.

"We also have to go now, Arjuna." I calmly uttered. "Parikshit is well-trained to take over. Let's handover this empire to him and renounce the world."

Arjuna looked up to me now, slowly nodding.

"You have said the words of my heart. Krishna used to say that he doesn't want to survive without me. Neither can I live without him." He looked determined. "Arrange for Parikshit's coronation, Jyeshtha."

"I shall talk with Aacharya Dhaumya. Let Parikshit rule Hastinapura and Vajra take over Indraprastha." I proposed. "We five shall leave after their coronation."

***

"It's your time to wear this now, son." I placed my crown on Parikshit's head. He bowed with joined palms, his eyes betraying sorrow.

"Remember, Parikshit, this is not a crown but a responsibility." I said. "A promise to the people of Bharata that I have struggled to fulfil for thirty-six years. Now it's yours to continue."

Parikshit touched my feet.

"Kulaguru Kripacharya, I'm leaving your disciple in your guidance." I turned to him. "Take care of him."

Guru Kripa nodded. I then turned to my only living cousin.

"Yuyutsu, stay with Parikshit as his mentor. Keep guiding him in the path of Dharma."

"Stay assured, Samrat. I shall not let anyone say that Parikshit could not become Dharmaraj Yudhishthira's worthy heir." Yuyutsu promised.

I exhaled, and addressed the wives of Duryodhana and his brothers.

"Sisters, you all have loved Parikshit like your own child. I leave him along with Uttara in your caring shelter. Keep showering your blessings on them. And," I joined my hands. "If I have ever done anything to offend any of you, please forgive me for that."

"Pray, do not say so, Jyeshtha." Bhanumati joined her palms. "The respect you have given to all of us is unimaginable for any victor to his enemies' widows. You have won our heartfelt admiration. Parikshit is not just your grandson but ours too. We promise to take care of him."

Exhaling, I left the court hall for preparing myself for the final journey.

It felt so relaxing to take down all gold and precious gems from my person. As if a heavy burden had gone down my heart.

I wanted to wear this deerskin long ago. Krishna did not let me. Today I had no more resistance. My way of salvation had finally opened!

Draupadi did not listen to any of us. She also was ready, wearing deerskin. Our wife, our Shakti, would never let us go alone to our final journey. With a lot of efforts she had somehow managed to convince a grieving Subhadra for staying back, to guide Parikshit and Uttara along with Vajra in Indraprastha. The responsibility of both the kingdoms would be hers from now on.

I approached the palace gate, followed by my brothers and Draupadi. Subhadra, Uttara and other ladies followed us till the gate and stood there looking at us. Their eyes were moist.

*How fast the time flies, doesn't it?*

Through this way, one day our mother and other elders went to vanaprashtha. Today it was our turn!

The citizens stood on our way, weeping and pleading not to go. I raised them who lay on the path and consoled them.

We walked towards the north. Our lives had begun in the lap of Himalaya. They were to be ended there only. At that abode of Gods and Rishis.

I promised you, king of mountains, that I would return to you when all my work would be over. I am coming to you for fulfilling my promise. Washing off all my sins, take me in your eternal peace now!

*Let that peace be mine today which I have craved for!*

*Om! Shanti! Shanti! Shanti!*

# References And Inspiration


1. *The Mahabharata*, translated by Kisari Mohan Ganguly

2. *The Mahabharata*, Critical Edition, translated by Bibek Debroy, Bhandarkar Oriental Research Institute

3. The Mahabharata, A Modern Retelling by Ramesh Menon

4. *Mahabharat* by Rajshekhar Basu

5. *Krishnaa, Kunti Ebong Kounteya* by Nrisinghaprasad Bhaduri

6. *Mahabharater Bharat Juddho O Krishna* by Nrisinghaprasad Bhaduri

7. *Mahabharater Chhoy Probin* by Nrisinghaprasad Bhaduri

8. *Mahabharater Pratinayak* by Nrisinghaprasad Bhaduri

9. *Mahabharater Ashtadashi* by Nrisinghaprasad Bhaduri

10. *Katha Amritasaman* (volumes 1-4) by Nrisinghaprasad Bhaduri

11. *Mahabharater Katha* by Buddhadeb Bose

12. *Krishna Charitra* by Bankim Chandra Chatterjee

13. The Difficulty of Being Good by Gurucharan Das

14. Marvels and Mysteries of the Mahabharata by Abhijit Basu

15. Mahabharata Now: Narration, Aesthetics, Ethics edited by Arindam Chakrabarti and Sibaji Bandyopadhyay

16. *Krishnavatara* by K. M. Munshi

17. The Great Golden Sacrifice of the Mahabharata by Maggi Lidchi-Grassi

18. *Pancharatram* by Bhasa

19. *Benisamharam* by Bhattanarayana

20. *Kiratarjuniyam* by Bharavi

21. Pandab Gaurab by Girish Chandra Ghosh

22. Pandober Agnatabas by Girish Chanra Ghosh

23. Articles by Indrajit Bandyopadhyay in Boloji.com

24. ancientvoice.wikidot.com

25. The Aryavarta Chronicles by Krishna Udayasankar

26. Bhima lone warrior by M. T. Vasudevan Nair

# About The Author

After majoring in Physics, Semanti Chakraborty turned to her area of passion - The Mahabharata. She hopes to revive and rekindle interest in the knowledge of Bhagavan Vyasa through her reimagination of the story of Yudhishthira. A teacher by profession and a writer by passion, she balances between science and spiritual wisdom in her daily life.

Samrat Yudhishthira trilogy is her debut work. Triumph of Dharma is the third and final book of this series. Apart from this trilogy, she also has plans to write on some underrated epic characters in future.

www.ingramcontent.com/pod-product-compliance
Ingram Content Group UK Ltd.
Pitfield, Milton Keynes, MK11 3LW, UK
UKHW040604210726
13854UKWH00009B/2424

9 798899 847103